An unforgettable saga of the
Southern Cheyenne's fight for survival . . .
from the Spur Award–winning
author of *Warrior's Road* . . .

THE WEEPING MOON

*Since the day his foot had been caught in the iron
jaws of the white man's trap, the boy had been called
Three Toes. He was a man now, and he would take
the name of a man. . . .*

"Once I ran like the antelope and led all the Elks after
Bull Buffalo."

"We remember," Two Claws said somberly.

"Now the years on my winter count are nearly finished.
Hanging Road's close. Once everyone knew Buffalo Horn
. . . Brave heart, take my name. Do it honor, as the dead
sons who should have taken it from me might have, had
they lived."

"Grandfather, I will," the new Buffalo Horn
vowed. . . .

Praise for G. Clifton Wisler's
Jericho's Journey

"Sound, traditional historical fiction."
—*Publishers Weekly*

THE WEEPING MOON

G. CLIFTON WISLER

JOVE BOOKS, NEW YORK

THE WEEPING MOON

A Jove Book / published by arrangement with
the author

PRINTING HISTORY
Jove edition / August 1995

ISBN: 0-515-11678-5

A JOVE BOOK®
Jove Books are published by The Berkley Publishing Group,
200 Madison Avenue, New York, New York 10016.
JOVE and the "J" design are trademarks
belonging to Jove Publications, Inc.

PRINTED IN THE UNITED STATES OF AMERICA

10 9 8 7 6 5 4 3 2 1

remembering Margie Prater
who shared her love of books

1

Heammawihio, the Great Mystery, taught the people that from his earliest moments a man must walk within the sacred hoop of the world. He must be in harmony with the four-leggeds and the two-leggeds, the trees and the plants, the rocks and the sky. He can only be what he is, and he should not consider himself more. If his feet remain on the sacred path, and his life is in conflict with no living thing, then his world will know perfect harmony. All his life he must struggle to achieve that harmony. He may come to know many things, the good and the bad. If he is unfortunate, pain and death become part of that path.

The boy came to know both well.

His mother, Gooseberry Woman, passed six days and six nights in Woman's Lodge, suffering the torment only women know as she waited for him to step out and begin his life. His father, Swift Antelope, danced and prayed in the hills of *Motoshe*, the place where the ash trees grow thick, hoping that he might at last have a son to keep him company when the deep snows choked the world, a boy to follow him when the days came to hunt Bull Buffalo.

"I shared my pain with the old women," Gooseberry Woman once told her son. "Your father suffered alone. He cut the flesh of his arms and chest. He starved himself. Finally he collapsed, and a dream filled his head."

Swift Antelope never shared the vision he saw the night of his son's birth. The spirit creatures told him much, though, and when he returned to the *Omissis* camp, he knew a child was waiting for him there. Most men gave their sons a name sent to them in such dreams, but the Antelope did not.

"He looks like a frog," the Antelope told the old woman who presented the child. "We will call him Frog."

Gooseberry Woman later complained that it was no fit name for a proud warrior's first son.

"He will be our only son," Swift Antelope explained. "The name is nothing. He will soon gain another."

The boy rarely spoke of his beginnings. His mother and father appeared troubled by the recollection of that time, and he had no wish to add to their pain. He knew they often thought of the other children, the stillborn ones, the little sons and daughters who never took their first breath before climbing *E kut si him' mi yo*, the Hanging Road walked by the spirits of the dead. As the only child Gooseberry Woman would ever bring into the world, Frog felt the burden of expectation. As for the name, he would soon leave it behind and take another.

Seven times Frog had watched the coming of the winter snows. His father kept him close to him each time the Hard Face Moon appeared in the sky, and Frog was filled with apprehension. Swift Antelope's face was normally calm, and his eyes boasted the confident glow of a *Tsis tsis tas* warrior. The snows brought with them a sense of dread.

Perhaps he knows something, Frog told himself. He remembered the mysterious dream and wondered if maybe the spirit creatures had whispered a warning. Even though Frog was small, he had heard of such visions. The old medicine man, Two Claws, had them. But boys rarely walk the world with an old man's cautious gaze, and Frog eluded the protective eyes of his father.

That winter the *Omissis* band was camped in the southern country, along *Mahohevaohe*, Red Shield River. Many *Wihio*, the strange pale-skinned people with the hairy faces, walked that country, and some had taken *Omissis* wives. Frog considered their words odd, and they didn't behave in the traditional manner of the *Tsis tsis tas*. Even the *Suhtai* band, the northerners who dressed and acted differently, walked the sacred path. These *Wihio* argued and fought among themselves. They treated their women and children harshly. Even Two Claws and the old man chiefs had no words capable of quieting them.

"*Naha'*, you've heard of Sweet Medicine, haven't you?" Frog's father had asked him that morning.

"Yes, *Ne' hyo*," the boy had replied. "He brought the people *Mahuts*, the sacred arrows. He gave the soldier societies their power, and he guided the people through difficult days."

"He warned us of these strange ones, these *Wihio*. He told us of the sickness and death they would bring."

"Then why do we allow them in our camp?"

"Because the guns and lead they trade us allow us to fight our enemies," Swift Antelope had explained. "We remember Sweet Medicine's warning, though. You must be careful of them. They can bring you harm."

An older, wiser boy might have taken the warning to heart, but Frog's mother's youngest brother, Pony Leg, had promised to take him hunting for deer in the thickets north of the river. What boy ever refused such an invitation to adventure?

Pony Leg himself was young back then. He was short of stature and terribly thin, more like a boy than a young warrior of seventeen summers. The Leg was a skillful hunter, though. He was always among the first to count coup on Bull Buffalo or drive the Pawnee scouts from *Tsis tsis tas* country. Frog was proud to call him *na khan*, uncle.

The snows were not yet deep, so Frog and his uncle walked together into the hills beyond the river. All the while Pony Leg spoke of the old ways, of hunting with the silent-killing bow and stalking game. They sat for a time on a slope and made the appropriate medicine prayers. Then Pony Leg with his man's bow and Frog with his shorter boy's weapon approached the thicket.

Heammawihio sent Frog many signs, but that morning he was blind to every one of them. The snow was torn by heavy tracks, the kind made by heavy *Wihio* boots, and the air was full of the damp, foul odor of *Wihio* cloth. Frog should have noticed the torn branches of the willows snapped off by careless-walking men. Instead he saw movement and hurried along.

The underbrush was thick, and Frog detected a faint trail. His eyes followed the movement ahead, and he failed to see the upturned leaves and boot tracks. The toe of his right moccasin struck something hard, and he stumbled. His left foot struck the ground. Then the iron jaws of a *Wihio* trap clamped on to the boy's left foot, and he yelped with pain.

"Ayyyy!" Frog howled. "*Na khan*, help me!"

The biting iron teeth chewed into his flesh, and his small hands were powerless to free the mangled foot. Suddenly a *Wihio* jumped out of the trees and stared angrily down at the trap.

"You've spoiled it, pup!" he shouted as he kicked snow into Frog's face. "Why is it you little fools have to mess with my trap lines?"

Frog only understood some of the words, but it was clear that the *Wihio* was angry. Frog asked for help, but the *Wihio* shook his head as if not understanding. Then another white man appeared.

"Caught yourself a Cheyenne whelp, did you?" the second man asked. "Better cut him loose 'fore his uncles start carving on you."

"Let him work his own way free," the first man grumbled.

The pain had surged over Frog like a wave, but now he was used to it. He shook away his tears and stared hatefully at the strange pale men with the hairy faces and hard eyes.

"Be a service to humanity if I cut his throat," the first man said, laughing. The second one scowled, knelt beside Frog, and drew out a sharp iron knife. With no more regard for the boy than a hunter might have for a wounded deer, the *Wihio* traced the edge of the trap's iron jaws and then sliced the two smallest toes from Frog's foot.

The boy had never felt pain of that sort before. It raced up his leg and exploded through him like summer thunder. Frog screamed across the river, into the sky, through the entire world. Then he fainted.

The first *Wihio* kicked Frog awake. The boy's foot lay in a mound of red snow, and only the cold stopped the bleeding. The trappers were laughing to each other. One held Frog's toes in his hand.

Suddenly, from out of the trees, an arrow came. It flew straight and true as if guided by *Heammawihio* Himself. The first *Wihio* stared in disbelief when it struck his chest. He tried to speak, but his mouth was full of blood, and he toppled backward into the snow.

"No!" the second man cried. He took one step toward the river, but an arrow struck his back, and he, too, fell. He managed to lift his head and stare back at Frog a moment before a second arrow entered his side and tore the life from him.

Frog sat up, dazed, and waited for Pony Leg. Who else could have cut down the two *Wihio*? His uncle came later, though. First a thick-necked warrior with a fierce scowl knelt beside the boy.

"*Na khan?*" Frog muttered.

"Quiet, Frog," the man said as he wrapped the boy's mangled foot in rawhide strips. Frog soon recognized him as Black Kettle, one of the leaders of the *Wu ta piu* band, those who eat like the Lakotas. They were camped on Red Shield River not far from the

Omissis camp that winter, and the Kettle had responded to Frog's screams.

"My uncle . . ." Frog began.

"Here he is," Black Kettle said, waving Pony Leg from out of the trees. "Take him to Two Claws. He knows the way to heal the wounds a *Wihio* makes."

Pony Leg inspected the bindings on Frog's foot and stared angrily at the dead trappers. The Leg wrapped the severed toes in a strip torn from one of the trapper's shirts. Then he lifted Frog in his powerful arms and carried the boy to the *Omissis* camp.

Frog lay for many days in Two Claws's lodge, undergoing the medicine cures. The boy's head remained hot with fever, and Two Claws danced and performed the iron curing rituals. Swift Antelope sat with his son most of that time, lamenting the boy's injuries and blaming himself.

"I saw it all in my dreams," he muttered. "I saw it all."

"*Heammawihio* warns us sometimes," Two Claws observed. "Some things will always happen. Didn't Sweet Medicine tell us of the sickness the *Wihio* would bring? Still we welcomed the hairy faces into our camps. Your son's wounds, those on the outside at least, will heal. It is the deeper hurt inside we must make well again."

Frog didn't understand that in the beginning. At the time he knew only pain and fever.

Pony Leg visited his nephew often in the medicine lodge, as did many of Frog's age-mates. They sat beside the boy, silenced by the awesome power of Two Claws's healing paints and medicine charms. His bear-claw rattle and raven-wing fan filled young eyes with dread, and the painted skins of a winter count warned the youngsters to respect the power of the old man.

Frog knew the boys had not come to share his pain. No, curiosity brought them. When Two Claws removed the bindings and cleaned the wound, the boys' eyes widened at the sight of Frog's mutilated flesh. Later, White Moccasin, Frog's closest friend, told of the jokes the other boys shared.

"I will never run like the others," Frog lamented when Pony Leg next visited. "You should have left me in the snow. What use is a cripple?"

"I don't see a cripple," Pony Leg argued. "The foot will heal. Do you know that I once saw a beaver chew an entire foot off to escape a *Wihio* trap?"

"Beavers have more use for tails than feet," Frog replied. "How can a boy grow tall enough to lead the hunt when he can't run?"

"I'm not tall myself," Pony Leg pointed out. "Black Kettle is far from the tallest or the swiftest, but the *Wu ta piu* follow him. Be patient, *Na tsin' os ta*. *Heammawihio* decides the path a man must walk. Yours may be steep, but you will walk it as Swift Antelope's son should. When it's too steep for you to manage alone, your uncle will help you. I'll never be too far away."

The boy knew, as surely Pony Leg did, that all boys eventually have to climb Man's Road alone. Frog had heard of boys who faltered. Some left the people and wandered the world alone, outside the sacred hoop. Others adopted the strange ways of the *Hohnuhk'e*, the contraries. They carried the two-stringed contrary bow in battle, and their power led to many *Tsis tsis tas* victories. Even so, they walked a difficult path, and

Frog sometimes overheard the young men describing a contrary going willingly to his death.

There were also the he-she men. These people never wore warrior's clothes or rode to hunt Bull Buffalo, but they were great healers. They acquired much power which they employed for the benefit of others. Broken Shell was such a person. He had visited Frog when the fever was at its worst. The Shell sat, sang, and made his healing dances. Frog grew better. When he was healthy enough to return to his father's lodge, Broken Shell gave him a small medicine charm, the tooth of an elk wrapped in horse hair.

"Such charms are usually given to young men riding into battle," Frog observed.

"Then it's appropriate, little one," Broken Shell replied. "You have a difficult enemy to vanquish."

"What enemy?" the boy asked.

"That's for others to say," the Shell whispered as he tied the charm behind Frog's ear. "I am a healer and charm-maker, not a guide who helps boys understand their paths."

Two Claws, however, had never hesitated where offering advice was concerned.

"Your heart is full of anger," he warned. "No man can walk the sacred path who has lost the harmony of his own being. The *Wihio* who hurt you are dead. They can trouble you no longer. Give up their memory or their ghosts will bother you."

"How can I forget when each time that I look at my foot, I recall their grinning faces?"

"Turn your heart away from these bad-heart recollections," the medicine man urged. "If you retain them, they will devour you with sharper teeth than any iron trap ever knew."

The boy stared hard into Two Claws's eyes, searching for some power that might convince a troubled soul of the truth in an old man's words. Frog felt only bitterness swelling up inside him.

"Perhaps in time," Two Claws whispered.

Frog considered it unlikely.

The day Swift Antelope and Pony Leg carried Frog back to their lodge, the boy studied the eyes of his agemates. Frog couldn't hear their words, but he read their thoughts. *There goes the mutilated one.* Frog wanted to scream at them. But they were only thinking what he already knew.

"You're back with us at last," Gooseberry Woman said when Pony Leg helped Frog onto a buffalo hide beside the fire. "They wouldn't let me into the medicine lodge, but I sang my own healing prayers."

"I know," Frog said, gripping her arm.

"I don't see why a woman's visit would spoil Two Claws's medicine," she added. "He often invites the help of his daughters, doesn't he?"

"He says the *Wihio* iron draws strength from women," Frog explained. "I didn't think I was abandoned, *Nah' koa.* How could my mother ever do that?"

She smiled, and Frog thought to himself that her warmth was more of a cure than any raven's-wing fan or bear's claw.

Gooseberry Woman's attentions soon had her son growing stronger. Her broths and teas could not grow new toes, but they hurried the mending of Frog's flesh and the recovery of his spirits. Before the Big Hard Face Moon of midwinter arrived, Frog was venturing outside. He had trouble walking, and he frequently fell, but Swift Antelope insisted that his son resume his duties. Frog helped his father work hides and tend the ponies. When the other boys invited him to join their games and contests, though, Frog stared at his malformed foot.

"Perhaps another day," he muttered.

By the time the snows began to melt, Frog's agemates had given up. They left him to his camp and raced off to scare some fat off the horses or hunt rabbits beside the river. Pony Leg, who sometimes led the young men to watch the maidens fetching water, noticed that his nephew had turned away from the others. Finally the Leg drew the boy to the river and pointed to a mound of earth on the far bank.

"That's where the *Wihio* trappers lie," Pony Leg explained. "Their friends piled rocks over their bodies. The ground was too hard to dig. Usually the *Wihio* bury their dead."

"Why?" Frog asked. "How can a spirit climb Hanging Road and reach *Seyan'* when he is covered with earth?"

"The *Wihio* have many strange ways, *Na tsin' os ta*. They walk the world with heavy feet, and they find no harmony. Maybe it's best that they don't find *Seyan'*. I don't think *Heammawihio* would welcome them."

"No, they are outside the sacred hoop," Frog agreed. "Man Above would find them troublesome."

"They can no longer trouble you, *Na tsin' os ta*."

"Not those two," Frog admitted. "There are others, though. We should have listened to Sweet Medicine's warning."

"It's too late to do that now," Pony Leg declared. "Not all *Wihio* are bad. Just as not all *Tsis tsis tas* are good. I don't think those men meant to cause you harm."

"They should not put their iron traps in our country," Frog complained.

"They have been doing that for as long as I have walked the earth. It's a bad thing, maybe, but others do it. No, I fault them for enjoying your suffering. Nothing more. And they have paid a price for their bad hearts."

"Black Kettle killed them."

"He also gave their relations four ponies," Pony Leg pointed out. "Most thought they earned their deaths, but Black Kettle saw that his actions had disturbed the harmony of the world. He will be a man to lead all the people one day."

"I would follow him," Frog said, sighing. "If only I had two good feet."

"You will never have all your toes again, but that is no reason for you to stay in the shadow of your father's lodge."

"What use can I be to anyone?"

"You must discover that, *Na tsin' os ta*. It won't come to you in a dream. You must join the others, play the old games. If you can't run, walk. If you fall, get up. There have been lame *Tsis tsis tas* before. Many have fallen from their ponies or been hurt fighting."

"They laugh at me, *Na khan*!" the boy objected.

"Yes, they say, 'There sits Three Toes. Are you certain his toes were all the *Wihio* cut?' "

"Three Toes?" the boy cried. "They call me that?"

"It's as good a name as another," Pony Leg insisted. "You should carry it proudly, as One Eye and Lame Panther carry theirs."

"I never owned a proud name, but Frog was better than this."

"This one you earned."

"Like one earns a blind eye?"

"What honor can a man win if he's born tallest and strongest?" Pony Leg asked. "If he wins a race, the others will claim it's because he was the biggest. If he shoots his arrow farthest, they will say he was always stronger than his age-mates. A boy with a maimed foot has much to prove, but if he wins a race or triumphs over his wrestling opponent, everyone will see he has accomplished a great deal."

"Not if he never wins a race. It's a hard thing to do with only a foot and a half."

"I don't care if you never win, *Na tsin' os ta*," Pony Leg said, drawing his nephew close to his side. "I was never a fast runner, nor the best bowman. I always tried, though. That's all I ask of you. A man, no matter how tall or how lame, must try. Or he must walk off into the snows and climb Hanging Road. One who doesn't try is just as dead as those *Wihio* across the river."

"And if I try and fail?"

"I'll help you try again," he promised.

2

Thereafter the people knew him as Three Toes. The name stung at first, and he would stare down at his left moccasin as if the scarred flesh were in full view. That spring, when the ice choking Red Shield River melted and the boys went there to swim, Three Toes noticed the others gazing at his foot. But after a few times the missing toes lost their hold on his age-mates. They turned to other mysteries, and Three Toes was just another *Omissis* boy struggling up the path toward Man's Road.

As he had suspected, the injury held him back in foot races. He often stumbled and fell. In time he learned, with Pony Leg's help, to compensate for the toes. Three Toes devoted each morning to shooting arrows, and by the time he reached his tenth summer, his bow arm was as hard as *Wihio* iron, and his aim was sharp and true. No boy's arrows found their target half so often.

Three Toes had other talents, too. Old Two Claws took the boy aside and spoke to him of the mysteries of earth and sky.

"Listen to the heartbeat of the world around you," the medicine man advised. "Open your eyes to all you can see. Not only the rocks and trees, the four-leggeds and the two-leggeds, but all that lies beyond."

In the beginning Three Toes had understood very little. Gradually, though, he learned to listen to the song of the wind and know when *Heammawihio* would send Thunderbird into the clouds. He studied the plants and the animals so that he could locate hidden springs. Most of all he learned to speak to Wolf and Hawk, to understand their hunting ways so that he might feed his camp. Later he came to study Badger, who tenaciously fought the fiercest enemy.

"Learn from him, *Na tsin' os ta*," Pony Leg urged. "Badger's not the swiftest, but he wins his fights."

"He's like a lance carrier," Three Toes observed. "He makes his stand, and he won't retreat. Bigger animals may kill him, but they know they've been in a fight."

"It's a good way to be," Pony Leg said, nodding respectfully. "Sad, though. There are some fights Badger can't win, and so he dies."

"Yes," Three Toes agreed. "But the important thing to do is stand tall. Earn respect. After all, nothing lives long."

"No, nothing," Pony Leg said, frowning. "We shouldn't talk about dying, though. We're young. There's time left to taste the sweetness of life before we start the long climb up Hanging Road."

"I haven't tasted any sweetness," Three Toes complained.

"You will," his uncle assured him. "Later, when you grow chin hairs, I'll show you how to pluck them. Then we'll talk about the sweetness of life."

"Afterward you can carve me a courting flute."

"And what do you know of courting flutes?" Pony Leg cried.

"Only what I see from the river," Three Toes replied. "When the maidens go down to fill the water bladders, you . . ."

"Enough," Pony Leg said, hiding the grin on his face. "We'll talk more about it later."

"When I have chin hairs to pluck," Three Toes said, laughing.

Three Toes didn't spend all of his time spying on his uncle and watching badgers. He devoted every morning and most afternoons to his father's pony herd. Swift Antelope was a famous horse stealer, and many a Pawnee's favorite mount chewed grass outside the *Omissis* camp. Three Toes admired those sleek horses. They could run with the wind while he stumbled to trot up a hill.

"One day I'll have ponies of my own," he whispered to the animals. "You will be my legs."

The ponies seemed to sense the meaning of his words. They stomped their feet and dipped their heads when he walked among them, and they didn't shy away from his touch. Three Toes wasn't a stranger. He had grown accustomed to their habits, and they to his. As the grass greened and the winter chill departed, he was riding even the fiercest of his father's stallions.

"There goes Three Toes, the strange one," the other boys began whispering. "He doesn't run well, but once he mounts a pony, there's no catching him!"

Soon he was riding with his uncle and the other

young men through the hills, chasing wild ponies. His companions gazed with wonder as he approached the captured animals, offering a bit of salt and speaking softly. Another man might take half a moon's passing to gentle a pony. Three Toes would be on an animal's back in a few days.

"It's a great talent you have, *Naha'*," his father told him. "A man who can win the trust of horses will always win favor in a *Tsis tsis tas* camp."

"It's no great thing, *Ne' hyo*," Three Toes replied. "Horses are simple creatures. They only ask you not to hurt them. They don't wish a man to bend their spirit. No, if you're sincere and only wish to be part of their world, they don't fight you. No horse has ever harmed me."

"As men have?" Swift Antelope asked.

"Yes, *Ne' hyo*. Men have done it often, especially the *Wihio*."

"The hairy faces have much to answer for, *Naha'*."

"Yes, *Ne' hyo*," Three Toes agreed. "Much."

That summer no *Wihio* visited the *Omissis* camp. The previous year traders had introduced the coughing sickness to the plains, and the ten bands of the *Tsis tsis tas* had suffered severely. Men, women, and especially little children had died. Not one or two, but hundreds.

"Sweet Medicine warned us," Two Claws lamented. "Ayyyy! We should have listened to the wise words of the old one. It's always the same, though. Men never hear, never see."

Perhaps if so many hadn't died, the chiefs would not have been so eager to sign treaty papers with the *Wihio*. All the ten bands met near the *Wihio* fort up north at Horse Creek. Lakotas were also there.

Arapahoes, too. Even the old enemies, Snakes and Crows and Pawnees! Some *Wihio* in a tall hat spoke of peace among all the brother peoples, but Three Toes had his doubts. His cousins, Raven Feather and Curly, who camped with the Lakotas, said that the *Wihio* soldier chiefs only wanted to build forts and roads through the heart of the buffalo country.

"They come to steal more of our land," Curly grumbled. "Haven't they killed enough of us?"

The Oglala Lakotas had also watched many of their people climb Hanging Road. They were bitter.

"Hate is a heavy thing to carry in your heart, *Naha'*," Swift Antelope warned. "It can grow until there's no room for anything else. I've seen it choke men."

"It's hard not to hate the *Wihio*, *Ne' hyo*," the boy answered. "Even if I had all my toes, I would still count the lodges in our camp circle and notice how few we've become. What harm have we brought the whites? Why do they bring these terrible sicknesses into our camps? Why do they kill our young men and shame our women? You know it's true! I've heard you speak with the other men about it."

"Maybe now it will end," Swift Antelope said. "Maybe now that the chiefs have signed this paper, we can live in peace."

Three Toes wished he could share his father's dream, but he feared the treaty would just be another disappointment. Two Claws refused to smoke with the chiefs who touched the *Wihio* pen, saying the *Tsis tsis tas* had been fooled often enough. If the whites kept their word, he would be happy.

"I see hard days in my dreams," the old man told Three Toes. "I trust them more than *Wihio* promises."

The *Omissis* made their summer camp on Fat River the following year. It was good, rich country, but there were many *Wihio* wagon roads along the river, and Pawnees also hunted Bull Buffalo there.

"You've grown taller," Pony Leg said when he saw his nephew tending Swift Antelope's horse one morning. "This is your twelfth summer?"

"Yes," Three Toes grumbled. "You don't have to ask. I don't have any chin hairs yet, so your secrets are safe."

"That's good," Pony Leg replied. "There aren't enough pretty maidens for me to walk with now. When you begin walking the water trail, they'll all chase you. Old men like myself will have to capture a Snake or a Pawnee if we are to ever have a wife."

"There are plenty who would share a blanket with you, *Na khan*. I see them whispering whenever you walk past."

"Do you?"

"They ask me how many ponies you have."

"Not enough," Pony Leg said, sighing. "I will have more soon, though."

"How?" Three Toes asked. "Are you going to hunt some on Fat River?"

"I don't have your way with ponies, *Na tsin' os ta*. They don't come when I call. I have to chase them into mud or trap them in a ravine. Even then I can't always capture them. No, for me to get a horse, I have to be clever."

"You're going on a raid," Three Toes concluded.

"Five of us are going," Pony Leg explained.

"Five?" Three Toes asked. "Who?"

"River Hawk always rides with me."

"And the others?"

"Wary Dog and his brother, Painted Horse. Their mother lived with the Pawnees, and they know the enemy's ways."

"That's only four," Three Toes noted hopefully. "The other?"

"We have to have someone along to tend our ponies," Pony Leg explained. "Painted Horse has plucked his chin now and considers himself too old for the task. I thought I might invite . . ."

"Yes?"

"A relation."

"Me?"

"Who knows horses better? Besides, it's time you struck a blow at the old enemy. *Heammawihio* makes the Pawnees plentiful so there are enough of them to fight."

"You mean to fight them?" Three Toes asked. "The chiefs touched the treaty pen, and . . ."

"We don't mean to kill any," Pony Leg said, grinning. "Only take their horses. And if they ride out against us, it's only proper we should count coup on them."

"Yes," Three Toes agreed. "It will be a remembered thing, the five of us taking the Pawnee horses."

"Well, we won't take them all," Pony Leg insisted.

"Only the best ones," Three Toes whispered.

"Naturally," Pony Leg replied, grinning. They then set out to complete preparations for the raid.

A horse raid was no simple undertaking. First Pony Leg carried a pipe through the camp, inviting River Hawk, Painted Horse, and Wary Dog to smoke and plan. Finally they summoned Three Toes. The five young men selected good mounts and made camp a short distance from the main band. There Pony Leg led the warrior prayers, invoking the favors of *Heammawihio* and the sacred directions. He then checked his companions' ponies and inspected their bowstrings and arrows. When he was satisfied that everything was ready, Pony Leg led his little band east along Fat River.

Wary Dog rode out ahead, keeping a sharp eye out for sign of the Pawnees.

"He has the keenest eyes," Pony Leg explained to his nephew. "He won his name two snows past when he discovered a Crow raiding party approaching our winter camps."

"You don't need sharp eyes to tell the Pawnees are nearby," River Hawk insisted. "You can smell them two days away."

Painted Horse laughed, but Pony Leg frowned.

"Not so long ago the *Tsis tsis tas*, led by *Mahuts*, attacked the Pawnees," the Leg reminded them.

"Yes," Three Toes added. "The young men boasted and raced out ahead, breaking the medicine power. The Sacred Arrows were lost to us."

"Remember that," Pony Leg warned. "You younger men must hold back and follow. A single Pawnee rarely stands and fights, but we're coming close to his hunting camps. When they have enough men in one place, they fight hard. We've discovered that often enough. We don't come here to fight Pawnees, though. We're after horses."

"I intend to count my first coup," Painted Horse boasted.

"This is my band," Pony Leg barked. "You follow me or ride back. Understand?"

"Yes," the Horse said, shrinking from Pony Leg's blazing eyes. "I only . . ."

"Enough," River Hawk said, making the slashing sign with his hand that indicated talk was finished. "Wary Dog is coming."

The Dog nudged his horse along the trail toward his companions, then halted and waved them forward. He spoke only to Pony Leg, but the shine in his eyes betrayed the news before he could speak.

"I found them," Wary Dog explained. "Below, in the valley past the wagon road."

"How many?" Pony Leg asked.

"Twenty, maybe more," the Dog replied.

"Pawnees or ponies?" River Hawk asked.

"Pawnees," Wary Dog answered. "Hunters. Their women are nearby, butchering."

"And the horses?" Pony Leg asked.

"More than fifty," Wary Dog explained. "Left to graze while the men celebrate their kills."

"Guards?"

"Six," Wary Dog noted. "Pony boys. Now they are swimming in the river, and we can easily take the horses."

"Their brothers and fathers would come after us," Pony Leg grumbled. "I hoped they would be farther from our own camp. We will come when it grows dark, and we must run all the mounts. Only then will we have time to warn our people of the enemy. Taking fifty ponies is nothing if we expose the helpless ones to danger."

Pony Leg waited for someone to reply. His companions grunted their agreement, and Three Toes saw his uncle smile with approval.

They rested the remainder of the day beneath a tall cottonwood on the slope above Fat River. Then, as night fell across the land, they painted their faces and strung their bows.

"Remember, the horses are the important thing," Pony Leg insisted. "It's better to drive off the pony boys than kill any of them."

"We have to kill the guards," Painted Horse argued. "Otherwise they can spread an alarm."

"There are other ways," Wary Dog told his brother. "Follow. Watch. Learn."

It was good advice, Three Toes observed. He had always known Pony Leg's skill with a bow, but that night the Leg demonstrated an equal talent for stealth. The raiders rode to within a stone's throw of the Pawnee pony herd. Then Pony Leg, River Hawk, and Wary Dog dismounted. Painted Horse remained on horseback to guard against surprise while Three Toes climbed down and held the mounts.

"I don't remember a night half so quiet," Three Toes said as the older warriors vanished into the darkness.

"It's dark, too," Painted Horse observed. "That's good for us. The Pawnees won't see us."

"You forget," Three Toes said, sighing. "We saw their fires."

"My brother won't walk beside any fire," Painted Horse boasted. "No, the fire won't matter."

Three Toes didn't argue. Instead he concentrated his gaze on the darkness and tried to detect the slightest movement or the faintest sound. Finally he heard a dull thump. Then a second. Shortly, River Hawk emerged from the darkness, dragging two young Pawnees. Their wrists and legs were bound in rawhide strips, and cloth gags plugged their mouths. To add to their misery, the Hawk had cut away their breech-clouts, leaving them bare below the waist.

Three Toes gazed into the terrified eyes of the young Pawnees. They were perhaps a hair older than he, but not much.

"Come," River Hawk said, motioning Three Toes on. "Bring the ponies."

"What about them?" Three Toes asked, pointing to the captured guards.

"We could scalp them," Painted Horse suggested. "Or maybe cut some pieces off them?"

"Yes," the Hawk agreed. "I understand Pawnee liver is tasty."

Painted Horse repeated the remarks in the Pawnee tongue, and the two captives squirmed in a frantic effort to free themselves.

"They have suffered enough," Three Toes observed. "Or will when their fathers discover we've taken the ponies."

"Yes," River Hawk agreed. "We should hurry and take the horses, though, before the enemy discovers their guards are gone."

Three Toes led the ponies to where Pony Leg and Wary Dog waited. Pony Leg then waved his companions along the flanks of the grazing horses.

"Urge them westward along the river," the Leg explained to each in turn. "Be as quiet as possible. It would be best for us to remain undiscovered until we are past the next ridge. That way we can run the ponies in the shallows and conceal our trail."

"Protect our camp," Three Toes whispered.

"That's important," Pony Leg agreed. "Too often our warriors have failed to protect the defenseless ones. It's a heavy obligation. One you, too, must honor, *Na tsin' os ta*."

"I will," Three Toes promised.

They then set the herd into motion. Three Toes smiled as the fine Pawnee mounts trotted along. He sang softly to them whenever they appeared eager to break away. Later, when they passed the ridge, he galloped alongside the largest stallions, urging them westward.

They rode and rode that night. Three Toes ached with the pounding, and even his leathery thighs began to burn. Once daylight painted the eastern horizon amber, Pony Leg led the way into the low hills beyond the wagon road.

"Fifty horses!" he called to his companions. "Fifty! Wary Dog, your eyes are keen but your counting's not."

Three Toes laughed at the astonished Dog. Fifty, he had counted. The young *Tsis tsis tas* raiders drove closer to a hundred animals toward their camp.

"We're rich men!" River Hawk howled. "Rich!"

"Now you can invite a maiden to share your lodge, *Nah nih*," Painted Horse told his brother.

"You, too, Uncle!" Three Toes called to Pony Leg.

"If you think you can find one," River Hawk taunted his friend.

"With this many ponies you can buy five wives!" Three Toes exclaimed.

"One is enough if it's the right one," Pony Leg insisted. "And I think I know such a girl."

"He knows several," River Hawk announced. "But most are too smart to walk the river trail with an old man of twenty-two summers."

The raiders laughed and shouted and sang the remainder of the morning as they hurried homeward. Only when they approached the camp did Pony Leg gallop ahead to share his news. Wary Dog then hung back, keeping a watch for Pawnee pursuers. None came, though. Or if they did, they walked. Pony Leg had taken all their horses.

3

Not all the people were happy when they saw what the horse stealers had done. Some of the treaty chiefs complained that the young men had broken the agreement.

"Where were these arrow-stealing Pawnees?" Two Claws asked. "In our country, hunting Bull Buffalo. We didn't kill them. They should invite their relations to a feast to celebrate."

If the chiefs viewed the raid with concern, the young men flocked to Pony Leg's side.

"Brother, you have struck the old enemy hard," Black Kettle, the young *Wu ta piu* leader, declared.

When the warriors gathered in council, Pony Leg, River Hawk, and Wary Dog related their versions of the raid. When the others learned of the trick played on the Pawnee pony boys, everyone had a good laugh.

As for Three Toes, his age-mates regarded him with new respect.

"There he goes," they whispered whenever he passed. "The horse stealer. It's said all he has to do is call and the ponies follow."

"You have found power," Two Claws declared when he found Three Toes alone beside Fat River.

"It's found me," Three Toes replied. "I don't understand, but it appears I can talk to horses."

"To their spirits," the medicine chief explained. "Do they touch you?"

"Not physically, Uncle, but they seem to make their feelings known."

"Yes, that's how it was with me. Tell me, little frog, do your dreams tell you anything?"

"No," Three Toes answered. "I see things, but none of it makes any sense."

"No spirit creatures speak in them?"

"No."

"That will come later, then. When *Heammawihio* chooses to give you understanding, He will. Now you must listen and wait. Those are hard things to do when you're young, but have patience. Come to me when your sleep's disturbed. We'll talk. Maybe then you can see what it is that the spirits wish to tell you."

"You're certain they want to talk to me?"

"Yes," the old man said, laughing. "I knew that the day the *Wihio* trap stole your toes. I saw it in your suffering. Look here," Two Claws added, opening his shirt so that the boy could see the numerous scars that marked the flesh. "Each mark reminds me of suffering. Each time I've bled so that the people might escape some peril. No man attains power without suffering, and those who suffer often frequently find the greatest power."

Three Toes felt a chill seize him. Was that his future? In time would he know the sharp pain of another knife? Would he sacrifice additional flesh?

"Some men choose to walk the sacred path," Two Claws whispered. "For others, there was never any choice. Our feet are placed on the trail, and all we can do is walk it."

Three Toes scowled. The words froze his heart, but he knew the old man was right. Words could lie. The somber truth etched into Two Claws's forehead and the deep glow within his eyes could not.

"The dreams will come," Two Claws whispered. "You can only wait. Come and sit beside my fire then, and we can talk."

"I will, Uncle," Three Toes pledged.

The dreams were a long time coming. That summer Three Toes worked the ten ponies Pony Leg assigned as a proper share of the stolen Pawnee herd and readied himself for Man's Road. Daily he felt his cheeks for the first hint of hairs, but they, too, seemed intent on keeping him waiting.

"Next summer we'll ride together to hunt Bull Buffalo," Painted Horse told him. "You won't remain a boy much longer."

It seemed long to Three Toes, though.

That winter the snows came early. Whole mountains of white powder choked the skies and started the starving early. The fall buffalo hunting had been poor, and many among the scattered *Tsis tsis tas* camps were hungry.

"*Ne' hyo*, the helpless ones are suffering," Three Toes told Swift Antelope. "We have to find something for them to eat."

"Yes," the Antelope agreed.

But although hunters set off into the snowdrifts

daily, they returned cold and empty-handed. The *Omissis* hunters found an occasional rabbit. Nothing more.

Three Toes watched as one by one the camp dogs vanished. Then the people began killing ponies to eat. Pony Leg, who had become wealthy in horses, offered three animals to feed the children. Three Toes couldn't find it within himself to sacrifice one of his own ponies. They had each become as friends. Finally the wailing of the babies overwhelmed him, though, and he handed over a black mare with a splash of white across her face.

"She has a bad foot," Three Toes told his father. "I spoke with her, and she said she was prepared to give herself up."

"It's a hard thing to do," Swift Antelope observed. "A man's horses are his life."

"A man has to make sacrifices, though, doesn't he, *Ne' hyo*?" Three Toes asked.

"Often," the Antelope admitted.

As day followed day, the *Omissis* pony herd dwindled. Some men slaughtered their animals. Other horses, finding scant grass to chew, thinned past hope and collapsed in the snowdrifts. They were too thin to offer much nourishment.

"Something has to be done!" Pony Leg insisted. He and the other young men organized themselves into bands and headed out in search of game. They killed a solitary deer. Only that. Meted out among the band's many families, the venison lasted only a single day.

Three Toes tried to bear the suffering. He watched quietly the pain that flooded the eyes of parents when they set a child on its burial scaffold. He avoided the haunting eyes of his age-mates whenever they lost a younger brother or sister. Finally it overpowered him, though. He made his way to the medicine lodge and stood outside, making his presence known by stomping his feet on the frozen ground.

"He expected you, little one," Broken Shell said, emerging from the lodge. "Go in and sit with him. I am finished."

Three Toes hesitated. The Shell, for all his charms and curing knowledge, was as thin and brokenhearted as anyone in the camp. Perhaps more so.

"Come inside, frog," Two Claws called from the medicine lodge, and the boy turned away from Broken Shell in order to enter the lodge.

"The Shell . . ." Three Toes began as he closed the heavy buffalo-hide flap of the lodge.

"He mourns the children," Two Claws explained. "He has prayed with many fathers and mothers. Charms cannot stop this starving, though. A dreamer's needed."

"You've had a vision?"

"My eyes are clouded with old age now, frog," the old man explained. "It's for someone else to do."

"I've tried to see something in my dreams, but mostly I see wolves and eagles. Mountains and rivers."

"It's not always easy to understand what the spirits tell us," Two Claws explained. "I spoke to you before about it."

"You said to come when the dreams arrive. They haven't."

"You came anyway."

"You don't have to dream to hear the helpless ones crying. You have power, Two Claws. Why can't you stop this starving?"

"I haven't seen a path through this darkness."

"Maybe there isn't one."

"Have you sought one then?"

"No," Three Toes confessed. "I've walked the hills until my toes became numb. I'm too small."

"You won't find the answers there," the old man said, pointing toward the outside. "The truth lies here, inside," he added, placing a weathered hand on Three Toes's chest.

"Help me find it, Uncle."

"I will," Two Claws said, sighing. "It requires suffering, though. Pain. Are you prepared for that?"

"If it will stop the starving, I can bear it."

"No one can be certain what the spirits will tell you, little frog. There may be no end to the starving."

"I have to try, though, don't I?" Three Toes asked.

Two Claws nodded. He then motioned for the boy to sit beside the fire. Two Claws drew out a pipe and performed the ritual prayers. After offering tobacco to *Heammawihio* and the sacred directions, the old man began singing. Three Toes recognized only a few of the words. It was an old *Suhtai* chant, and he joined in awkwardly. They sang it three times. Then Two Claws removed his shirt. Three Toes removed his as well. The medicine chief drew out a knife and cut small pieces from the flesh of his chest. The old man then placed the old flint-tipped knife in Three Toes's fingers.

"Make only shallow cuts and let the bleeding purify your spirit," Two Claws explained.

"How many times should I cut?" Three Toes asked.

"Five," Two Claws explained. "You have prayed to the sacred directions, and they will expect you to suffer."

"As will *Heammawihio*," Three Toes observed.

He hesitated a moment. The tight brown flesh was smooth, unmarked. He thought of the mangled foot, of the stares and whispers.

"It's a difficult choice," Two Claws whispered. "Once a man steps onto the sacred path, he cannot step aside. You're young. No one expects you to . . ."

"I do," Three Toes said, wincing as he cut his chest the first time. The sting lasted but a moment. Then he felt the warm trickle of liquid running down his chest onto his belly. He cut a second time on the opposite side. Then he made the other cuts. He hardly flinched the final time.

"Listen to the prayers and learn them," Two Claws instructed. "You will make them yourself soon."

Three Toes nodded. He felt small, inadequate. He could not imagine why the spirits would choose a boy to speak through when there were so many good, tall men among the people. It did little good to wonder, though. He trusted Two Claws, and he followed the old man's instructions. Whenever the bleeding slowed, Three Toes rocked back and forth so as to open the small wounds. The singing and the rocking, or perhaps the bleeding, had a strange effect. Three Toes saw the fire grow hazy. He began to lose his balance. Inside the fire he envisioned Bull Buffalo, charging out of the flames and into his soul. He wavered a moment and fell backward, into the soft buffalo hides Two Claws had placed in readiness there.

"*Heammawihio*, hold him close to your heart," Two Claws pleaded. "He is small, but his heart is strong. Give him the far-seeing eyes."

The words echoed through Three Toes's ears as if

from some distant land. He seemed to float through the clouds, out of the medicine lodge, and past the snow-cloaked hills and valleys beyond. It was a strange, unearthly sensation, and it both thrilled and terrified him. He knew the dream, at long last, was coming. Only part of him truly welcomed it. The rest longed for the warm comfort of his father's lodge, for the reassuring touch of his mother, and the security they had always provided. Three Toes realized that, too, was coming to an end.

He floated on a cloud for what seemed a long time. Finally he saw below him a narrow clearing. Bull Buffalo was there, painted white with snow.

"So, *Na tsin' os ta*, you would end the people's suffering," the great beast bellowed.

Three Toes found himself shrinking from the terrible beast's flared nostrils and icy breath. *Na tsin' os ta*, he said? Nephew?

"Yes, *Na khan*," the boy replied, using the appropriate response a *Tsis tsis tas* boy was expected to give to an honored elder. "I have suffered. Now I hope to understand. Help me to see the vision you've brought me."

Three Toes saw himself alone in that clearing, his bare legs knee-deep in the numbing snow. He wore only his breechclout, and the bitter wind tore at his flesh. He had a long bow of polished ash in his fingers. Just ahead, stumbling through the drifts, was the grandfather of all elks.

He reached for an arrow, but his fingers lost sensation. The scene became blurred, and he drifted back into an enveloping cloud. Suddenly there was only darkness. Cold, bitter darkness.

He awoke to find himself wrapped in buffalo hides

beside Two Claws's fire. The old medicine chief sat nearby, bathing the boy's face with a cool cloth.

"I dreamed," Three Toes whispered.

"I know," Two Claws said, smiling faintly. "The spirits came to you. You suffered and they came."

"It was Bull Buffalo. I saw him first in the fire. Then in the dream."

"He will visit you often now," Two Claws explained. "He will be your spirit guide. A man with power needs such a guide to help him find his way. For me it has always been the red-tailed hawk. For you, then, Bull Buffalo. Now, tell me what you saw."

Three Toes managed to rise to a sitting position. The hides slipped off his chest, revealing an odd whitish ointment painted atop the five cuts.

"Keep warm," the old man chided, wrapping a heavy hide around his young companion's narrow shoulders. "Your work is only beginning."

"I know," Three Toes said, sighing. "The hunting. It's for me to do, too."

"Slow down and tell it all," Two Claws urged. "I can help you make sense of it."

"Yes," Three Toes agreed. But in truth he had already begun to understand. He would find the elk in that narrow clearing, and it would sustain the helpless ones.

Two Claws listened intently while Three Toes recounted his odd experience. First he told of the flying. Then he described the clearing. Finally he told of facing the creature with the ash bow, of notching an arrow.

"It's the way our people hunted in the grandfathers' time," Two Claws explained. "A man approached a creature bared, fearless, using only his bow. Sweet

Medicine warned of adopting the *Wihio* weapons, and the old Arrow-keepers scolded the people about using iron knives and rifles."

"The *Wihio* guns can kill from far away," Three Toes observed.

"They take the heart from the hunter, though. Once a man bonded with his prey. He took life only after making the appropriate prayers. He never killed the young. He took only what he needed to fill his belly and cover his nakedness. Now see what's happened. Trappers have emptied our streams of beaver. The wagon people shoot buffalo calves to collect their hides and tails. And what of the *Tsis tsis tas*? Their children cry from hunger and wonder why their path has become so steep."

"I know what's to be done."

"You know such a clearing? You've seen it before?"

"No," Three Toes confessed. "But I remember the hills that led me there. I can return."

"First you must rest. Eat. Grow stronger. Then . . ."

"And if the children die while I'm resting?"

"You face a great challenge, Frog. You won't feed anyone if you die in the snow."

"No," Three Toes admitted. "I'll rest today. Tomorrow I'll hunt the elk."

It was an odd thing, that hunt. Even as Three Toes rested, word spread through the camp that the boy had dreamed of elk. Young men formed hunting bands and prepared to leave camp. Others made the old prayers or repaired weapons.

It was Pony Leg who greeted Three Toes the following morning. He brought with him a quiver of stone-tipped arrows and a fine bow of polished ash.

"I saw it in my dream," Three Toes explained as he accepted his uncle's gift.

"The arrows are from your father," Pony Leg explained.

"Is he coming?" the boy asked.

"I come instead, *Na tsin' os ta*. Swift Antelope said to tell you that his own father once used those arrows to bring down a bear that was troubling the camp. They are made in the old fashion."

"It's appropriate," Three Toes observed. "I'm to hunt in the old way. Alone."

"Your dream showed you that, too?"

"Yes."

"Even a boy beginning a spirit quest is allowed a watcher," Two Claws explained. "It should be an uncle. He should go along, Frog. Not to hunt, but to watch. You will also need help bringing the meat back to camp."

"There's another who has asked to come along," Pony Leg explained.

"*Ne' hyo*?" Three Toes asked.

"It's not a father's place to guide his son while there are uncles at hand," Pony Leg muttered. "I speak, I think, of a friend."

Three Toes stared at his uncle, awaiting an explanation. Instead a solemn boy of twelve winters opened the flap and stepped inside the medicine lodge.

"Otter?" Three Toes asked, confused. The boy had never been friendly. Sad, sullen, and all too often taunting, but never friendly.

"You killed a horse to feed my brothers," Otter explained. "I owe a debt. I should come with you."

Three Toes avoided the other boy.

"His father has died," Pony Leg explained. "He has a hard path to walk now."

"Then he should come along," Three Toes agreed. "Listen to my uncle and keep back. I have a trial to face. Afterward there will be game for your arrows, too."

"Arrows?" Otter asked. "I have my father's rifle."

"We will hunt in the old fashion," Pony Leg explained.

"It's what I saw in my dream," Three Toes added.

"I'll do what's required," Otter vowed.

"I haven't seen him shoot, *Na khan*, but he runs much better than I do," Three Toes noted.

"It's not running that's needed, though," Otter insisted. "I can pull a man's bow."

"You'll have your chance," Two Claws declared. "Sit. We'll smoke. Then you must make your hunt."

4

That same morning the three of them, Pony Leg, Three Toes, and Otter, set off into the frozen hills beyond the *Omissis* camp. Three Toes led the way through the deep drifts, relying on the dream to guide his feet. He could hear the heavy breathing of his companions, and he knew that they were feeling the sting of the cold. Otter in particular labored to keep pace.

It will get worse, Three Toes told himself. Ahead they would ceremonially strip down to their breech-clouts. Meanwhile the heavy buffalo and elk hide robes protected their flesh from the icy teeth of the biting wind. So long as he kept moving, his toes retained some sensation, but gradually a numbing weariness worked its way up his spine and across his shoulders.

Nothing is easy, Three Toes reminded himself. Bull Buffalo offered to end the starving, but he required additional suffering. Well, who better to suffer than a wifeless young man, a fatherless boy, and a one-footed stumbler?

Three Toes lost all notion of time and distance as he forced himself onward. Pony Leg remained alongside, but Otter fell farther behind. There seemed a great urgency to the task. Three Toes knew that if he hesitated, he would collapse into the snow and freeze to death.

Suddenly he heard a noise from the bare cottonwoods up ahead. It was a deep, resounding bellow. For just an instant he thought he spied Bull Buffalo. His feet found firmer ground, and he hurried ahead. At last he saw the clearing. The great elk waited there, standing watch over a harem of cows.

"*Heammawihio*, I am here," Three Toes sang. He added the old half-remembered *Suhtai* words of a warrior song as he shed his robes and pulled his heavy deerskin shirt over his bony shoulders. Pony Leg gathered the discarded hides and quietly waited for his nephew to continue. Three Toes tightened his bowstring and notched an arrow. Then he approached the bull elk.

"Grandfather, the time has come," Three Toes called. "I come to you in the old way, bare, with only my arrows. The helpless ones are starving. I ask your life, but I take it reluctantly, with reverence."

He stood a moment and let the words roll through the clearing. They echoed through his mind. He had not practiced what he would say. Instead the words seemed to flow out of him. The elk stirred a moment. He dipped his great antlered head and trudged forward.

Pony Leg began singing a warrior song as Three

Toes took aim. The elk continued until within a stone's throw of Three Toes before halting. The great beast then dipped his head as if to interpose his antlers between himself and the polished ash bow.

It's time, Three Toes told himself. He shivered as the wind clawed at his bare chest. Then he took a deep breath, released the air from his lungs, aimed toward the center of the great elk's chest, and released the arrow. It flew swiftly across the clearing and struck hard and deep. The elk stumbled and fell.

"Ayyyy!" Pony Leg howled.

Three Toes himself uttered no sound. Instead he silently spoke a prayer as he surged forward through the snow.

The other elk began moving away, and Three Toes notched a second arrow. He shot a second bull, ignored a cow, and killed a third bull. Pony Leg joined in the killing. Together they slew five animals, enough for the purpose at hand.

As Pony Leg made the throat cuts to allow the blood to drain from the carcasses, Three Toes hurriedly dressed himself. His flesh was turning bluish white, and he had difficulty drinking in the icy air. Only when he managed to catch his breath did he glance around for Otter.

"*Na khan*, where is he?" Three Toes called.

Pony Leg turned, studied the clearing, and sighed.

"Maybe he went back to bring the others," Three Toes suggested. Parties of young men were following with horses on which to pack the meat.

"I'll look for him," Pony Leg declared.

"No, that's for me to do," Three Toes insisted. "This is my hunt."

"Be careful," Pony Leg urged.

Three Toes tried to smile a reply. Careful? Hadn't he just set out into the snows with only a bow and seven arrows? Guided by a dream!

Three Toes retraced his steps through the snow. It was easy enough to do. The trail they had torn through the frozen oceans would remain clear until the next snowfall. He walked cautiously, calling out for Otter. Finally he reached a point where a separate trail split off from the other.

"Otter?" Three Toes called.

Marching into the deep forest, following the path cut by Otter through the drifts, Three Toes grew ever wearier. At times he wanted to rest, but he recalled the stories of warriors found frozen in the snows. He had to keep moving. At last he came to a slight rise. Just ahead the snow was disturbed. Three Toes spied a smear of red, and a chill flooded his insides.

"Brother, wait!" Otter called.

Three Toes tried to step back, but he was suddenly confronted by a pair of ravenous dogs. They bared their teeth and approached slowly, cautiously. The animals had somehow escaped from the camp, but they, too, were starving. Hunger had driven off their natural wariness of humans, and the dogs continued to close on Three Toes. He managed to shake off his elk robe, string his bow, and notch an arrow before the first one could charge. He shot it through the side, and the creature whimpered as it died.

The second animal was the larger. It had waited for its companion to move. Then as Three Toes fired an arrow, the other dog raced forward. As it leaped toward Three Toes's throat, the boy managed to raise his bow and deliver a glancing blow. The weight of the dog threw Three Toes back into the snow, though, and the bow flew from his hands. The dog regained its feet and began a second charge. That was when Otter arrived. With a fierce howl that resounded across half the world Otter shot a solitary arrow past Three Toes that pierced the dog's vitals. A second arrow finished the creature.

"I came to rescue you," Three Toes explained as Otter helped him from the snow.

"You did," Otter replied. "I became lost. Snow-blind. Then the dogs came, forcing me into the branches of that tree," he added, indicating a nearby cottonwood. "I would have frozen there."

"So we rescued each other," Three Toes observed.

"It's a good way to begin a friendship," Otter said, clasping Three Toes's wrists. "You found the elk?"

"Yes," Three Toes replied. "We killed five."

"The starving's over then."

"For now," Three Toes said, sighing. "We'll have to make other hunts."

"We will," Otter vowed. "You and I."

Three Toes read new confidence in his companion's eyes. Somehow he knew Otter was right.

As the starving faded into memory, and the sun again warmed the plains, the country began to green. Snows melted, and rivers thawed. The *Tsis tsis tas* met to remake the world and organize the summer buffalo hunt.

For Three Toes it proved to be a remembered time. Chin hairs had finally arrived, and Pony Leg showed him how to pluck them. Afterward the boy departed his father's lodge to join the other young men.

"I'm going out to scout Bull Buffalo," Pony Leg explained as Three Legs helped ready his uncle's horses. "We'll need to provide much meat. The people are still hungry from the winter's starving, and it's necessary to fatten the children."

"Yes, *Na khan*," Three Toes agreed. "We need to dry enough to last this year, too."

"We'll do better."

"I hope so," Three Toes said, gazing hopefully into his uncle's eyes. "Maybe if there were more of us hunting."

"Yes, good men have died," Pony Leg observed. "Some of the people had trouble with the Pawnees. Alights on the Cloud's dead. Many others."

"It's not because we stole the Pawnee ponies?" Three Toes asked.

"No, the Pawnees need no excuse for killing us. We're old enemies."

"*Na khan*, I'm taller now. You remember I killed three elk last winter."

"I remember," Pony Leg said, grinning.

"Don't you think I've earned the right to hunt Bull Buffalo?"

"No one's invited you then?" Pony Leg asked. "Ah, I thought for certain the Elks, or maybe . . ."

"No one's spoken to me, *Na khan*," Three Toes lamented. "It's not proper for me to ask to go, is it?"

"You should be invited. Still, you sleep in Young Man's Lodge now, and Two Claws says you have power. I suppose you could come along with me and the other scouts."

"Can I?"

Pony Leg cracked a smile. Then he began laughing.

"*Na khan*, were you going to ask me anyway?" Three Toes growled.

"I was asked to discuss the matter with you. Your father said you were ready, but I . . ."

"You what?" Three Toes asked.

"I thought perhaps you enjoyed watching the maidens at the river and wouldn't wish to leave their company."

"There will be time for them later," Three Toes declared. "After all, I don't expect to be an old man of twenty-five before I invite a woman to share my blanket."

"It's not the sharing of blankets that makes a man cautious," Pony Leg insisted. "It's the sharp tongues."

Three Toes only laughed. Not all the maidens had sharp tongues, after all.

That morning Three Toes followed Pony Leg to the scouts' camp north of Fat River. Five other young men waited there. Otter greeted Three Toes warmly, and the two of them spread their blankets beside a small fire.

"It will be good to have a brave heart nearby when we charge Bull Buffalo," Otter remarked.

"Buffalo are harder to fight than dogs," Three Toes warned.

"I hope there's more meat on them," Otter replied.

"More than on those two we killed last winter. A stick has that much meat."

In the days that followed, the two thirteen-year-olds formed a deep bond. If it were possible for two people born of different mothers to be brothers, then Otter and Three Toes had become just that. It wasn't unusual among the Lakotas for young men to become *kolas*—brother-friends. Both Otter and Three Toes had Lakota kinsmen, so they accepted the new relationship without ceremony or discussion.

"It's a good thing," Pony Leg told his nephew. "Otter's brothers are still small, and he lacked uncles or a father to hunt with."

"I don't have any brothers," Three Toes noted. "I can't expect my uncle to take me everywhere. We took enough Pawnee ponies for you to buy three wives."

"It's true," Pony Leg admitted. "After the hunting's finished, you can help me carve a courting flute."

The hunting had not yet even begun, though. Each soldier society sent parties of scouts out onto the buffalo range, but the Elk band led by Pony Leg had little success. From time to time he spotted other scouts, the Foxes and Crazy Dogs in particular, but Bull Buffalo eluded everyone. The scouts finally turned back to seek the aid of medicine prayers. Two Claws sponsored a feast, and the men fasted and prayed. Finally the old medicine chief suggested a new direction.

"There are Pawnees out there," Black Kettle pointed out.

"Good," Wary Dog declared. "We can hunt Bull Buffalo and steal more Pawnee ponies. It will be a good summer."

"The Pawnees have many new *Wihio* rifles," Two Claws warned. "They killed many of our people last summer up north. Feed the helpless ones before considering any war councils."

"Yes," Black Kettle agreed. "We must watch our camps, too."

"You stay back and watch the lodges," Yellow Nose suggested. "I have dead relatives to avenge. If we see Pawnees, I'll carry a pipe."

"Not until the hunting's finished," Two Claws scolded. "Hunger and sickness have killed more of us than all the Pawnees that ever lived could manage."

Three Toes took the old man's words to heart, as did Black Kettle and many of the leaders of the soldier bands. Some did not, though. Pony Leg worried no one was looking after the helpless ones, and Three Toes noticed that the Elk scouts hung back more and more often.

"*Na khan*, the best way to protect the camps is to find Bull Buffalo," Three Toes finally argued. "We have to make the hunt before we find the Pawnees."

"I know," Pony Leg agreed.

"We'll go ahead," Otter volunteered. "Three Toes and I. He sees things in his dreams. Maybe we can find a herd."

"We'll stay together," Pony Leg insisted. "It's important that when we find a herd, men can ride back and summon the other hunters. Others have to stay and watch the animals."

"Still, it wouldn't hurt to invite a dream," Otter suggested.

"No," Three Toes agreed.

The Elk scouts continued riding east and north. Three Toes rode with his uncle and Otter. At night, though, Three Toes ignored food and only drank a little water. He dragged his blankets a short distance from the others and performed the old *Suhtai* prayers Two Claws had taught him. The first night, hunger and exhaustion brought on a deep, untroubled sleep. The second night Three Toes cut his flesh and added new, personal prayers.

"*Heammawihio*, look down and see your suffering people," Three Toes pleaded. "Protect us from our enemies. Guide us to good hunting."

Three Toes also prayed silently to Bull Buffalo, hoping to receive a vision. It came that very night.

It was different from the other in every way. There was no flying, and the landscape was completely familiar. In a valley not far from Fat River, near the *Wihio* wagon road, a great herd of buffalo chewed the summer prairie grasses. Three Toes found himself creeping toward a low rise, bow in hand.

"Give me your children, Uncle," he called to Bull Buffalo. "The helpless ones are hungry. We come in the old way, with honor and respect. Our hearts are heavy with the killing we must do."

Bull Buffalo then emerged from the dark dust that rose from the herd, nodded his great ponderous head, and mournfully sang a song with odd, half-understood words.

"Yes," Three Toes said, rising and facing the great herd bare-chested. The wind seemed to claw at his flesh, and the hair flew back from his forehead. Bull Buffalo turned and shook the very earth as he charged. Three Toes waited silently as the spirit creature's horns pierced his chest. Then he awoke.

"Three Toes?" Otter said, crawling over beside his brother-friend.

"I know where the buffalo will be," he whispered. "Tomorrow we'll find success."

Three Toes slept the remainder of that night. The next morning he prepared a pipe. The scouts smoked and sang old warrior songs. Then Three Toes spoke of the dream.

"I know that place, too," Wary Dog said, sighing. "*Wihio* wagon people camp there. The Pawnees ride that country, too. You're certain we have to go there?"

"No," Three Toes replied. "But my dream showed me buffalo there."

"His dreams," Painted Horse muttered.

"He saw the elk," Otter reminded the others. "Follow him and we'll see buffalo."

"What choice is there?" Pony Leg asked. "If we don't begin the hunting soon, we can't hope to complete it before our enemies. If they strike when the men are still in the hunting camps, the helpless ones will be at risk. We have to go."

"Yes," Wary Dog admitted. "But we should be careful."

Three Toes thought that, too. There was an unseen, unspoken sense of danger in the dream, and he told Pony Leg of it.

"We'll take precautions," Pony Leg promised. "First we have to find the herd."

That didn't prove difficult, though. The animals were spread out along the wagon road, exactly where Three Toes had seen them. Pony Leg quickly sent riders to summon the others. He, Three Toes, and Otter remained behind to watch the buffalo. Only when the other hunters arrived did the chiefs organize the hunt.

Three Toes and Otter met with the *Himoweyuhkis*, the Elks. Pony Leg had escorted the brother-friends to the council fire. With Otter and Three Toes on either elbow, Pony Leg sat among the Elks. Two Claws performed the pipe ceremony, and the Elks sang the old warrior prayers. When they finished, the men set off to make their own preparations. Some tied charms in their hair or painted themselves.

"It's time," Pony Leg announced.

The honor of riding ahead to strike the first blow had been given the Elks, and Pony Leg suggested it was appropriate that the young friends who had first sighted the herd go first. Otter had allowed Pony Leg to paint his chest, but Three Toes had refused.

"I'm going as in the dream," Three Toes explained. "Unadorned, carrying my bow and stone-tipped arrows."

Some of the older men laughed at the notion of a boy trying to slay a bull buffalo with stone-tipped arrows.

"Get yourself a good rifle from the traders," Yellow Nose suggested.

"No," Three Toes said, scowling. "I'll never have any power using *Wihio* weapons."

"He sees things," Otter explained, and the others merely grinned.

Once the hunting began, no one laughed. Three Toes made the first charge. He turned the herd and raced alongside the lead bull, counting coup on the rampaging beast with the tip of his bow. He then notched an arrow and shot a single arrow through the animal's heart.

Otter went next. He, too, carried stone-tipped arrows. He hated the notion that Three Toes could manage something he could not, so he charged the first bull to emerge from the leaderless herd, tapped its side with his bow, and then fired an arrow into its side. The bull ignored the first arrow, so Otter shot a second and a third. Finally the bull collapsed.

As the others closed in and began their own killing, an odd thing happened. Three Toes had dismounted and was making the required throat cut to drain the blood from his dead bull. The herd suddenly reversed its path and thundered directly toward him.

"Ayyyy!" Pony Leg shouted, turning his pony in an

effort to rescue his helpless nephew. The herd blunted his charge, though.

Three Toes never flinched. Instead of running, he stood behind the slain bull and began singing the words of the song from his dream. The singing appeared to transfix the other hunters, and when Two Claws heard the words, he froze in disbelief.

As for the buffalo, whether it was the singing or the sight of their fallen brother, they parted as they approached Three Toes and raced past, leaving him unharmed except for a world of swallowed dust. As the air cleared, the other *Tsis tsis tas* saw with relief that their young dreamer remained unhurt.

"Ayyyy!" Pony Leg howled. "He's a brave heart!"

"Yes," Two Claws echoed. "That and more."

5

As the hunt concluded, Three Toes found reason to hope for better days. The people had plenty of meat, and the women began sewing hides into new lodges.

"It's a good thing you've done, *Naha'*," Swift Antelope observed. "I'm proud to see a son of mine understanding the obligations a *Tsis tsis tas* man accepts."

Others among the *Omissis* and even some of the other bands also recognized Three Toes. Sometimes it was only a gesture, or perhaps an invitation to smoke. Other days an important man would appear in the morning, when the younger men were swimming, and join Three Toes and Otter.

"It's good that the people have strong young men in their camps," Black Kettle, the *Wu ta piu* chief, declared. "Difficult days are coming. We'll need you."

"Difficult days?" Three Toes asked. "I hoped the hard times were in the past."

"No, there's no end to them," the Kettle insisted. "No end."

Three Toes was still pondering the Kettle's sobering words that evening when Pony Leg called to him.

"*Na tsin' os ta*, someone's looking for you," the Leg announced.

"Someone?" Three Toes asked. "For me?"

At that same instant four hands grabbed him from behind, threw a hide over his head, and dragged him from Young Man's Lodge.

At another time, on another day, Three Toes might have been afraid. That night he was pleased. For days he had watched as the various soldier societies had abducted young prospects from the camp circle. He hoped it was now his turn to be introduced to the mysteries of the Elks. His father and uncle rode with the Elks, and he had gone with their scouts to hunt Bull Buffalo. If it was as he expected, he would finally be one of them.

In spite of the darkness, the rude slaps from his abductors, and an odd sense of bewilderment, Three Toes managed to keep his feet as he stumbled along. At last his guards slowed his progress. He could hear the noise of older men laughing a short distance away. When he recognized Swift Antelope's voice, Three Toes sighed. Surely it was the Elks.

A rough voice then called out a challenge, and Three Toes waited for his escorts to reply. They had seemingly vanished, though. Heavy footsteps approached. Hands tore away the hide, and large eyes stared angrily at Three Toes's confused face.

"Do you have business with us?" Wary Dog demanded.

"I . . . don't know," Three Toes replied. "Some men . . . brought me here."

"You can't come among Elk warriors like that," the Dog declared scornfully. "Wearing a boy's shirt! Frayed moccasins!"

"I didn't know . . ." Three Toes tried to explain. At that moment the two escorts reappeared, dragging a second young man to the Elk council.

"It's no excuse," River Hawk, the other council guard, grumbled. "Who sponsors this thing?"

"I sponsor him," Pony Leg announced as he marched out from behind the other abducted youngster. "And the other one, too, Brother. They're brother-friends, like we are ourselves. It's right they should come here together."

Otter managed to cast off the hide covering his face, and Three Toes directed a slight nod of recognition toward his friend.

"You'll have fewer horses tomorrow," Wary Dog observed.

"I'm rich in horses," Pony Leg boasted. "We Elks grow fewer, though. It's necessary for us to invite good men to join us."

"Yes," River Hawk agreed. "Bring them among us, but first make them ready."

Pony Leg muttered a reply. The others then walked on toward the fire.

"I have better clothes to wear," Three Toes said as Pony Leg pulled the worn deerskin shirt off his nephew's back.

"These are all I have," Otter said, sighing.

"Take off everything but your breechclout," Pony Leg instructed.

"Ah, I understand," Three Toes said, slipping off

his weathered moccasins. "We should go bare before the others."

"Modestly," Otter added. "Like you hunted Bull Buffalo, Brother."

"That's right," Pony Leg replied. "Later, when we celebrate, you'll receive better things to wear."

Three Toes sensed Otter's relief, and he gripped his young companion's wrist.

"Now listen," Pony Leg urged. "Approach silently, and listen to what you're told. Be respectful. I'll do what's needed. All you have to do is wait and watch and listen."

"Yes, *Na khan*," Three Toes agreed.

"I'll do it," Otter added.

The two thirteen-year-olds then followed Pony Leg through an opening in the circle of Elks that led to a great blazing fire. Three Toes noted that the Elks wore their best clothing. Those entitled had tied coup feathers in their hair, and the soldier chiefs wore their down-feather headdresses. Among the *Tsis tsis tas* Elks there were four lances, and three of the lance carriers sat at that council. A tall man of thirty-five or so, wearing blue paint on his chest and a bonnet of twenty feathers atop his head, stood in front of the fire, gazing seriously at his encircling companions.

"Blue Racer," Pony Leg called, halting Three Toes and Otter with a motion of one hand. "Here are the young men I spoke of. They've hunted Bull Buffalo and provided meat for the helpless ones. We should ask them to join us."

"Is there anyone else with something good to say?" the Racer asked.

"I will," Wary Dog said, rising from his place well back from the fire. "These young men rode with us to the hunt and counted coup on Bull Buffalo. They rode in the old manner, even as they stand before you now, bare, humble."

"Are they named?" Blue Racer asked.

"This first one's Otter," Pony Leg explained. "The man who was his father also wore that name. He was a good hunter and a fine fighter against the Pawnees and Crows. The *Wihio* sickness killed him."

"Your father was a Crazy Dog," Blue Racer recalled. "You come among us today to be our brother. Do you want to be *Himoweyuhkis*?"

"Yes," Otter declared, stiffening his spine so as to appear taller. "I've not had a man to guide my feet onto Man's Road, but I know that I won't ever be far from the Sacred Path if I follow Three Toes."

"What name is this?" Blue Racer asked, frowning. "No name for an Elk, surely."

"It's a worthless name," Pony Leg said, reaching down and scooping a bit of dirt in his fingers. "I'm his uncle, and I speak for him today. He has no use for such a bad-heart name and throws it to the wind."

Pony Leg turned his hand over, letting the dirt blow away in the light breeze.

"It was never a good name," Swift Antelope said, rising. He carried three brightly painted sticks in his left hand. He walked halfway around the circle, passing one stick at a time to some young man in need of horses. The sticks would later be exchanged for ponies.

"He should have a better one," Two Claws argued.

Finally a white-haired old man rose and smiled at the nameless youngster standing before the Elk chief.

"I heard you shot a big bull with flint-tipped arrows," he shouted. "Did you sing the old prayers?"

"I did," the nameless one answered.

"Ayyyy! It's good to hunt!" the old man cried. "In my father's time, we had no *Wihio* iron or lead bullets. We had to rely on *Heammawihio*, to make the proper preparations and sing the brave-heart songs. Now we're nothing. If we are to be great again, it will require sacrifices."

"Yes," others agreed.

"I'm old and withered like a spring plum left to greet winter. Once I ran like the antelope and led all the Elks after Bull Buffalo."

"We remember," Two Claws said somberly.

"Now the years on my winter count are nearly finished. I won't see New Life Lodge erected again. No, my days are over. Hanging Road's close. Once everyone knew Buffalo Horn. Now those who watched the sun of my youth rise are all on the other side. Ayyyy! Brave heart, take my name. Do it honor, as the dead sons who should have taken it from me might have, had they lived."

"Grandfather, I will," the new Buffalo Horn vowed.

"It's a good name," Swift Antelope observed as he handed two other sticks to the old man. "Uncle, you've honored my son. Let me honor you."

"That's best done by giving the horses to others," the old man insisted, rejecting the gift. "There are poor women among the people. Make the gift to them, saying it comes from Dirt in the Wind. That's me."

Buffalo Horn thought to offer the old warrior some comfort, but when he read the proud fire in those ancient eyes, he swallowed his words. The naming made the old Elk as proud as Swift Antelope and Pony Leg.

"Now it's time to speak to you two," Blue Racer said, motioning the brother-friends closer. "You come to us like children, naked and small. There's no room in our council for faint hearts or saplings. To be *Himoweyuhkis* is to serve the people. The Elks ride into the heart of danger, and they stand to fight when the helpless ones are in danger."

"Ayyyy!" the Elks shouted. "We stand."

"To be one of us requires a heavy obligation. Suffering. Even sacrifice. Can you accept such burdens?

"I have already," Buffalo Horn said, touching the scars on his chest.

"And you?" Blue Racer asked, turning to Otter.

"I go where he leads," Otter explained. "It's brought suffering before."

"Then join us, little brothers," Blue Racer said, embracing them both. He then waved to Wary Dog. The Dog presented a beaded doeskin pouch from which Blue Racer drew out two pieces of elk horn carved like small snakes. The tops were blue and the bottoms yellow, much as a blue racer is. The horns were notched, and a piece of bone was attached so that when the horn was shaken, it made a hard rattling sound.

"Shake them," Blue Racer said, and the Elk council was suddenly drowned in a cascade of peculiar rattling.

"I take my name from the no-legged that the ancient ones asked for power," Blue Racer explained. "It helps us to remember that even the greatest among us is nothing."

"Yes," Buffalo Horn whispered.

"Others have brought things to give you, and to give others in your name," Blue Racer explained. "Greet them as brothers now. A man may see a father die," he added, clamping his hands firmly onto Otter's thin shoulders, "but an Elk is never without relations. We are *Himoweyuhkis*! Ayyyy!"

The others echoed the cry. Soon men were bringing fine shirts and good moccasins of stout buffalo hide to the young men. The families of the Elks soon joined the celebration, and everyone had plenty to eat. Later they danced and sang and recalled brave-heart deeds.

Buffalo Horn felt aglow. He observed the respectful attitudes of the other Elks, and even though he tried to remain modest as he accepted their many fine presents, he couldn't help marveling at his good fortune.

The time for celebrating proved short, though. Even as the soldier societies were conducting their dances, young men from the northern bands arrived in the *Omissis* camp carrying a pipe.

"Bad hearts," Two Claws grumbled when Buffalo Horn walked with him beside the river. "They followed Alights on the Cloud in his fight against the Pawnees. While the men were needed in the hunting camps, these fools rode to war. They broke the power of *Mahuts*, and the helpless ones went hungry. Good men who tried to lead them died."

"Yellow Nose said they fought to keep the camps safe," Buffalo Horn noted. "I think maybe our raid on their horses stirred them against us. We concealed our trail, and the Pawnees found the northern people instead."

"It wasn't Pawnees riding anywhere," Two Claws assured the Horn. "No, our people were hungry to strike the Pawnee camps. They're rich in horses, and they have new, far-firing guns. It was greed that led our young men astray, and even a great man like Alights on the Cloud lacked the power to prevent many from dying."

"You counsel against going then?"

"We remain weak," Two Claws observed. "If the Pawnees leave us alone, we shouldn't bother them."

"Some will go."

"Yes, too many. It's always easy to carry a pipe and stir up the young men. It's why there are so few of us left."

"If you were younger, you'd go yourself," Buffalo Horn declared. "I saw your eyes when the old Elks recounted your many coups."

"Fighting was different then," the old man said, staring off northward into the distant hills. "Men challenged each other, and no one did much killing. Even the arrow-stealing Pawnees counted coups. Now they've got *Wihio* rifles. They've lost the old ways. They give their women to the bluecoat soldiers, and their sons will never find Man's Road."

"It's a sad thought, even for Pawnees."

"Yes, soon the old ways will be dead. It won't be so hard on old men like me. Our walk is coming to an end."

"You can still pull a bow, Uncle," Buffalo Horn argued. "I saw you drop a bull."

"I won't hunt next summer," Two Claws insisted. "Soon younger men will conduct the healing cures. Already others have to do the dreaming."

"We still need a guiding hand."

"Soon you'll have to find your own way."

Two Claws continued to warn against joining Yellow Nose's raiders, but his voice could hardly be heard among the shouting and singing of younger men determined to avenge the death of Alights on the Cloud and other brave men killed the previous summer by the Pawnees. Tall Bull and Little Wolf had brought in many men from the northern bands. Yellow Nose had sent relatives out to smoke with the Lakotas and Arapahoes. Soon men from those other bands arrived. A few Crows even rode up, but they didn't stay long. Two bands of Kiowas came up from the south, though, and they remained.

"It's said the Pawnees have many good ponies," the Kiowa chief, Satanta, said. "I wouldn't like to burden a neighbor with such a difficult task as taking all those horses himself."

Finally Wood and Two Thighs, chiefs of the Fox soldiers, led a scouting party out in search of the Pawnees.

"Doesn't anybody know the proper way to organize a war party?" Blue Racer cried when he learned of the scouts' departure. "No one should leave before we meet and discuss what's to be done. We've neglected the prayers. No one's invited a vision. Are we *Tsis tsis tas*? Have we forgotten everything?"

The Elks held considerable power among the *Omissis* after finding the buffalo herd that summer, but the Foxes and Crazy Dogs held sway among the other bands. Yellow Nose, glad to have so many men in his party, ignored the warnings of older men.

"We've done all those things before, and the enemy has run us," he complained. "I have my own power. It will bring us success."

Buffalo Horn didn't expect the Elks to join the fight, but River Hawk's young cousins carried a pipe to his lodge, and he couldn't refuse them.

"I'm also obligated to go," Pony Leg told Buffalo

Horn. "Stay and watch over the helpless ones, *Na tsin' os ta*. I don't think we're all coming home from this raid."

"It's for me to follow you," the Horn insisted. "You let me ride to hunt Bull Buffalo. I'm an Elk, aren't I? If my brothers are going to fight the Pawnees, I should come, too."

Other Elks also smoked the war pipe. Wary Dog and Painted Horse agreed to go. Even Otter touched his lips to the pipe.

"We can't stay behind," Otter explained when Buffalo Horn asked his reasons for going. "If there's hard fighting to be done, shouldn't we do it? And if the Pawnees are as careless with their ponies as when you stole their herd, I may be able to get some good ones. A young man needs ponies if he's to get a wife."

"What use do you have for a wife?"

"I'm not a pony boy any longer," Otter insisted.

"Have you chosen someone then?" Buffalo Horn asked.

"No, but the Kiowas have some pretty women."

"I don't speak the Kiowa language. Do you?"

"No," Otter confessed. "Maybe there's an Arapaho who knows our words."

"Maybe," Buffalo Horn said, warily eyeing his brother-friend. "I could speak with my Oglala cousin, Curly. Maybe he knows of a Lakota who wouldn't mind a young husband. Still, what will you do with your mother? You know the Lakota laws. No Lakota would accept a husband's mother into her camp."

"My brothers are getting bigger. I've been in Young Man's Lodge a long time now. It's their obligation to . . ."

"No, it's yours," the Horn insisted.

"You're right," Otter admitted. "There's time to court, though. I wouldn't want to make a mistake. I should start now so that I am good at it when I'm ready. I wouldn't want to be as old as Pony Leg before walking the river with a girl."

"He walks with plenty of them," Buffalo Horn said, frowning. "I think he'll ask my father or perhaps me to take some ponies to Iron Belt. Summer Cherry Maiden's caught his eye."

"The *Wu ta piu?*"

"There's no one else that looks like her," the Horn said, hiding the smile creeping onto his lips.

"She's one of Black Kettle's relations, I think."

"A cousin. It's a good family, and they'll welcome a man of good reputation like my uncle."

"She's got sisters, too," Otter pointed out. "When we have our Pawnee ponies, we can . . ."

"You intend to go then?"

"Brother, we can't stay behind," Otter said, growing serious. "If your dreams lead you away from it, I'll follow. If they don't, we should join the other young men."

"Many are staying behind."

"I'm not wrinkled with age like Dirt in the Wind or Two Claws. Blue Racer cautions against leaving the camps defenseless, but he's going to lead the Elks. Black Kettle's been chosen to carry *Mahuts.*"

"The Arrow-keeper has been consulted then?" Buffalo Horn asked.

"*Issiwin* will be there, too. The Medicine Hat and Sacred Arrows, the two great medicine powers of our people, will be together. Ayyyy! This will be a remembered fight! We can't stay behind."

"I suppose not," Buffalo Horn said, sighing. "I think I'll speak to Two Claws about it, though."

"Search your dreams for a vision," Otter urged. "If there's danger, we should warn our brothers. We must be with them, though."

6

When the scouts returned with word of the Pawnees, the *Omissis* camp, like that of the other bands, was astir with war preparations. Wood and Two Thighs led the way into camp, and their companions howled like wolves to mark the success of the venture. War Bonnet spoke first, but he left the task of informing the people to Wood.

"We've found them," Wood explained. "Many Pawnees. Many horses! Ayyyy! We'll strike them a hard blow. We'll be rich in ponies!"

The *Omissis* warriors shouted their approval. Then Wood urged them to ready their horses and weapons.

"We're close, brothers," he added. "We can't throw away this chance to avenge Alights on the Cloud."

Soon men, young and old, scrambled to assemble their weapons and ready their ponies. The soldier bands gathered to make plans while the scouts satisfied their hunger.

Buffalo Horn noticed Two Claws's concern, but the excitement pulsing through the Horn's veins overwhelmed his natural caution. Even Wary Dog, never one to take chances, was caught up in the madness. As Wood and Two Thighs headed away to alert the other camps, Buffalo Horn turned to Pony Leg.

"What's to be done, *Na khan*?" the young man asked.

"Much," Pony Leg explained. "Find Otter and bring six ponies from our herd. I'll show you how to paint them."

"There's no time to waste," River Hawk added. "We have to strike the enemy before he discovers our own camps."

"No!" Two Claws cried. "There are preparations to make."

"You trust your old *Suhtai* prayers," a young Fox named Red Root muttered. "We have power. Our chiefs have dreamed, and we carry *Mahuts* and *Issiwin*. They will blind the Arrow-stealers, and we'll kill them!"

"It's like before," Dirt in the Wind lamented. "The young ones never listen, never learn."

"Their hearts are brave, and their bow arms are strong," Two Claws observed. "They don't understand that courage isn't enough."

Blue Racer was also concerned.

"Brothers, we'll make proper preparations!" he shouted, waving his *Himoweyuhkis* lance. "We'll do what's required, even if the others don't."

But as it turned out, the experienced chiefs insisted on observing the proper ceremonies. Each of the soldier societies formed into a line. The soldier bands then paraded in impressive columns around the as-sembled camps. The Foxes and Crazy Dogs went first. They were followed by the Crooked Lances and Bow-strings. Lakota, Arapaho, and Kiowa parties also joined in. The Elks, perhaps because so many of their best men seemed unconvinced of the success of the raid, were placed at the end of the column.

It was a sight Buffalo Horn would long remember. Pony Leg and River Hawk had instructed their young companions in the proper manner of painting war po-nies, and the older Elks had then painted the brother-friends' faces. The long column of brightly painted men, many of them adorned with eagle and hawk feathers, and all dressed in their finest clothes, was an imposing sight. Each band sang its own warrior songs, and the very earth seemed to tremble before the as-sembled might of the people.

When the ceremony was over, Buffalo Horn and Otter were among the younger men who drove the war ponies to the stream to wash away the war paint.

"We have prayers to make," Pony Leg had ex-plained. "We can't break the paint's medicine power by returning the ponies to the herd."

Afterward the young men bathed themselves. Their elders joined them later, for the face paint also had to be washed away. Buffalo Horn did not fully under-stand the preparations, but he trusted his uncle and the older men to know what needed doing. Two Claws joined them at the river, and the sight of the medicine chief calmed any remaining misgivings.

The following day the camps began moving east. Chiefs met in council to plan the raid while young men helped maintain order within the temporary camps. There were straying children to mind and hunting to do, so Buffalo Horn kept busy. Later he found time to chase Otter's younger brothers, Snow Bear, Rabbit Foot, and Sparrow, through a nearby stream. It was an unequal contest. The boys ran with the wind, and, skilled horseman that he was, the Horn remained a three-toed runner.

Another time he would have remained at the river, swimming or wrestling, but Pony Leg rode by with a summons to the Elk council.

"There are things to do," the Leg announced.

"Yes, *Na khan*," Buffalo Horn replied. "We're coming."

Otter nodded and waved his brothers back toward the makeshift camp. The two young Elks then dressed themselves and joined the council.

Blue Racer addressed the Elks in a serious manner that evening. He recounted other fights and reminded them of the recent deaths of Alights on the Cloud and other good men.

"Remember your obligations," he urged as he passed a pipe among the younger Elks. "Safeguard your brothers. Protect the helpless ones."

"We're Elks!" the others shouted. "We'll do it."

"Will we be last again?" Painted Horse asked.

"Other soldier bands will lead the raid," Blue Racer replied. "The Foxes and Crazy Dogs are scouting the enemy."

"There will be no one left to fight," Painted Horse complained.

"There will be plenty of fighting," Wary Dog snapped. "It's good we're hanging back. We can protect the camps."

"It's the Pawnees who will need protecting!" Painted Horse exclaimed. "We'll steal their ponies and kill their men."

"We have ponies enough," Blue Racer grumbled.

"We'll take their women, too!" the Horse boasted. "Ayyyy! A Pawnee woman will give me strong sons!"

"You have to catch her first, *See' was' sin mit*," Wary Dog said, laughing. "Even then it's far from easy."

The others continued their boasting, but after a time Buffalo Horn no longer paid any attention. His ears followed his eyes to where old Dirt in the Wind was sitting beside Two Claws. Both old men's faces revealed concern.

Buffalo Horn tried to forget that concern as the others boasted of coups counted against other Pawnee bands. He tried to recall the ease with which he and Pony Leg had taken the Pawnee ponies. Even amidst the war songs the Horn could not entirely erase a creeping sense of danger.

"Remember," Blue Racer said as the embers of the fire began to dim. "We're Elks. We are obliged to protect the helpless ones."

"He'll hold us back," Painted Horse grumbled when the younger men rose to leave the council.

"A chief never forces a man to do anything," old Dirt in the Wind growled. "It's for you to decide when to ride, when to fight, and when to stand."

"Is that how you came to be so old?" the Horse asked. "Choosing wisely when to ride?"

The old man merely laughed. He tore open his shirt so that his companions could see the many scars etched in his leathery flesh. There were the long, jagged marks left by lance and knife. Two smaller holes left by lead balls marked his hip and side. Higher up, on each side of his breastbone, were twin scars that marked him as a man who had suffered in New Life Lodge for the welfare of all the people.

"Ask me about it when you have something other than air between your legs," Dirt in the Wind growled. "Count coup. Then come and ask me how I have won *Heammawihio*'s favor!"

Buffalo Horn tried not to grin.

"And you!" Dirt added, clamping an amazingly strong hand onto the Horn's bare shoulder. "You carry a good name. Show you deserve it."

"I will," Buffalo Horn vowed.

"Remember your obligation," Dirt in the Wind urged. "You're *Himoweyuhkis*. Show the others what an Elk can do!"

"We will," Otter pledged, leading his brother-friend away.

"He may not have many teeth left," Buffalo Horn whispered when they were out of hearing, "but he's lost nothing of real importance."

"No," Otter agreed. "I thought Painted Horse was going to wet himself."

"With nothing between his legs?" the Horn asked. "How could he manage it?"

The brother-friends shared a brief laugh. Then they hurried to their sleeping pallets to find an uneasy rest.

Weary as he was, Buffalo Horn expected a vision of the approaching fight to come to him that night. Instead the morning sun stirred him from his slumbers. He shook off the temptation to crawl beneath the warm buffalo and elk hides. The eastern sky was already striped with reds and yellows, and men were painting their horses and preparing their bows and lances.

"Up," the Horn said, nudging Otter with one toe. "The Elks are already gathering."

"What?" Otter asked, throwing off his covering and jumping to his feet.

"We don't want to be left behind, do we?" Buffalo Horn asked.

Otter frowned and helped the Horn rise. They rolled up their belongings and dressed themselves. Otter wore a fine shirt of elk hide with strips of weasel fur attached. Buffalo Horn chose only his breechclout.

"It's good for a man to ride modestly to war," he said.

"Why not go naked?" Otter asked, laughing. "If a Pawnee kills me, I want him to think he's killed someone of importance."

"You won't die," Buffalo Horn insisted. "Your brothers need your hands to help them onto Man's Road."

"I'm not certain which would be less pleasant," Otter muttered, "climbing Hanging Road or staying behind to look after them."

Buffalo Horn started to reply. Then he stopped. Instead he pointed past a slight rise to where Snow Bear and Rabbit Foot were leading four horses from the pony herd. It was a difficult task for the youngsters. Snow Bear had only seen nine summers, and Rabbit Foot was even younger.

"Yes," Otter said, sighing. "Brothers can't help being burdens, but they have good hearts."

"We'll take them to the Elk council when it's time," Buffalo Horn vowed. "Until then we'll guard the camp from Pawnee arrows."

"We'll run the Arrow-stealers from this good country."

The boys brought more than ponies that morning. Otter's mother had prepared food. The brother-friends ate hungrily while Otter's brothers saddled the ponies. By then Swift Antelope and Pony Leg had joined them.

"I see you've already eaten," the Antelope said. "You can put this food pouch away for later needs."

"We came to help with the paint," Pony Leg explained.

"Thank you, *Na khan*," Buffalo Horn said. "*Ne' hyo*," he added, turning to his father, "it's generous of my mother to think of our needs. We'll kill a deer for her later."

"You've brought much meat into our camp," Swift Antelope said. "At times like these, the people must see to the needs of the younger men. Now, we'll make you ready for the Pawnees."

Swift Antelope drew out a small pouch and began to wet a reddish root. At that moment Two Claws walked over, and the Antelope stepped back.

"This is for me to do," Two Claws argued. "I have pounded a bull's horn and made medicine. You, Frog, will wear it to fight the unseen ones."

"The unseen ones?" Otter asked nervously.

"It's never difficult to fight what you see," Two Claws explained. "It's always the ones you don't see that can kill you."

"You've had a dream?" Buffalo Horn asked.

"I've seen nothing," the old man replied. "As I said, it's the unseen things you should fear."

"He's right," Swift Antelope agreed. "Let him paint you, *Naha'*. His power will protect you."

"No, it holds no such power," Two Claws said as he smeared a whitish powder onto Buffalo Horn's chest. The paint gave the skin an eerie, unsettling appearance, and the medicine chief likewise painted the young man's face.

"If it won't protect me, why are you painting me?" Buffalo Horn asked.

"It's a blinding paint," Two Claws explained. "Good for confusing the unseen. It can only protect a man who sees his danger, though."

"Paint me, too," Otter said, baring his chest.

"It's good that you have a brother-friend today," Two Claws said, painting red lightning bolts through the white circle occupying Buffalo Horn's chest. "I'll make you twins. That should confuse the unseen ones even more."

"Uncle, what danger have you seen?" Pony Leg asked, sitting at the medicine chief's feet. "We bring *Mahuts* and *Issiwin* to bend the Pawnee bullets."

"You need not fear Pawnees," Two Claws whispered. "Look for the unseen, though. Be prudent."

"What worries you so, old friend?" Swift Antelope asked.

"I look into the hungry eyes of the Fox chiefs," Two Claws explained. "They're eager to kill. Killing should always be done slow, with reluctance. These men who hurry into it break the medicine power and bring our people into danger. Ah! They've often done it. Why are we so few? Because the bad hearts are so many!"

"We'll protect the camps," Pony Leg promised. "Blue Racer has vowed to do it, and when did he ever break a promise?"

"It's good to hear," Two Claws admitted, "but it may not be enough. Watch the young men. Too often they've ridden ahead and broken the medicine power."

"We'll do what we can," Swift Antelope declared.

"Yes, I know," the old man muttered. "I couldn't stop them, either."

The Elks nevertheless did more than most to insure the safety of the camp. Swift Antelope personally escorted the women and children to a low hill where they were shielded from view. Up ahead the Arrowkeeper was unwrapping *Mahuts*, the four Sacred Arrows given to the *Tsis tsis tas* by Sweet Medicine in the grandfathers' time. Nearby *Issiwin*, the Sacred Medicine Hat, emerged from its protective covering.

Long Chin stepped forward and accepted the obligation of wearing *Issiwin*. Black Kettle tied the Arrows to his lance. While the chiefs were occupied with the medicine preparations, a small band led by Big Head slipped away and hurried toward the Pawnee camp. They were hungry to avenge their relatives killed the previous summer and eager to count the first coup.

"Look," Otter grumbled, pointing to the dust thrown up by Big Head's pony.

"Two Claws saw it," Buffalo Horn noted. "They've gone on ahead. The medicine power's broken."

Many of the older men began to urge caution, and some set their weapons aside, unwilling to fight without the protection of *Issiwin* and *Mahuts*. The young men were hot to fight the Pawnees, though, and they hurried on to where Wood had spied the camp. Buffalo Horn followed his uncle in that same direction, but they halted in disappointment at the sight of two hundred *Tsis tsis tas* warriors overrunning the abandoned Pawnee camping place.

The war party began breaking up into twos and threes, searching for signs of Pawnees. Then Big Head came up, waving a scalp and shouting that he had struck the enemy.

The Crazy Dogs made a charge on the Pawnees, but the old enemy had witnessed Big Head's charge. Soon the women and children were back among the lodges, and the pony herd was shielded by a high bank on the far side of a muddy stream. The Pawnee warriors formed a line there, fighting not as individuals on horseback but in the *Wihio* manner, using their good guns to kill from far away.

Blue Racer held the Elks back as other bands made futile charges against the well-protected Pawnees. The few young men who reached the stream safely had their horses killed. Some of the warriors screamed out in pain as Pawnee bullets struck them. Others managed to crawl back to safety, only shaken.

"When will they learn?" Swift Antelope howled as Big Head and his companions turned to ride away. They had counted two coups and killed a man, but the success that might have avenged Alights on the Cloud and made the people rich in horses had been thrown away.

"Look there!" Red Root called out, and Buffalo Horn turned to study a swirl of dust approaching from the north. A party of men carrying long-barreled rifles hurried up toward the milling *Tsis tsis tas* and Lakota horsemen. Arapahoes and Kiowas were only just arriving then, and they turned to face the newcomers.

"We know these people!" a Kiowa chief called. "They're *Savane'*, our friends."

The *Savane'* apparently failed to recognize the Kiowas, though. They began firing their rifles, and a Kiowa was the first to fall.

"Ayyyy!" the Kiowas screamed, turning away from the furious fire of the newcomers. The Crazy Dogs and Foxes, once so eager to fight, fled from the enemy. A Bowstring chief thought he could form a line, but it melted away as the howling *Savane'* grew closer.

"Run!" Red Root shouted, and the Elks, too, took flight.

It was a shameful thing, running away like that, and it tore at Buffalo Horn's soul. He ground his teeth and turned his horse back toward the enemy. Otter also turned. Old Dirt in the Wind saw the youngsters and gave a shout. He, too, stopped.

A band of Arapahoes was taking a stand on a nearby hill, and Blue Racer waved his lance in that direction. Then, shaking his Elk rattle, he called on his brothers to run no farther.

"What's your hurry, brothers?" the Racer shouted. "Have you got something better to do? Let's stay for a time. We have an enemy to run."

"Ayyyy!" River Hawk screamed as he and Pony Leg swung around to face the charging *Savane'*. "Nothing lives long."

"Only the earth and the mountains," others chanted, finishing the words of the *Tsis tsis tas* death song.

For a time the opposing horsemen exchanged insults and managed disorganized charges. Then two *Savane'* dismounted in order to steady their aim. With a fierce shout a Kiowa chief, Satanta, raced toward the first one and lanced him through the chest. Blue Racer, singing the ancient *Suhtai* words of a war song, charged the second *Savane'*, drove a lance through his side, and stepped down to take a scalp.

"Ayyyy!" the Elks cried. "He leads us."

The Elks then mounted a new charge. Buffalo Horn and Otter were on the right end of the line as it hurried toward the confused *Savane'*. The enemy didn't run, though. They began swinging their rifles and firing at the approaching enemy. First one and then another Elk fell. More than ten died in that charge alone, and four Arapahoes fell as well. Buffalo Horn felt the fiery heat of *Savane'* lead whine past his left shoulder. Then something struck his saddle. Another bullet tore a piece from his left ear.

"Ayyyy!" he shouted, rising up in his saddle as he steadied his bow. Just ahead a young *Savane'* raised his rifle. Buffalo Horn loosed his arrow, and it struck the *Savane'* in the throat, killing him. A second *Savane'* moved over to shield his companion's body, and Buffalo Horn slapped the second man's chest with the tip of the ash bow. The second *Savane'* gasped and stared with wide eyes as he fell from his horse, stunned.

"I was first!" Buffalo Horn shouted, celebrating his coup.

Otter jumped down and prepared to cut away the slain man's hair, but three *Savane'* spotted him and galloped over.

"No!" Buffalo Horn cried, notching a new arrow and firing it into the *Savane'* leader's knee. The wounded man grunted and turned away. Old Dirt in the Wind shot an arrow into the chest of the second man's horse, and the others retreated.

"Brother, leave it," Buffalo Horn pleaded as Otter cut at the dead man's forelock.

"I'm almost finished," Otter replied, tearing at the hair and scalp.

By then the stunned *Savane'* had regained his senses

and turned toward Otter. Buffalo Horn leaped from his horse and drove the enemy into the ground.

"Kill him!" Red Root urged, galloping up to collect his companions' ponies.

Buffalo Horn drew his knife, but when he turned to finish the *Savane'*, he stopped. The youthful face that stared up at him was no older than his own, but the eyes showed no fear. Indeed this boy had turned back to protect the body of his brother.

"I see," Buffalo Horn said, frowning. "You and me, we're the same."

The Horn counted a second coup on the *Savane'* youngster, then clubbed him with the elkhorn handle of his knife.

"You didn't kill him?" Otter called as he finally ripped the forelock from the dead enemy.

"A man can't kill himself, can he?" the Horn asked.

Otter gazed up, confused, but accepted it as another of his brother-friend's peculiarities.

The *Savane'* had collected themselves, and now they began a fresh attack. Red Root, who was minding the horses, saw the new danger and rode off, taking the ponies along.

"Root!" Buffalo Horn shouted in disbelief.

"He's gone," Otter said, dashing over and grabbing an abandoned *Savane'* pony. The one animal would never allow both of them to get away, though, and neither would mount first.

"Here, take mine!" a familiar voice shouted.

Buffalo Horn turned in time to see Dirt in the Wind climb down from his pony. The animal was a good, sound horse, and Otter took it in hand.

"We can't leave you, Uncle," Buffalo Horn argued.

"I have one foot on Hanging Road already," the old

man said, lifting his shirt to reveal a bloody wound in the right side. "Use your medicine paint to disappear. Leave me to find a remembered death."

"No," the Horn argued. "You've given me enough."

"Sing of me sometime," the old warrior said as he pointed his lance at the approaching enemy. "Leave!"

"Ayyyy!" Buffalo Horn shouted, mounting the *Savane'* pony. "He's *Himoweyuhkis*. He stands!"

"Nothing lives long!" the old man said, smiling faintly at the departing youngsters.

As they rode away Buffalo Horn looked back twice. The first time he saw Dirt's lance knock a tall *Savane'* with many feathers in his hair from his horse. The second time he saw a circle of men cutting the life from the old Elk.

"He's shown us all what an Elk does," Blue Racer told them later. "He was always the first to stand and fight."

"He gave us our lives," Buffalo Horn said, dropping his gaze.

"Next time we'll do the rescuing," Otter vowed.

7

It was a remembered fight, but Buffalo Horn found no joy in his part of it. Old Dirt in the Wind, the name-giver, was dead. Many other good men had also fallen. Women wept, and little children ran around searching for their dead fathers and uncles.

"You knew what would happen," Buffalo Horn told Two Claws. "You didn't stop it!"

"No one listens to me now," the medicine man growled. "Ears are wasted on them. They taste the sweetness of their dreams and close their eyes to danger. Who discovered the enemy? Who struck the first blow? Those same ones were the first to run away. Who stood to meet the enemy? Who protected the helpless ones in our camps? It's like before. We mourn them while the boasters tie feathers in their hair and recount brave-heart deeds performed against pony boys and women!"

"Someone should do something about it," the Horn declared.

"You can't scold a dog for barking," Two Claws observed.

"Even if he reveals your camp to the enemy?"

"He's only walking his path, frog," the old man argued. "It's for you and your brother Elks to guard against the consequences. You accept the obligations of men while the others play boys' games. Be careful. There are always some of us who will get the rest killed."

It was all too true. As Buffalo Horn and Otter grew taller, they tried to honor their obligations. It proved difficult. *Wihio* diggers had found the precious yellow powder they called gold in the streams and mountains beyond the Red Shield River country, and swarms of them flooded the good buffalo range on their way to the gold country. Soon trouble broke out between the newcomers and the *Tsis tsis tas*. An army of bluecoats arrived, and the people decided to fight them.

Fire and Ice, two medicine chiefs, provided strong protection for the soldier bands. Buffalo Horn and Otter had ridden out with confidence that the *Wihio* bullets would find no target. Trickster must have whispered a warning to Sumner, the bluecoat soldier-chief, though. The *Wihio* horsemen set aside their rifles and took up their long iron knives instead. The sight of those weapons, against which Fire and Ice offered no protection, stunned the warriors. Even the Elks fled. The *Tsis tsis tas* ran away, leaving many good horses behind. The *Wihio* soldiers captured some of the camps, too, and that next winter was a time of great suffering.

The lost battle broke the hearts of many old men. Worse, fevers brought by the *Wihio* diggers hung over the plains like a dark cloud, and a forest of burial scaffolds rose from the hillsides above the people's winter camps. Those were the most difficult days of Buffalo Horn's young life. He watched, helpless, as Swift Antelope took to his lodge, weak with fever. Gooseberry Woman tried to provide the healing cure, but she only brought the sickness into her own weakened body.

"What's to be done?" the Horn had asked Two Claws.

"Prepare them a resting place," the old man had replied. "Their hard walk is almost over."

Otter helped erect the scaffolds. They built three. His mother was also sick, and the brother-friends brought all three of their parents into the hills above Fat River.

"A day has died with them," Otter observed as he stood with his smaller brothers.

"Yes," Buffalo Horn agreed. "They are gone, but we are the continuing. It's for us to do the hard things now."

The Horn found it difficult to accept a world without Swift Antelope.

"I've seen eighteen summers now," Buffalo Horn told Otter. "I've taken horses, counted coup, and even killed the enemy. I always knew that whatever happened, *Ne' hyo* would be nearby, watching. Now there's nobody."

"Pony Leg?" Otter asked.

"My uncle's with the *Wu ta piu*, courting Summer Cherry Maiden. It's time he took a wife. The people will need his strong sons to lead them."

"We also should find wives," Otter said.

"Soon enough," Buffalo Horn said, eyeing Snow Bear, Rabbit Foot, and Sparrow. "First we have brothers to guide onto Man's Road."

"Yes," Otter agreed.

Buffalo Horn knew what his brother-friend was thinking. Would Otter and the Horn be strong enough, wise enough, to guide anyone? Only *Heammawihio* could know.

"We'll do it," the Horn whispered. "There's nobody else."

As the sun rose and set those next three days, Buffalo Horn's words took on a greater truth. He and Otter conducted the mourning prayers and made the required giveaways. There was no one else to do that, either. They broke down the lodges that had sheltered them as boys and abandoned the comforting buffalo and elk robes that carried the remembered scents of their parents. It seemed that there was nothing left of the past!

Winter's end found Buffalo Horn a changed man. The good men he had relied upon as a boy were vanishing. One by one they climbed Hanging Road and left the cold heartless plain for younger men. Even Two Claws had grown faint of heart.

"It's time for me to join the grandfathers, Frog," he declared one morning when he joined Buffalo Horn, Otter, and the other young men at the river. "My flesh is shriveled with age, and my heart is broken with too much remembering."

"We need you," Buffalo Horn insisted.

"My dreams are empty," the old man replied. "Once I held great power in my hands. Now I've given it all away. There's nothing left. I have no sons to take me into the hills. My grandsons are among the Lakota. I ask a favor."

"I'll be your son, *Ne' hyo*," Buffalo Horn volunteered.

"I could ask no better," the medicine man said, sighing. "When I'm gone, make the giveaway. Keep nothing of mine. You'll be tempted, but don't hold my ghost here. You have enough to haunt you. Find a good woman. Bring children into your lodge. Their laughter makes a man strong enough to endure what's sure to come."

"What's that?" the Horn asked.

"Your dreams will show you," Two Claws observed. "Trust them. Find some good men to ride at your side. Remember the old ways, and be careful who rides at your back. You won't be harmed by any enemy you can see. Most of all, guard the helpless ones. I won't be here to do it, and the ones I once trusted to guard our camps have started the long walk up Hanging Road. I trust you. Promise me that you will do it."

"I will," Buffalo Horn vowed.

"I'll help him," Otter added.

"He'll need you," Two Claws said, turning toward Otter a moment. "A man of the people acquires enemies. Some will be envious. Others will be ashamed of their own weakness. No one is more dangerous than a weak heart. Watch them."

"We will," Otter promised.

"Don't linger long in this camp," Two Claws said, gazing at the few lodges that remained in the *Omissis* circle. "Find a good man to follow—one that has the heart to lead and the wisdom to see the dangers awaiting our people."

"I know such a man," the Horn said, clasping the old man's hands.

"There's another," Two Claws whispered. "Once before when you knew pain he saved you from the icy laughter of the *Wihio* trappers. Now he leads the *Wu ta piu*."

"Black Kettle," Otter noted.

"Your uncle is there already," Two Claws pointed out. "He's another good man. Perhaps four of you will be enough."

"Soon there will be more," Otter said, pointing to where his younger brothers were wrestling in the soft grass along the river's bank.

"More, yes," Two Claws said, shuddering. "And fewer."

The medicine chief stepped away and began removing his clothing. Buffalo Horn did likewise. The two were a contrast of age and experience. The old man's withered frame bore a lifetime of scars and suffering. Buffalo Horn's flesh remained taut, and his muscles surged with an eagerness to accept his weighty new responsibilities. Only the missing toes and the mutilated ear spoke of his troubled youth. And there were the faint lines left on his chest by his own knife.

It was strange how the chill waters of Fat River brought new life to Two Claws that morning. A hundred burdens seemed to drift away from the old man, and he laughed and swam with the boys. Otter and Buffalo Horn watched in disbelief as the wrinkled old man outraced Rabbit Foot to the far bank.

Four days later Two Claws closed his eyes a final time. Buffalo Horn did as the old man had instructed. The Horn spoke the required prayers, and Otter erected a scaffold near Swift Antelope's resting place.

The brother-friends placed the old medicine man there and then cut their already short hair even shorter. Snow Bear and Rabbit Foot, who had plucked their chins, also cut their hair in mourning. Only Sparrow, who had only walked the world ten summers, left his hair long. Otter considered it disrespectful for a boy so young to join in the ritual mourning of a nonrelation.

All the *Omissis* and some of the other bands as well joined in the required three days of mourning. For a brief time the small camp circle grew to its former size. Following the giveaway, the others departed to join their separate bands, though. Buffalo Horn and Otter also broke down their makeshift shelter and prepared to leave.

"You should stay," Blue Racer argued. "Our people need strong young men to hunt and gather ponies. Take some of Two Claws's possessions. We'll erect you a proper lodge."

"A man should take a wife first," Buffalo Horn pointed out. "I can't take anything from the giveaway. I promised that man that's gone now that I wouldn't."

"Then you have to honor your vow," Blue Racer observed glumly. "If you want to find a wife, though, there are maidens here in this camp. I would happily speak to their fathers for you. You only have to ask."

"It won't do," Otter grumbled. "I'm related to most of them, and Horn is related to others. I have to think of my brothers, too. Who would take them in? So many families are overburdened now. No, we should leave."

"Is that how a man of the people acts?" the Racer asked.

"It's not because we don't feel our obligations. The

old one urged it," Buffalo Horn said, sighing. "I see your needs, Uncle, but there's nothing we can do to lessen the burden."

"If he told you to leave, you have to do it," Blue Racer admitted. "I came to invite you to stay with me and smoke about the future, but there's no disputing things now. The old one had far-seeing eyes, as you yourself do, Horn. Go and find your path. When the Elks ride to hunt Bull Buffalo, though, we'll be glad to see you."

"It won't be long," Otter assured him. "Perhaps then we'll invite others to join us, too."

"We're few," Blue Racer said, following Otter's eyes to where Rabbit Foot was readying ponies. "We need strong hearts like your brothers."

"Then we'll hunt together when the grasses grow taller," Buffalo Horn declared. "Maybe the trouble will be over then. Some of the men have noticed camps of Kiowas and Arapahoes nearby. There will be too many for the bluecoats to bother."

"We were many before," Otter lamented. "And now? Every summer there are fewer of us and more of them."

"Yes," Blue Racer agreed. "It's hard to know what to do."

"We can only walk the world," Buffalo Horn observed. "We decide nothing. Only *Heammawihio* sees tomorrow."

"Yes, only He," the Racer agreed. "Be careful, brothers. I hate to think of some Pawnee wearing your hair."

"If one does, he will have to mourn many of his dead brothers," Otter insisted. "We're only going to ride to the *Wu ta piu* camps, though."

"They have some pretty maidens there," Blue Racer said, brightening. "Tell your uncle, Horn, I expect to hear he has sons soon."

"He will," Buffalo Horn replied. "Pony Leg has never been one to put off his obligations."

They all shared a laugh. Then Otter and Buffalo Horn finished packing up their belongings. Afterward the brother-friends and Otter's three younger brothers left the *Omissis* camp and rode eastward along Fat River. The five of them drove their thirty horses along and hoped for better days.

The sun rose and set twice before Buffalo Horn observed pony dung and horse tracks near Fat River.

"Our friends are near," Otter declared when he spied a broken arrow with *Tsis tsis tas* markings. "Maybe we should kill a deer and take it along to them."

"It's a good idea," Buffalo Horn agreed. "Have you seen anything to shoot? It's still cool. Bull Buffalo will be farther south. We won't find deer in open country. If you want, we can hunt in the thickets."

"It would be better to find the camp first," Otter said, sighing. "We wouldn't want to drag meat very far."

"*Nah nih*, Rabbit Foot and I could scout ahead," Snow Bear suggested. "Maybe we can find an elk."

"Horn?" Otter asked, turning nervously to his brother-friend.

"We haven't ridden this country since the snows began to melt," Buffalo Horn declared. "We should stay together. After we find the *Wu ta piu*, there will be plenty of time for hunting."

"Soon we'll hunt Bull Buffalo with the Elks," Otter added.

That seemed to ease some of the boys' disappointment. Otter turned his pony eastward and waved his brothers along.

The *Wu ta piu* winter camp spread in a ragged circle across three low hills overlooking the northern bank of Fat River. Buffalo Horn knew the site well. He had camped with his Lakota cousin Curly in those same hills, and the two had shot a large bull elk near the river one morning.

As the little party approached the camp, Buffalo Horn scowled. Where were the watchers? He saw only two boys minding a hundred horses. Were all the others asleep? Had the sickness struck down all the men?

"Wait here," the Horn told Otter. "I'll go ahead and see what's wrong."

Buffalo Horn nudged his pony into a trot and drew out his Elk rattle. He managed to alert one of the pony boys, but the other ignored the noise.

"Ayyyy!" Buffalo Horn screamed. "Is everyone dead? Are there no men to guard the helpless ones?"

The anger in his words surprised him. They also drew a response. A boy of twelve summers named Grouse appeared, notched an arrow, and pointed it at the noisy intruder.

"Have you brought us all these ponies?" the boy asked. "Can I have them if I kill you?"

"Do I resemble an Arrow-stealer?" Buffalo Horn shouted. "Have I cut the hair above my ears like a Crow? Maybe my skin has turned white and you imagine me a *Wihio*!"

"Put the bow away, Grouse," a voice boomed out from the cover of several willows. "He's no enemy."

"If I were, someone would be sorry to lose his horses," the Horn observed. "My brother-friend Otter, his brothers, and I have come to speak with my uncle, Pony Leg. We thought we would be welcome among the *Wu ta piu*, but we never expected to ride into a camp unseen."

"I saw you," the voice insisted. "Things aren't always what they appear to be."

The Horn glanced back at Otter, only to find his companions surrounded by twenty warriors carrying *Wihio* rifles or bows.

"I intended to trap a Pawnee, or maybe a *Savane'*," the voice continued. "I didn't know the noise that broke the harmony of my morning belonged to a three-toed frog!"

Buffalo Horn finally identified the voice. It was Black Kettle himself. The *Wu ta piu* chief stepped out from the willows and motioned for his visitor to dismount.

"Is Pony Leg with you?" the Horn asked.

"Hunting," Black Kettle explained. "He has a wife to provide for now. If you had come earlier, you might have danced at the wedding feast."

"I couldn't," Buffalo Horn explained. "I had a son's obligations."

"Swift Antelope would have been welcome."

"He that was my father is gone," the young man explained.

"Ah," Black Kettle said, frowning. "I understand why your hair's cut short. That bothered Grouse. He brought word to us that strange men were coming, but I told him it was only our *Omissis* relations. The one who was your mother?"

"Her, too," Buffalo Horn explained. "Our old friend who made medicine has also begun the long walk up Hanging Road."

"We are less, all of us, without them."

"The old one sent us to you. I hope you can find a place for us in Young Man's Lodge."

"The brothers, too?" Black Kettle asked.

"Otter's obligations are mine," the Horn explained. "We can hunt. We won't be a burden on the band, any of us."

"There's time to talk about it later," Black Kettle observed. "Leave your ponies to chew the soft river grass and come with me. My wife will cook something. We can hear your news, and you can hear ours."

"It's a good notion," Buffalo Horn agreed, waving Otter up the hill.

"I'll enjoy your company," the Kettle confessed. "Pony Leg and Summer Cherry Woman will steal you away when they learn of your arrival. First, though, I will hear what you want to say."

Buffalo Horn, Otter, Snow Bear, Rabbit Foot, and Sparrow shared the task of unsaddling the ponies and unpacking their belongings. Then the five young men entered the *Wu ta piu* camp circle and joined Black Kettle beside a small cooking fire. The Kettle's wife had boiled some elk meat, and she offered each of the visitors a good piece.

"You're all too thin," she complained.

"Winter's a starving time," Otter observed.

"Boys should have some fat on their bones," she grumbled, pinching Sparrow's side. "I would eat a dog before allowing him to grow so thin!"

"Be careful she doesn't cook you," Black Kettle warned. "She's tasted *Wihio* pig meat. A person who can stomach such an unnatural beast is certain to enjoy chewing a boy's rump."

Sparrow squirmed uncomfortably, but the woman just laughed.

"We had fever," Otter said, lowering his eyes. "I haven't protected my brothers as well as I should have, but . . ."

"There's no avoiding *Wihio* fevers," Black Kettle insisted. "We are fewer, too. Soon we'll fatten the young ones on roasted buffalo."

"Yes," Otter agreed. "Soon."

They then devoted themselves to eating. Buffalo Horn found the meat surprisingly tasty. The ride had seemed to empty his belly as well as his heart, and he ate hungrily. Afterward he spoke of the *Omissis* hardships and learned the *Wu ta piu* had also experienced sickness and death.

"Summer's coming now," Black Kettle observed. "We'll hunt and grow stronger. We've made medicine and invited dreams. Our trail won't be without danger, but if we remain within the harmony of the sacred hoop, we can expect better days."

"It's never an easy thing to do," Buffalo Horn pointed out, "but I've always struggled to do it. It's the *Wihio* who bring us trouble. How can we find peace when the crazy ones scar the land and shoot our young men?"

"It's a difficult task, I admit," Black Kettle said, staring hard into the fire. "Not so long ago I carried *Mahuts* against our enemies, the Pawnees and *Savane'*. When you were no bigger than a rolled elk hide, I killed *Wihio* trappers who harmed you. It didn't stop them from coming into our country. Nothing will. We have to treat with them and learn to walk the world in harmony in spite of them. I've been to talk to Trader Bent at his fort. There's talk of a new treaty council. Maybe we can make a better peace."

"With the *Wihio*?" Otter gasped.

"With everyone," Black Kettle explained. "I'm only a single voice among the chiefs, but I will lead my band away from war. I've smoked and dreamed, and I can find only death on the other trail. We must make peace."

"All of us?" Buffalo Horn asked.

"If those young ones are to grow as old as I am now, we must put aside our bad hearts and seek a new way," Black Kettle argued. "The *Wu ta piu* will do it. So long as you share that path, I welcome you. Stay. Hunt. We'll teach your brothers what they need to know. If you remain hungry for revenge, find another camp. I've seen too much death already, and I'm not yet an old man. I want to see grandsons swim Fat River. I'm hungry for laughter, not dying."

That evening Pony Leg returned to the *Wu ta piu* camp. He led a small band of hunters, and they brought three freshly killed deer with them. Buffalo Horn approached his uncle from the side, unseen.

"It's good the *Wu ta piu* have a man of the people with them," the Horn said when he reached his uncle. "Now the helpless ones can grow fat."

Pony Leg turned quickly, saw his nephew, and drew the young man close.

"*Na tsin' os ta*, you've grown tall!" Pony Leg exclaimed.

"Taller," Buffalo Horn argued. "Not so tall as he who was my father."

"Was?" the Leg asked. The smile faded from his face as he studied the sadness sweeping across Buffalo Horn's face. "He's started the long walk, then?"

"Yes," Buffalo Horn replied.

"And my sister?" Pony Leg cried.

"She who was my mother didn't wish to linger," the Horn told him. "We made the proper prayers and conducted the giveaway. Everything that should have been done was accomplished. Otter and I have brought his brothers here to learn what a man needs to know."

"And why have you come, *Na tsin' os ta*?"

"You taught me that an Elk should follow a good, wise man," Buffalo Horn noted. "My uncle's always been such a man."

"Black Kettle leads us," Pony Leg pointed out.

"He's also highly regarded, *Na khan*," the Horn declared. "Who else would I follow? Too many chiefs have led the people into danger and death. I'm tired of fighting. Black Kettle has far-seeing eyes."

"You have them yourself," Otter added.

"It isn't easy, following the Kettle," Pony Leg warned. "We kill no *Wihio*. When they come among us, bringing sickness and death, we don't raise our lances in anger. We're still alive, though. Others aren't."

"I promised to heed his admonitions," Buffalo Horn said, sighing. "If I can't, I'll leave."

"It's only proper," Pony Leg replied. "It's what a man of the people should do."

Buffalo Horn managed a faint smile of agreement. Then he began assisting the other men as they removed the meat bundles from the backs of Pony Leg's horses. The Leg himself made his way around the camp circle, distributing venison to hungry families. Later Otter and Snow Bear dragged a lodge skin across the camp and began erecting poles near Pony Leg's lodge.

"You can't camp here," Grouse growled when Buffalo Horn joined his brother-friend.

"It's appropriate," the Horn argued. "Pony Leg's my uncle."

"He's also my sister's husband," the boy declared. "If Black Kettle has invited you to camp with us, you should go to Young Man's Lodge."

"And where would they sleep there?" a slender young woman demanded to know. "You know too many are already there. Soon you'll want to go to Young Man's Lodge yourself. You'll be glad they're not there then."

Grouse glared at the woman, but Buffalo Horn smiled. He remembered Summer Cherry Woman from the times he had spied on the women carrying water along the river path.

"He's right about putting up a lodge, though," she added. "We don't have children yet. There's only Pony Leg, me, and my brother. The others have all started the long walk."

"Yes," Grouse grumbled. "We're fewer this summer."

"Few that we are, we shouldn't quarrel," Summer Cherry declared. "Grouse, greet Buffalo Horn as you would any relation."

"We share no blood," the youngster objected.

"The son I will bring into the world will call you uncle. He will know Horn as a cousin," she observed. "He'll be the blood link between you."

The boy remained sullen, and Buffalo Horn motioned for Otter to drag the lodge skin away.

"I didn't come here to disturb the harmony of the *Wu ta piu* camp," the Horn explained. "Otter and I will find another place."

"No," Pony Leg said, joining them. "Our lodge is big enough, and I welcome the noise of boys."

"Who am I then?" Grouse cried.

"You're far too serious to have ever been a boy," Pony Leg complained. "*Na tsin' os ta* and the others will teach you how to laugh again."

Grouse only muttered to himself and walked away.

"He worries you won't have time for him now, husband," Summer Cherry Woman told Pony Leg. "Go and tell him he can go with you to hunt Bull Buffalo."

"He's young," Pony Leg observed.

"I was young myself that first summer," Buffalo Horn pointed out. "When we approached the camp, others hid. He took up his bow to defend the camp."

Summer Cherry Woman nodded and pointed to where Grouse was sitting beside the river. "Go tell him," she whispered.

After Pony Leg departed, Buffalo Horn respectfully addressed his aunt.

"It might be better for us to camp elsewhere," he suggested. "It's not only me, you see. Otter, my brother-friend, is responsible for three brothers. With so many men, you may reconsider having sons."

"I had four brothers," she said, sighing. "Now there's only Grouse. Before I bring my first son into the world, you and the others will find wives."

"I may wait as long as my uncle," Buffalo Horn warned.

"Ah, he didn't wait long after visiting our band," she observed. "I'll find a wife for you, and another for Otter. When the time's appropriate, we'll even locate a companion for Grouse."

She spoke with a cheerfulness and confidence Buffalo Horn had considered lost to the *Tsis tsis tas*. He accepted her words for the truth they carried, and that same night he slept for the first time in the lodge of his uncle and aunt.

In the days that followed, Buffalo Horn found a degree of the peace he had sought for so long. Black Kettle and the other older *Wu ta piu* men maintained order in the camp and saw to the needs of the helpless ones. Pony Leg often led a band of younger men out to hunt. Horn and Otter often rode along, and most times Snow Bear, Rabbit Foot, Sparrow, and Grouse accompanied them. Rabbit Foot, who was a summer older than Grouse, soon befriended the younger boy, and the two of them began to ride and swim and wrestle together.

"They're much alike, those four," Pony Leg told Buffalo Horn as the *Wu ta piu* began breaking down their lodges for the move to Red Shield River. "After we remake the world, we should take those young men to hunt Bull Buffalo."

"Otter and I already promised his brothers," the Horn explained. "From the day their mother climbed Hanging Road, they have hurried their feet onto Man's Road."

"It shouldn't surprise anybody," Pony Leg observed. "You and Otter were impatient, too. Sparrow's still small, though."

"His brothers will watch over him," the Horn insisted, "the way you watched over me."

"I was never a very good watcher," Pony Leg muttered. "I didn't keep you from the *Wihio* traps. I didn't shield you from the *Savane'* bullets."

"*Heammawihio* determines a man's path, *Na khan*. Not you. Not me. You gave me the strength to endure the pain and the heart to take my stand. A nephew couldn't ask more."

"Sometimes, when I look out over this good land and see it changing, I wonder if either will be enough."

"They're all a man has," Buffalo Horn said, sighing. "They have to be."

It seemed to the Horn that summer that strength and courage and honor were once again enough. The *Wu ta piu* joined with the other bands to erect the New Life Lodge. Afterward he and Otter joined Blue Racer to scout Bull Buffalo. That summer Buffalo Horn sought no dream, for a large herd was nearby. The Elks, like most of the other soldier bands, found success. Much meat and many good hides were dragged to the main camps, and it seemed as if, for once, *Heammawihio* had given the *Tsis tsis tas* an easy path to walk.

It was only after the hunting was over that the dancing and celebrating began. Young men like Snow Bear and Rabbit Foot, who had counted coup on Bull Buffalo for the first time, joined the Elk council. The Elks also summoned Grouse, but the younger boy chose to join the Crazy Dogs instead.

"There are too many bad hearts in their council," Rabbit Foot had warned his friend. "Come with us instead."

"The Dogs will punish the *Wihio* for bringing death to our camps," Grouse grumbled. "I'll ride with them."

"His heart still aches for his mother and small brothers," Summer Cherry Woman told Buffalo Horn later. "He can't understand how anyone can find harmony when white men ride this country, killing and stealing."

"There's no understanding some things," the Horn noted. "You can only live with them or die."

It wasn't long after that conversation that Summer Cherry Woman invited Buffalo Horn and Otter to join her for a visit to her cousins' lodge. Their father, White Goose, was a *Wu ta piu* chief and a nephew of Black Kettle. His two daughters, Bright Swallow Maiden and Feather Dance Maiden, had become old enough to attract husbands, and even a blind man could see Summer Cherry's intention.

"We have brothers to lead onto Man's Road," Buffalo Horn had argued.

"Snow Bear and Rabbit Foot have joined the Elks," Otter pointed out. "Sparrow will soon be old enough to live with them in Young Man's Lodge. It's time we walk the river path, brother. A woman can chase away winter's chill."

"Too many maidens have no husband to provide for them," Summer Cherry Woman added. "It's not right that young men wealthy in horses should ignore them. You've been alone too long, Horn. You should open your heart and let someone inside."

Buffalo Horn started to object, but the conviction in her eyes silenced him. What could it hurt to meet these cousins? She was right about obligations. Wasn't he a man of the people? How long could he busy himself feeding the helpless? He would only help the people grow by inviting sons into the world.

After they had made their way halfway around the camp circle, Summer Cherry Woman stopped. She then approached a large, brightly painted lodge and called out to her uncle. White Goose greeted Summer

Cherry warmly. She then motioned Otter and Buffalo Horn nearer and introduced them to White Goose.

"I've heard of you," the chief said, clasping Buffalo Horn's wrists. "You killed three bulls with stone-tipped arrows. It's said that you carry power in your bow arm, that you know the old *Suhtai* songs, and that *Heammawihio* walks in your dreams."

"Who can say about such things?" the Horn replied.

White Goose smiled. He was obviously pleased at the remark.

"What about you?" White Goose added, turning to Otter. "You have only small brothers for family. Are you a dreamer, too?"

"I follow him," Otter said, stiffening. "My brothers and I ride and hunt with Horn. We trust him to know what to do."

"He and I fought the bluecoats," Buffalo Horn boasted. "When we fought the *Savane'*, others fled. We stood."

"I heard about it," White Goose said, nodding. "It's said you have good horses."

"The best the Pawnees could raise," the Horn said, grinning.

"Are they many?" the Goose asked.

"Thirty," Otter replied.

"Enough so that you can honor any man's daughter and still remain a wealthy man."

"Yes," Otter agreed. "And later we can always take more."

"There are few Pawnees nearby," White Goose observed. "Black Kettle isn't pleased when men steal from the *Wihio*."

"There are horses running free in this country,"

Buffalo Horn insisted. "I've captured them before. I can again. Now we have all we can watch. Later, if we need ponies, I can find others."

"You may need them," White Goose whispered. "I only have two daughters, and I prize them. I will need five good ponies for each of them."

"It's a high price," Otter said, scratching his ear. "I would have to see them first."

"The horses aren't all there is to our bargain," White Goose insisted. "I could never sell my daughters as some men do. You must court them, make them happy. Only then, when they agree, can you send someone to speak to me. Only then."

"I've never been one to break a pony's spirit," Buffalo Horn said, swallowing a trace of anger. "I speak to a pony's heart. Only when he agrees to carry me will I climb onto his back. I wouldn't want a woman who didn't want me."

"It's a good way to be," White Goose observed. "I'll ask my daughters to meet you."

"My brother and I think alike," Otter added. "But you should know I have younger brothers. I'm not as free of obligation as Horn."

"I know," the Goose admitted. "It's good you told me, though. It's always best to treat with honest men."

White Goose finally turned toward the lodge. He made only the slightest motion with one hand, and Summer Cherry Woman slipped through the lodge door. She returned with two slender young women.

"This is my cousin, Feather Dance Maiden," she told Otter. "She has walked the world sixteen summers. You might walk with her to the river."

White Goose nodded.

"I brought no blanket," Otter said, staring at his toes. "I forgot to carve a courting flute."

Feather Dance chuckled, and the Goose grinned.

"There's plenty of time for that later," White Goose insisted. "It's too hot to sit in a blanket anyway. Get acquainted. Pick some plums. Talk."

"Yes, *Ne' hyo*," Feather Dance replied obediently.

"Buffalo Horn, my nephew, this is my cousin, Bright Swallow Maiden," Summer Cherry Woman explained as the second young woman turned to greet the Horn.

"She's older by fourteen moons," White Goose whispered to Buffalo Horn. "She has a sharp tongue, but she cooks good food."

The Horn felt the woman's heavy gaze examining every inch of him, and he instinctively retreated a step. He couldn't help noticing, though, that Bright Swallow had a pleasant shape to look at and eyes as deep and thoughtful as anyone he'd ever known.

"Well?" White Goose asked.

"I don't have a flute, either," Buffalo Horn explained.

"Maybe you should walk past the camp toward the hills," Summer Cherry Woman suggested. "I believe you should leave the river walk to the others."

Buffalo Horn turned and caught a glimpse of Otter and Feather Dance. They seemed to merge into a single figure. The Horn envied his brother-friend's easy manner.

"I always prefer a walk in the hills," Bright Swallow declared. "On summer days there are always too many children running around the river."

"I like high places myself," Horn confessed.

"That's how it often is with medicine men," Bright

Swallow observed. "*Ne' hyo* walks into the hills every morning to greet the sun. When he's troubled, he seeks a dream up there."

"The spirits find a man more easily when he's in a lonely place."

"Do they find you often then?"

"Once," Buffalo Horn admitted. "I've had few dreams since joining the *Wu ta piu*."

"Since making the mourning prayers for those others?"

"Yes," he agreed.

"Have you invited a dream?"

"I've been busy," the Horn said, frowning. "Otter's brothers needed guiding, and . . ."

"*Ne' hyo* has always said that a man with power owes an obligation to his people. If *Heammawihio* favors you, you . . ."

"Favors me?" Buffalo Horn gasped. "Do I appear favored? I walk with a lame foot, and a piece of my ear's gone. Those good people I knew are gone."

"Look around you," she said. "Is anyone different? All the *Tsis tsis tas* suffer. Only a few can do anything about it."

"What do you think I should do?"

"Seek dreams. Use your far-seeing eyes to find a path for us all to walk. I've heard what some of the old ones say about you. They've seen your power. My father's spoken of what the chiefs say. You and Otter are valued men. You stood and protected the helpless ones against the Pawnees and *Savane'*. When others fled from Sumner's bluecoats, you remained."

"Fighting's gained us nothing," Buffalo Horn muttered.

"That's what our chiefs say, but there are many

who speak for revenge. If you join your voice with *Ne' hyo* and Black Kettle, some of the young men will listen."

"Is that why Summer Cherry Woman invited me to your lodge?"

"No," she said, sighing. "My cousin thinks you are lost. She says she hears you speak in your sleep, troubled by dreams you can't remember. I have walked the medicine trail, and I understand the healing cures. I'm old enough to go to a husband's lodge, but we aren't visited by many young men from other bands. Most of the young *Wu ta piu* are relatives of mine."

"You believe I could be the husband of a chief's daughter?"

"You'll lead the people yourself one day," she observed. "Many of our people think so. *Ne' hyo* says if war comes, Blue Racer will offer you an Elk lance."

"I'm too young," the Horn objected.

"When did age count for anything? I've heard of how you bled to invite a dream of Bull Buffalo. You were still small then."

"I had guidance."

"Now it's for you to guide."

"And you?"

"I may be able to help. Search your heart to see what we should do."

"I've walked the world alone a long time."

"Alone? I never see you without Otter nearby."

"We're brothers," the Horn noted. "We ride together. We share danger. There's an emptiness inside me I share with no one, though."

"I see it," she said, frowning. "It's a troubling thing."

"Yes," Horn agreed. "I've always been afraid I

would die young. I never considered taking a wife or making children."

"They'll be needed," she said, taking his hands in her own.

"I know," he said, scowling. "Maybe I should carve a flute and ask to see you again."

"I would welcome it."

"Then I'll do it," he promised. "I don't know all the things a man should do, but I'll ask my uncle."

"First ask your heart," she advised.

"I already have," he replied, easing her head onto his shoulder. "I won't hurry you, Swallow. It's best two people know each other before sharing a common path. There's an emptiness in me that's hungry to be filled, though."

"I can fill it," she said, gazing up into his eyes.

"I know," he whispered.

9

When Buffalo Horn returned to Pony Leg's lodge that evening, he found his uncle waiting for him.

"Should I speak with White Goose?" Pony Leg asked. "Or has my wife done everything that's required?"

Buffalo Horn grinned, stared at his toes, and laughed.

"I never thought about taking a wife," he confessed. "Bright Swallow is different from other girls, though."

"The one you take to your lodge is always different, *Na tsin' os ta*," Pony Leg observed. "I waited a long time myself. Then I wondered how I had ever have been content without a woman's company."

"River Hawk rode with you," the Horn pointed out.

"We still hunt together," Pony Leg noted. "Now he, too, has taken a wife, and we ride in different bands.

It's good to have a trusted man at your side, but you can't make sons with him."

"Summer Cherry Woman hasn't given you one, either."

"The child will come before winter," Pony Leg announced. "The old women have read the signs."

"That's good news, *Na khan*. There'll be another brave heart among us."

"He'll want cousins to ride with."

"He'll have them," Buffalo Horn vowed.

"Only if you choose a wife," Pony Leg mumbled.

"I will," the Horn vowed. "Soon. I admit that I like Bright Swallow. She knows the healing cures, too."

"Ask her," Pony Leg urged.

"There's more to be done than ask her father," the Horn argued.

"Yes," Snow Bear added, grinning as he and Rabbit Foot made their way over beside Buffalo Horn.

"Well?" Pony Leg asked.

"We made this for you," Rabbit Foot explained as he handed over a courting flute.

"We made two," Snow Bear added. "I already gave *Nah nih* his."

"He's already using it," Rabbit Foot added. "You shouldn't waste time here. Go back and see the woman. Make music for her."

"I'll do it later," the Horn promised. "First I have to consider things."

"What is there to consider?" Snow Bear asked. "She's pretty. Her family's as good as any. You wouldn't want to waste your life leading your young brothers along Man's Road."

"No, I wouldn't," Buffalo Horn agreed, laughing at

the youngsters. "There will be time tomorrow, though."

Snow Bear and Rabbit Foot scowled, but they accepted Buffalo Horn's decision.

"It's a good flute, Horn," Snow Bear boasted. "Don't wait too long to play it."

As long summer days grew shorter, Buffalo Horn did put the courting flute to use. He was surprised at how natural he felt walking the river trails or riding into the hills with Bright Swallow. Even so, he didn't ask Pony Leg to treat with White Goose.

"It's an important step," Horn declared. "I have to consider many things."

Otter didn't hesitate. The cherry-ripening moon of late summer hung high in the sky when Snow Bear led five good ponies to White Goose's lodge.

"You said it yourself, brother," Otter told Buffalo Horn. "We are too few. Good men need to bring new sons to the people."

As for Bright Swallow, she waited patiently.

"Ask your dreams," she told the Horn. "Ask *Heammawihio* what we should do."

Buffalo Horn found his thoughts crowded with other concerns. Black Kettle had traveled south to visit the trader George Bent, who had married a niece of the Kettle. Bluecoat soldiers were building a new fort near Bent's old stone store, and the *Wihio* chiefs had sent someone to ask the *Tsis tsis tas* and Arapahoes to make a new treaty.

"It's a mistake," Grouse complained. "All the Dog Soldiers say Black Kettle closes his eyes and lets the whites steal everything we own. Already the diggers have taken the mountains. They build roads beside our rivers and scare the game away! We should fight them!"

"We fought Sumner when he came to build his road," Pony Leg noted. "Did we stop him? No. He killed many of our best men, and he broke our medicine power. There are too many bluecoats to kill."

"It's said the bluecoats have their own trouble," Grouse argued. "Soon they'll be fighting each other. The traders talk about it. They say things will return to the old ways when all the soldiers leave."

"Nothing lasts long," Buffalo Horn observed. "And once life changes, it rarely turns back to the old way."

"We'll help restore the power of the tribes over this good country," Grouse boasted.

"It's not our nature to question the path we find in front of our feet," Pony Leg insisted.

"We can only walk it," Buffalo Horn agreed.

A short time later Buffalo Horn, Otter, Snow Bear, Rabbit Foot, Sparrow, and Grouse set off to hunt. It wasn't that the people were hungry. Plenty of buffalo meat had been dried against winter's need. Although fresh meat was always welcome, Buffalo Horn sensed his young companions had a greater need. They had grown restless, and the hunt would provide a welcome release from the graying days of autumn.

The *Wu ta piu* had moved their camps just west of Bent's Fort, and many of the older men rode in to trade hides for powder and lead. Buffalo Horn led his small party away from the trader's fort. He hoped to locate a small buffalo herd. When he found no tracks or dung trail, he pointed to a small hill to the southwest. Trees topped the slopes, and he expected to spy deer there. Instead, as he approached the hill, Horn noticed two distant puffs of powder smoke. An instant later he heard the unmistakable crack of rifle shots. A heavy lead ball tore into the yellowing sod a few feet to his left. Then Grouse cried out, clutched his bare side, and fell off the side of his pony.

"Ayyyy!" Otter howled, stringing his bow. "Enemies!"

Buffalo Horn quickly moved to shield Sparrow from the danger. Rabbit Foot jumped down to tend to Grouse, and Snow Bear collected the horses.

"How badly is he hurt?" Buffalo Horn asked as a third shot shattered the peaceful morning air.

"I can't tell," Rabbit Foot replied, gazing up with frightened eyes and holding his bloody hands in the air. "There's too much blood!"

"It's always the same," Otter muttered.

"Yes," Horn agreed as he pulled his pony alongside his brother-friend. "I'll go right."

"Then I'll ride left," Otter declared. "Nothing lives long!"

"Only earth and mountain!" Buffalo Horn added.

The unseen enemies continued to fire from the hillside, but the two *Tsis tsis tas* riders hugged their mounts and wove their way toward opposite flanks of the ambushers. Horn charged with rare abandon. He tried to spit the sour taste from his mouth. It wasn't possible. All the old bitterness surged through his insides, and he notched an arrow in anticipation of ending a life.

It wasn't like him to feel such unbridled hatred. Old Two Claws had cautioned him about disturbing the harmony of the sacred circle, and Buffalo Horn had tried to accept each peril as a new challenge given by *Heammawihio*. The sight of his brother-friend and the brothers shrinking from the long-firing rifles, the memory of Rabbit Foot's bloody hands, and the concern over Grouse's wounds had trampled that harmony as flat as the prairie grass under his pony's hooves.

"Brother, I see them!" Otter shouted from the left. "Three men afoot. Ayyyy! I have their horses!"

A fresh rifle shot split the air, and Buffalo Horn followed the sound to where three hairy-faced *Wihio* stood among large rocks, firing frantically.

"Ayyyy!" the Horn shouted as he turned his horse. He then raced toward the rocks, steadying his mount by squeezing its ribs with his knees. Then he fired his first arrow. It struck the tallest *Wihio* in the throat.

The wounded *Wihio* collapsed, spitting blood and clutching his throat. The others discarded their rifles and fled toward the far slope. Otter blocked their retreat, and Buffalo Horn struck down each in turn by clubbing them across the head with the old ash bow.

"Go," Otter then urged. "I'll do what's necessary here."

"Your brothers . . ." Horn started to argue.

"You know the healing cures, brother," Otter insisted. "Help Grouse!"

Buffalo Horn knew that Otter ached to return to his brothers, but there was no arguing with him, either. Otter had never been a man to speak much, and what he said carried both wisdom and weight. Horn turned his horse and nudged it into a trot. Soon he was back with the younger men.

Snow Bear, Rabbit Foot, and Sparrow had gathered around Grouse. Their eyes betrayed their anxiety.

"Grouse?" Rabbit Foot whispered. "Our brother's here. He'll help you."

Buffalo Horn dismounted. Snow Bear took charge

of the Horn's pony, and Rabbit Foot hopped over to make a place for Horn beside the injured Grouse.

"You're not feverish," Buffalo Horn observed as he felt the boy's forehead. "It's only the wound in your side?"

Grouse managed to mutter a feeble yes.

Horn then pulled a blood-soaked cloth away from the boy's side and gazed at a five-inch tear in the youngster's side. It was still bleeding, but there was no penetration of the youngster's vitals. The ball had grazed Grouse and left him shaken and weak from loss of blood. The boy would survive, though.

"You're fortunate," Horn said as he replaced the cloth. "The *Wihio*'s aim was bad."

"He should have shot at you," Grouse replied. "You're a bigger target."

"He probably *was* shooting at me," Buffalo Horn admitted. "He shot poorly."

"Maybe he'll be more accurate next time," Rabbit Foot suggested.

"There can be no next time," Snow Bear growled. "Our brother has remained behind to watch them die."

"Yes?" Sparrow asked.

"Only the last two," Buffalo Horn told them. "I killed the first."

"It's the only thing you can do with *Wihio*," Grouse said, raising his head enough to look at his injured side.

"You can't think that way," Rabbit Foot argued. "You've heard Black Kettle talk about them. We're different from the Pawnees. *Wihio* are also different, one from the other."

"We should have killed them all when they first came onto our land," Grouse insisted.

"It would have changed nothing," Buffalo Horn declared. "They're like a swarm of locusts. You can stamp your feet and kill some of them, but they'll still spread over the prairie, eating all the grass."

"And you stand by and watch them eat everything?" Grouse asked. "If we had fought, we would now be able to say that we at least tried."

"The bullet the *Wihio* shot into you must have been carrying a poison tip," Horn observed. "What else could make you so bitter?"

"Tell me that when the *Wihio* shoot you!" Grouse complained.

"Once, not so long ago, I was also hurt by them," Buffalo Horn said, gazing at his foot. He slipped off his moccasin and watched as the contempt left Grouse's face. In its place was the beginning of understanding.

"You killed the ones that did that?" Grouse asked.

"I was a small boy," Horn confessed. "I was powerless to help myself. Another man killed them."

"Another man?" Grouse asked.

"Black Kettle," Buffalo Horn explained. "I owe him a great debt."

"For avenging your toes?"

"For disturbing the harmony of his world. Killing does that," Buffalo Horn explained. "It's a difficult task to regain that harmony. It's easy to ride out against an enemy and kill him. A man can do it without thinking. When he considers what he's done, the hard time begins."

"You killed a man on that hill," Rabbit Foot observed.

"It will be a hard thing to forget," Horn admitted. "I had to do it, though."

"What about our brother?" Snow Bear asked.

"His road's also difficult," Horn told them. "We'll need good company to restore our spirits. Maybe we'll take a sweat and seek a vision. You could come along as watchers."

"Watchers for what?" Grouse asked.

"A man who seeks a vision must have someone along to guard his camp from enemies," Rabbit Foot told his wounded friend. "Otter's done it often. We're old enough to watch now."

"Maybe I'll come with you," Grouse suggested. "I'll be stronger soon."

"It would be a good idea," Buffalo Horn agreed. "After all, we'll soon be related."

"Once I turned away from you," Grouse recounted. "Now I owe my life to you. I'd be happy if you let me repay my obligation."

"It's settled then," Horn said. "We'll speak no more about it."

Otter returned then, bringing along the long-barreled *Wihio* rifles and four good horses. Bags of corn flour and sugar were packed on the back of one animal.

"We've taken horses," Snow Bear observed. "No meat, but we've won some distinction."

"The ponies are nothing," Otter grumbled.

"We'll take a sweat, brother," Buffalo Horn promised. "We'll ponder your marriage, and I'll seek a dream. Maybe *Heammawihio* will show us a better road to walk."

"I hope so," Otter replied. "This one smells of death."

*   *   *

Grouse's wounds healed, leaving only a thin whitish scar on the bronze flesh of his side. Once the young man left his blankets and regained his feet, he began joining Rabbit Foot, Snow Bear, and Sparrow each morning. They swam and wrestled, and sometimes all four of them accompanied Buffalo Horn and Otter when the brother-friends made the morning prayers.

As the hard-face moons of winter approached, Summer Cherry Woman's belly grew larger.

"Your son wants to come out and meet you," she began telling Pony Leg. "You should go out and make the proper prayers. Winter's never a good time to be born, but it's easier on the little ones born before first snowfall."

Pony Leg knew that, and he summoned Buffalo Horn.

"*Na tsin' os ta*, it's time for me to ride into the hills," Pony Leg announced. "It would be wise for me to have a watcher."

"I thought I might invite a dream myself," Horn replied. "We could go together."

"Who would watch?" Pony Leg asked.

"We would," Otter explained. "I and my brothers."

"Some of them are still small," Pony Leg pointed out.

"It isn't a man's size that makes him a good watcher," Otter objected. "We'll keep you safe."

"*Na tsin' os ta*?" Pony Leg said, turning to his nephew.

"I've considered it, and it seems the best plan. We'll take a sweat this morning and prepare to ride out at dusk," Buffalo Horn explained. "I trust Otter with my own life. I would also trust him with yours. I value it more highly."

Pony Leg smiled and nodded his silent thanks.

Buffalo Horn wasn't certain whether it was the sweat itself or the companionship of Otter, the brothers, and Grouse that chased the gloomy recollection of killing the *Wihio* from his and Otter's minds. By the time they readied the horses and prepared to set out into the nearby hills, the little party was in high spirits.

"Remember, brothers, we're not riding out to count coup on Pawnees or hunt Bull Buffalo," Otter warned. "Our task is to watch for danger and keep the dreamers safe."

"We know," Snow Bear agreed, "but if we discover trouble, we won't run away."

"We won't welcome it, either," Otter said sternly. "We watch and listen. Warn and protect."

Otter's brothers nodded their understanding, but Grouse remained silent. The youngster's brooding concerned Buffalo Horn, but he knew that words weren't capable of curing every wound. Sometimes time was necessary.

Pony Leg led the way at first, but he stopped at a low hill overlooking a meandering stream.

"This will do," the Leg said, turning to his brother.

"No," Buffalo Horn argued. "Let's find a higher place."

He knew the others were satisfied with the hill, but he sensed the place lacked the power he needed for his vision. Otter read his brother-friend's thoughts and silenced the grumbling.

They continued north and east for a considerable time. Finally Buffalo Horn saw a narrow ridge. Near the top of the southern face a heavy rock slide had torn away all plants and trees. A narrow ledge remained. Horn pointed the way, and Otter rode ahead. The watchers encircled Pony Leg and Buffalo Horn as they rode up the ridge and made their way to the ledge. Once there, Horn explained that the place would suffice.

"We'll build up a fire and begin the medicine prayers," he added.

Snow Bear and Sparrow hurried to gather firewood while Grouse helped Rabbit Foot unpack the horses and tether them to some nearby trees. Only then did Buffalo Horn produce a pipe and begin the ceremonial pipe ritual. He sprinkled an offering of tobacco to each of the four directions and invoked the power of all the spirits. Then he turned to Pony Leg, who made the traditional father's prayers. Horn and Pony Leg concluded the ceremonial by singing old medicine chants and dancing.

It wasn't until later, when the sun slid behind the western horizon, that Buffalo Horn stripped himself and began singing to *Heammawihio*. The young man joined his voice to that of his uncle's in praying for a strong son to be born to the people, but there were other, very ancient songs he sang alone.

> Man Above, I'm nothing;
> Even the birds can fly above me.
> Bear is stronger, and coyote is smarter.
> Only with your help do I live.

> Man Above, hear me,
> I know my voice is small
> But my heart's strong.
> Set my feet on the sacred path.

Again and again Buffalo Horn sang the words. As he sensed a weariness flooding his being, he drew out a knife and cut the flesh of his arms and legs and chest. Bright crimson blood flowed across his belly and ran down his bare thighs. He felt his eyes begin to blur. His legs grew heavy, and he finally collapsed into the soft comfort of an elk robe.

The dream came that same night. It was unlike the ones he had previously experienced. Instead of buffalo spirits charging out of swirling mists, Buffalo Horn saw a low flat plain scarred by ravines and small creeks. It was morning, and a blanket of eerie white snow clothed the land.

The world seemed frozen. There wasn't a sound to be heard. No one moved. Finally a hawk appeared. It was a beautiful bird, gray-feathered with a reddish tail. Its sharp, tearing beak moved as it screamed a terrifying cry that rent the heavens.

Buffalo Horn then felt a chill seize him. He inhaled deeply, but recoiled as an odor of death entered his nostrils. The earth shook with the hooves of a hundred horses, and rifle fire tore into the circle of peaceful lodges.

"Ayyyy!" an old man screamed as he leaped out of his lodge. Wrapped in a buffalo hide, with only a lance for a weapon, he briefly held a swarm of blue-coated horsemen at bay. Then one of the riders pointed a pistol and blew three bullets through his chest.

Elsewhere women and children scrambled out of their lodges, only to be struck down. Death was everywhere! The very ground began to run red with the blood of the dead and dying. It was a nightmare scene brought all too vividly to life.

Buffalo Horn searched the scene for some sign of

himself, his relations, his friends. None of the dying people had faces, though. As for the bluecoats, they were more ghost than human. As the dream continued, more brave hearts died in the futile effort to protect the helpless ones. In the end, all seemed to perish.

"No!" the Horn screamed, throwing off the elk hide and rising to his feet. "We've suffered enough!"

A wary Otter shook himself awake and stared at his brother-friend, confused.

"What's wrong?" a fretful Pony Leg asked. "*Na tsin' os ta*, have you seen something?"

"Seen something?" Buffalo Horn gasped. "I've seen everything!"

"What was it?" Otter cried. "What did you see?"

"Everything," Horn replied. "Everything."

10

When they returned to the *Wu ta piu* camp, Bright Swallow brought word that Pony Leg had a son.

"He's small, and he looks like a mole," she added. "Still, he has a strong appetite, and he cries like a wolf."

To Buffalo Horn that seemed to be adequate reason for calling him Wolf or some other appropriately inspiring name. Instead Pony Leg chose to name the child Mole.

"It will be a hard name to carry," Buffalo Horn observed. "His age-mates will torment him!"

"He has all his toes," Pony Leg replied. "How can a boy grow strong without challenges? The name will be a burden, but it will make him strong. Later, if he walks man's road honorably, he'll win a new name."

"As I did?"

"It's all a father could wish, *Na tsin' os ta*. If you

heard a different name in your dream, you can give it to him."

"I didn't, *Na khan*," Horn admitted. He stared at the ground, and Pony Leg sighed.

"I suspected as much," Pony Leg said. "What did you see? Was it so terrible that it woke you?"

"Yes," Buffalo Horn muttered.

"Then you should go and speak to the medicine chiefs."

"I would have told the old man," Horn said, referring to Two Claws. "He's on the other side now. There's no one who would understand."

"Bright Swallow might."

"I want her to share my life, not my nightmares."

"Was the dream that dark?"

"More than I imagined possible," Buffalo Horn confessed. "I saw the death of our people."

"Then there's only one man for you to find, *Na tsin' os ta*," Pony Leg observed. "Black Kettle. He's had dreams himself, and he has far-seeing eyes. Talk to him. He needs to know what *Heammawihio* has shown you."

"I'll go and talk to him," Buffalo Horn promised.

As that first day flowed into another and another, though, Buffalo Horn avoided the Kettle. In fact Buffalo Horn avoided all the chiefs. He felt their eyes on his back. He noted the sense of expectation etched across the faces of Grouse, Rabbit Foot, and the other young men. He had no desire to share the dream, though. It frightened him. He only wanted to imagine it had never come.

The first snows of winter were peppering the hills north of Red Shield River when Black Kettle finally visited Pony Leg's lodge.

"You seem troubled, Horn," the chief said, sitting in an honored position between Buffalo Horn and the fire. "Your uncle says you've seen something in your dreams. I remember how you found Bull Buffalo when you were still a boy. *Heammawihio* tells us things sometimes that we fail to understand."

Buffalo Horn tried to avoid the chief's words, but Black Kettle clasped the younger man's shoulders and held them firmly.

"Not everyone enjoys Man Above's favor," the Kettle said. "You know something. How can I find the path our people should walk when I can't know what lies ahead?"

"It's a hard thing to explain," Horn said, sighing. "I don't like to remember it."

"I have to know."

"It will only make your burdens greater."

"No, it will help me understand. I know you intend no harm. I remember how I once found a small boy, bleeding, mutilated by the steel jaws of a *Wihio* trap. I already knew from my own dreams that I had a choice to make. If I accepted the bonnet of a chief, my path would prove difficult. If I didn't, and turned away, you would not be the only one to suffer for it. Yes, my burden may be heavier, but it was my choice to bear it, just as it's my choice to hear of your dream. Tell me about it."

"It won't help," Buffalo Horn insisted. Black Kettle remained determined to hear, though. Eventually Horn surrendered and shared his daunting vision of the future. It chilled the chief.

"I see," Black Kettle finally whispered. "I understand why you appeared troubled, but don't you see?

This is what may come to happen if we walk the world blindly. Instead we can work to prevent it."

"Can we?" Buffalo Horn asked hopefully.

"We have to do it. My heart's already troubled by the many who died from the *Wihio* fevers."

"I'm an Elk," Horn said, swallowing hard. "I've sworn to protect the helpless ones. Each summer we grow fewer, though. I try to fight our enemies, but how can a man hold off a fever? If the bluecoat soldiers come, hundreds of them like Sumner had, how can we stop them?"

"To stop a bad thing from happening, you don't always have to fight," Black Kettle argued. "Sometimes by turning your own path, you can prevent a confrontation."

"With the *Wihio*, you mean?"

"Especially the *Wihio*. My own dreams told me long ago that we could never avoid them. They come like a flood, and one man or an entire people can only stand and be drowned or find a way to go to safer ground and outlast it."

"You think they'll go away?" Buffalo Horn asked.

"They'll grow tired of scratching yellow powder out of the mountains. Their log houses are too hot in summer and cold in winter. The trader Bent says they're fighting each other in the East. They have plenty of trouble. We should learn what we can of them so that we can avoid their sicknesses or find cures for them. We can also turn their thinking. Once they see that our way is a good way and that we will bring them no harm, their angry eyes will clear, and we can all be friends."

"Friends?" Horn asked, refusing to believe it was possible to befriend such bad hearts.

"It's the only way I can see to avoid the bluecoats."

"And if you're wrong? If they will come anyway?"

"We can only walk the road that lies before our feet, Frog," Black Kettle said mournfully.

"Yes," Buffalo Horn agreed. "It's all we can do."

The hard-face moons of winter came and went without illuminating the path ahead. Amid the snow and ice, Buffalo Horn found it difficult to forget the chilling dream. Each time he glanced into the hopeful eyes of Otter's brothers or watched the peace that Grouse found sleeping in Pony Leg's lodge, he recalled the faceless victims of the bluecoat attack.

His relationships with others began to sour. Even Otter complained that he was losing his way.

"It's time you talked with White Goose," Otter suggested. "Bright Swallow has missed your walks. A wife's comfort can fill a man's emptiness."

"How would you know?" Horn grumbled. "You and Feather Dance Maiden remain apart."

"I've spoken to White Goose," Otter replied. "He believes in the old ways, and he insists the oldest daughter should take a husband before the younger one leaves his lodge."

"Ah," Buffalo Horn said, managing half a grin. "I'm surprised you haven't told me about this before."

"Then you only think you know me," Otter muttered. "For a long time now I've ridden at your side like a brother. We've stood together, facing the same dangers. I'll always follow you, even when your heart turns bitter and you lose your way. I only want to help you find the sacred path again so that all our people can benefit. You can't be so blind to not understand that!"

"I do know," Buffalo Horn said, clasping his

brother-friend's arm. "Sometimes I climb so deep into my thoughts that I forget the brave hearts that are always nearby, eager to help."

"We could help, brother, if only you'd ask."

"No," Horn insisted. "It's for me to find a path out of my despair."

"Go and walk with Bright Swallow Maiden," Otter urged. "She can help."

"She might," Horn admitted.

"Then go and talk with her," Otter pleaded. "Put the darkness behind you. Try and find something better than dark dreams and old memories of pain and death."

"I'll try," Buffalo Horn promised. But he wasn't sure it was possible.

He waited only a short time before trudging through the snowdrifts to White Goose's lodge. Bright Swallow was outside, cooking, but she avoided Horn's gaze. He, in turn, continued past her to where her father stood shaving the hair from an elk hide.

"I thought I might talk with your daughter," Buffalo Horn declared.

"She expected you before," the Goose replied. "I thought you might come with presents when you returned from seeking your dream. Instead we heard nothing. You dishonor my daughter and my family by ignoring us."

Buffalo Horn hung his head.

"I never intended to bring you any unhappiness," he explained. "It's only that my world is full of disharmony, and I chose to avoid everyone."

"If that's so, you're a foolish young man," White Goose grumbled. "Did you expect my daughter to smile at your neglect? Was she supposed to enjoy the taunts of the other maidens? What about me? You know Otter wishes to take my second daughter, but I can't give her up while my eldest remains unwed. You've thrown my world into the air and let it smash against the rocks!"

"I never suspected that," Horn said. "I'd rather die than harm you, or especially Swallow. I may seem to be old and experienced, but I'm still finding my way up a difficult climb. The old ones that used to help me understand things are gone, and my dreams warn of peril I can't begin to comprehend."

"I see the truth in your eyes, Horn, but only a fool takes such a burden upon himself. Bright Swallow knows the medicine trail. She can understand far more than you suspect."

"Now that I've shamed her . . ."

"Nothing's so damaged that it can't be repaired," White Goose observed. "Bring me a good pony from your herd, and I'll talk with my daughter. Your gift will show the people your strong feelings. I don't believe Bright Swallow could remain angry at you for long anyway."

"I'll come back tomorrow then."

"Will it take so long for you to find a pony?" the older man asked, grinning.

"No," Buffalo Horn confessed. "Not nearly so long. I'll return as soon as I have a suitable pony."

The Horn felt oddly rejuvenated as he made his way across the snow-covered landscape to where Otter and the brothers had driven the pony herd. The *Wihio* miners had had with them a good sure-footed buckskin mare, and Buffalo Horn slipped a loop over its head and led the animal back toward the main camp.

As he approached White Goose's lodge, women exchanged knowing looks. Men nodded approvingly.

"I bring this horse to White Goose," Horn said, loudly enough that all could hear. "My thoughts have pulled me from the sacred path, and I have neglected my obligations as a man of the people. I hope you and your daughter can understand and forgive my behavior."

"Yours is a difficult trail to walk," White Goose observed as he accepted the pony.

"Maybe I could walk to the river with your daughter?" Horn added hopefully.

"I'll ask her," the Goose replied. He approached Bright Swallow, whispered to her, and she allowed Feather Dance to assume responsibility for the cooking. She walked out, took Buffalo Horn's hand, and led the way toward the river.

"You should have told me," she grumbled as they walked. "What was I to think?"

"You should realize that a wife of mine will know difficult times," he explained. "My dreams are different from the ones others have."

"Yes, and you should be glad of it," she scolded. "It's a rare gift, seeing the way ahead. It's not something that should trouble you."

"It does," Buffalo Horn confessed. "I often wish that I was ordinary, more like Otter and the others."

"You're not," she noted. "*Heammawihio* has chosen to favor you with far-seeing eyes. Whatever the reason, it's not something you can turn away from. The people need your guidance."

"They need a man who can make sense out of confusion," Horn argued. "They need someone who can glimpse peril and know how to avoid it."

"You'll learn to do that."

"Will I? There was an old man who shared that confidence, but he's started the long walk. I look around, and I see men as troubled and confused as I am."

"Not Black Kettle."

"I try to believe he's chosen the correct path, but who can be certain? He urges me to make friends of the *Wihio*, but when have they sought our people as friends? Those three who shot Grouse gave no hint of warning. Even a Pawnee will ride out and challenge you! These *Wihio* are spiders waiting to trap us in their webs!"

Bright Swallow took two steps back and stared fearfully into Buffalo Horn's fiery eyes.

"We've had white men among us since my grandfather's time," she said, sighing. "Some have brought sickness into our camps, but most are people much like you and me. They have married our cousins and learned our language. The Bents are *Wihio* traders, but their children are *Tsis tsis tas*, related by their mothers' blood. They've done us few wrongs and often carried our words to the bluecoat soldier chiefs. Bent saved our treaty goods from the *Wihio* when you and the other young men fought the bluecoat chief Sumner."

"We fought because he, like the rest of the *Wihio*, considers us good only for killing."

"They're not all that way, Horn!"

He started to reply, but instead he swallowed the words. He didn't want to share the dream, the nightmare of killing that had come in the quiet night to tear apart his very soul. How could he tell her that even as they stood beside the river on that silent winter morning, his eyes searched the heavens for sign of the hawk that would warn of the approaching bluecoats?

"Otter says that your father has refused the horses he's offered for Feather Dance Maiden," Buffalo Horn said instead. "They should be married soon. They've bonded their hearts, and it's right they should share a path. Raise strong-heart sons."

"I agree," she said. "*Ne' hyo* believes in the old tradition that the older daughter should be first to leave her father's lodge."

"And what do you think?" he asked.

"I agree that often the old ways are best, but there's only a small difference between our age. Feather Dance is ready. She should go with Otter."

"Are you also ready?"

"Do you ask for yourself or someone else?"

Buffalo Horn was stunned. He dropped his gaze and tried to compose himself.

"I always believed that you felt as I did," he told her. "I know you are the person I want to pass my life beside. It's your child I will take hunting. When we're older, it's you that I want to sit with as we watch our grandchildren swim the rivers and run through the tall grasses. I can't imagine anyone half so pretty, and I . . ."

"I wish you had said all this to me when you and Pony Leg returned from the hills."

"I planned to," he explained. "Then the dream came."

"It darkened your heart, Horn," she observed. "Have you spoken to White Goose?"

"I will," he offered.

"Don't," she said, turning away.

"Swallow?" he called.

She tried to avoid him, but he drew her closer. He peered into her deep, thoughtful brown eyes.

"I don't understand," he told her. "How am I supposed to act? What am I supposed to do? Otter tells me that you desire me as a husband, and your father scolds me for ignoring you. Then when I suggest a permanent relationship, you turn away."

"It shouldn't be hard for a prophet to notice," she grumbled.

"There's another man?"

"No," she insisted.

"I'll bring five good horses. If your father's lonely, he can easily find a good young girl to come and tend his fire. For three ponies he could have half the maidens in this camp."

"I admit that I care about you, Horn. I even admit that I have seen myself in a dream, walking at your side."

"Then what's preventing our joining?"

"You are," she said, sighing.

"How can I be the cause?" he cried. "I just asked how you felt about being my wife. I spoke of taking ponies to your father. I'll do it, too."

"No, you won't," she insisted.

"Why not?"

"Because you won't share your heart with anyone, Horn. You speak of obligations, but you're afraid. Your mother and father are gone. You said it just now. The old ones you trusted have started the long walk up Hanging Road. I saw how worried you were when Grouse was hurt. You're afraid of the responsibility."

"Shouldn't I be?"

"I've heard my father say it a thousand times. A man of the people has obligations."

"I accept them."

"Do you? Your dreams warn of danger, but do you share the news? Only when our chief demands to hear of the dream do you tell him. He's a man who once saved your life, too. No, Horn, you can't be the husband I'll require."

"I'll change," he insisted. A sudden fear of losing her drove him to plead.

"You still don't understand," she cried. "How can I be one with you when you aren't one with yourself? You have to find some sort of peace with the world and with that vision in particular before I can agree to a mating."

"You can't," he agreed. "I see now. I've wandered farther from the sacred path than I imagined."

"Yes, you have," she agreed.

"How do I find my way back, Swallow?"

"I can't tell you that," she replied. "No one can. You have to find where the disharmony came from and send it away."

"It's the dream," he said, sighing.

"It's more than that," she argued. "Go to the medicine men and ask their help. Take a sweat. Lead the buffalo hunt. Whatever obligation you sense inside yourself, it's gone unmet."

"I've always done what was required, Swallow."

"Nothing more? That's what is needed now. A brave-heart act from you that can be long-remembered."

"What can I do?"

"Consult Black Kettle," she advised. "I don't know, but it's said that the *Wihio* doctor needs help. Maybe you could go to Bent and live with this strange medicine man. You can learn how to fight the spotted sickness and the fevers that the strange ones have brought among us."

"I'll do my best," he vowed. "I don't see how this will draw us closer, though."

"Perhaps it won't now," she relented. "It may turn your heart back to us later."

"It's a good idea," he admitted. He just wasn't sure it could happen that easily.

11

"It's a difficult thing, getting to know anyone," Black Kettle told Buffalo Horn. "You can never be certain just how well you understand even a brother. To acquaint yourself with an enemy requires all the cunning of Coyote, and good fortune as well."

Buffalo Horn thought the Kettle should know. In the two years that had passed since Horn had dreamed of bluecoats attacking the *Wu ta piu* camps, Black Kettle had often ridden out with the *Wihio* peacemakers to talk of bettering relations.

"Each time he listens to them," Otter observed. "When we are in the right, they ask us to understand and forgive. When we are in the wrong, they demand payment or seek to place some young man of ours in an iron box. They shoot our children and laugh. We come across a horse on the prairie that has their mark burned into its rump. We keep it and they call us thieves. Who stole the land? Who cheats us of our possessions and shames our women?"

It tore at Buffalo Horn to see such injustice, but the dream was never far from his thoughts.

"Some part of us must survive," Black Kettle had insisted.

"I'll do what I can to help you find peace with the crazy ones," Buffalo Horn had vowed. "I'm not certain we can manage it, though."

"We have to," the Kettle had replied. "Otherwise we are like last summer's rain—gone and forgotten. A world without us? It isn't possible!"

More and more, Buffalo Horn suspected that was exactly what the whites had in mind. He lived and rode among the *Wihio*. He passed his winters at the Bents' fort on the stream that the *Wihio* had renamed Arkansas River. Recently the bluecoats had built a second place, calling it Fort Wise.

"To protect the settlements against the Kiowas," the soldier chief said.

"They spend no time chasing Kiowas," the Arapaho chief Left Hand observed. "They're here to watch us."

"Well, perhaps we'll watch them instead," Buffalo Horn said.

And so he had erected a small lodge along Arkansas River near the Bent store. Mostly he stayed there alone. Otter had finally persuaded White Goose to allow Feather Dance Maiden to wed, and the younger brothers now rode with the young *Wu ta piu* and slept in Young Man's Lodge.

"It's the way of things," Horn observed. "They have their own path to walk."

Recently Grouse had come to Bent's Fort. He

passed his days with the traders, and he joined Buffalo Horn after sundown.

"My sister said that you hope to restore the harmony of your world by understanding the men who hurt you," Grouse explained one morning when they walked together to the river to swim. "Maybe I can also put my hate behind me."

"I haven't been very successful," Horn confessed. "You might learn more from someone else."

"There isn't anyone else," Grouse insisted. "Your uncle's son is my sister's son. That ties us together. Besides, who else has felt the sting of *Wihio* iron?"

In Grouse's case, it had been lead, but Buffalo Horn didn't argue. He accepted Grouse's good company and greater need. The two young *Tsis tsis tas* accompanied the Bents on visits to the nearby army camps, picking up bits and pieces of the English language as they haggled over the merits or value of a buffalo or elk hide. Horn found little honor in the work, for the bluecoats enjoyed stealing from the unwary.

"We're nevertheless learning a great deal about them," Horn told Grouse. "There's time to learn more, too."

One of the great puzzles of *Wihio* life was the fight they were having over who would own the black *Wihio*. Sometimes the white men who visited Bent's Fort brought along their slaves. These weren't captive enemies who might hope to win acceptance by their captors or expect to be ransomed by their families. They were people born and bred as slaves. Their sad songs and long faces troubled Buffalo Horn. Only occasionally did a family of them gather around a cooking fire and sing lively songs or dance to the tune of a fiddle.

During Buffalo Moon's twenty-first summer, the *Wihio* living in the north went to war with the ones in the south. Some of the traders said it was about the black slaves, but others said it was about who told whom what to do. None of the tribes understood, but except for some Pawnees who hung around the bluecoat forts, everyone was glad that the *Wihio* soldiers were leaving the plains to fight somebody else.

Buffalo Moon marked the two summers that followed as a time in which the world itself seemed to turn upon itself. While the *Wihio* war to the east kept the bluecoats preoccupied, it also sent an army of scoundrels westward. Some, like the young trader Isaac Guthrie, became friends. More often the newcomers rode the land blindly, robbing and killing until someone ended their lives.

Guthrie, on the other hand, wasn't like most white men. He was only a year older than the Horn, but no one would have guessed it. The young *Wihio* was terribly pale, and the sun streaked his dark hair with lighter streaks.

"He's like a frightened rabbit," Grouse insisted the first time Guthrie visited Horn's lodge.

"Rabbit?" Guthrie asked, surprising Horn with a knowledge of some *Tsis tsis tas* words. "I know I'm not much to look at, but I'm not afraid."

Buffalo Horn didn't know how Guthrie would fare in a fight, but he accepted the young *Wihio*'s self-appraisal. Not many whites came to Buffalo Horn's lodge, and those few came armed. Guthrie arrived with a mouth organ, a buckskin pouch filled with paper and drawing pens, and a dark gaze Horn recognized all too well.

"It's pleasant here," Guthrie announced as he sat

beside the modest fire Grouse had kindled that morning. "Quiet, too."

Grouse picked up a stick and glared at the intruder, but Buffalo Horn only sighed.

"You wouldn't chase away a ground squirrel," Horn declared. "Let him stay."

Guthrie remained beside the fire all that morning. Sometimes the strange young man would blow music out of his mouth organ—mostly sad melodies that drifted hauntingly along the river. Later he took out his paper and began sketching the countryside. When Buffalo Horn finally walked over to have a look at the drawings, he found himself struck by the dark shadows that seemed to choke the life out of earth and sky.

"He left out the people," Grouse grumbled. "The birds, too."

"You don't understand," Guthrie said, setting his sketches aside a moment.

"No, he does," Horn insisted. "You see the world that I dream. Everything's dead. Grouse knows pain," Horn added, lifting the boy's shirt so that Guthrie could see the crude scar left by the *Wihio* bullet.

"You, too," Guthrie said, pointing to Buffalo Horn's ear. "My scars are all on the inside, where no one can see."

"You can't hide the darkness," Buffalo Horn insisted. "It's in your pictures. In your eyes."

"I hoped to leave it behind," Guthrie said, sighing.

"It follows," Horn muttered. "You can't ever get far away from it."

"No," Guthrie agreed. "It's always there."

Only later, after Guthrie erected a small tent beside the river and they grew more accustomed to each other, did Buffalo Horn share the tale of the *Wihio* trap. Guthrie then explained how his own mother and father, together with three sisters and a brother, died at the hands of *Wihio* raiders in Kansas.

"I might have stopped them, but I ran," Guthrie confessed.

"It's a heavy burden to bear," Buffalo Horn observed. "You should take a sweat and leave it behind. The path's ahead of you, not behind."

"And where are your ghosts, Horn?" Guthrie asked.

"Out there," Buffalo Horn explained, waving his hands across the land. "Everywhere."

Early the following morning Buffalo Horn began constructing a sweat lodge. Two Claws had taught him the ritual prayers, and he thought it a good idea for Guthrie to sweat the pain from his life. Grouse hoped to revive his own spirit, and Buffalo Horn hoped he might also be able to restore the harmony of his world.

The sweat did seem to help. It purged body and soul of ill humors, but it did nothing to erase the haunting memory of Buffalo Horn's dream. Grouse appeared less sad, though, and Guthrie actually smiled.

"You never asked me why I came here," the young trader noted afterward when the three of them swam together in Arkansas River.

"Who can ever know why?" Horn asked. "*Heammawihio* turned your path toward us."

"No, Charlie Bent suggested I come," Guthrie explained.

"He also has a difficult path to walk," Buffalo Horn noted. "He's part *Wihio* and part *Tsis tsis tas*. He's never at home in either camp."

"I'm not, either," Guthrie told them. "Haven't you wondered how I know some of your language?"

"You listen and learn," Grouse explained. "We know *Wihio* words."

"I didn't learn here," Guthrie told them. "My mother's mother was *Suhtai*. She taught me. I was luckier than my brothers and sisters. They looked Indian. It wasn't an accident, the fire that killed them. A crazy man whose brother was killed on the Santa Fe Trail came to our house. He shot my father and mother. Then, while the rest of us hid in terror, he set the house afire. I dug my way out, but the others . . ."

"I suspected it," Grouse said, touching Guthrie's shoulder. "You don't grow hair all over you like the other traders. At first I thought it was because you're so skinny, but then I wondered if you might be one of us."

"I'm not," Guthrie declared. "I can't ever be. Your people wouldn't accept me any more than they accept Bent. I'm nobody."

"You're Guthrie," Buffalo Horn insisted. "It's not important what other people imagine. So long as you know your own heart, you can walk the mountains, knowing who you are."

"And who are you, Horn?" Guthrie asked.

"A man lost," Horn said, sighing. "Once I knew, but now my dreams disturb any harmony I find."

"You can't get rid of everything with a sweat, can you?" Guthrie asked.

"No, but it helps," Horn explained. "The heat reminds us of the sun that warms the earth, and the suffering revives the heart. I have some searching to do, but I'm determined to find my way."

"Me, too," Guthrie added.

They left Bent's Fort that next morning. Buffalo Horn wasn't certain where he was headed, but he decided he had spent enough time on the Arkansas. He and Grouse led the way north and east, into buffalo country, and the three young men devoted their time to hunting. In the evenings Guthrie sketched the country, the buffalo, and his companions. The drawings took on a cheerful, almost comical appearance.

"You've found your way," Horn said, nodding solemnly. "It's good you came to us."

"I've given you nothing in return," Guthrie observed. "Maybe the pictures?"

"No," Horn said, declining the offer of a sketch. "I'm a modest man and need only a few possessions. I want something else."

"If I have it to give, it's yours," Guthrie insisted.

"Teach me about the *Wihio*," Buffalo Horn urged. "Help me understand him."

"There's no understanding him," Guthrie said, frowning. "Not for a *Tsis tsis tas*. I'll tell you what I know, and I'll help you learn his words. Maybe you don't need to understand so much as you need to know."

"Know what?" Grouse asked.

"How to keep him from killing you," Guthrie explained. "It's the worst part of it, too. He'll most likely do it in spite of everything. He won't even intend to. He'll do it with his sicknesses, his ignorance, and by choking the people with roads and towns and progress."

"Progress?" Horn asked, not fully understanding the strange word.

"Change," Guthrie declared. "I'm not certain people who trust in dreams and content themselves with hunting, praying, and trying to find peace have a place in the world that's coming."

"There's no place for us?" Horn asked.

"Maybe not," Guthrie confessed. "Maybe we can change, though."

Buffalo Horn started to reply, but he swallowed the words. Only a man who was part *Wihio* could fail to see that when a man changed what he was, he was as dead as those climbing Hanging Road.

Isaac Guthrie did his best to keep the promise, but it was difficult. Buffalo Horn could roll the *Wihio* words off his tongue, but the meanings behind them never touched his heart. The words were empty, colorless, lacking in passion. The whites could name a rock or a tree, but they failed to grasp the life within the thing. There was no melody in the strangers' language.

"They're a people good at counting," Charlie Bent, the old trader's mixed-blood son explained. "A *Wihio* needs straight lines and hard rules. It's why he can't understand a man who follows the wind and listens to his heart."

Guthrie also tried to explain the white man's road, but even though Horn lived near the traders and visited the soldier fort, he couldn't fathom their odd ways.

"Sweet Medicine was right," Horn told Grouse. "Long ago, in the time of the grandfathers' grandfathers, he warned of treating with the pale people. A rabbit may as well treat with a wolf. The two may get along for a time, but when the wolf becomes hungry, there can be only one result."

"The difference is that Wolf never hides his teeth," Grouse pointed out.

"Yes," Buffalo Horn agreed, laughing.

As the summer grasses began to brown and the wind grew colder, Buffalo Horn began to be hungry for the company of his own people. He missed Otter and the brothers. He wanted to see his little cousin and hear of his other relations. Most of all he ached for the comforting embrace of Bright Swallow Maiden.

"Winter's hard here," Grouse observed that same day. "The traders sit and drink whiskey. Even the bluecoats that are left find it a difficult time. There's nothing for us to do, either."

"You want to return to the *Wu ta piu?*" Horn asked.

"Yes," Grouse confessed. "If you're worried about Guthrie, we could take him along."

"You think he would be welcome? No, he looks too white. He's better off with the Bents."

"When do we leave?"

"Soon," Buffalo Horn promised. "Maybe we can ride out and hunt Bull Buffalo one final time before the hard-face moons arrive."

"My old coat's too small for me," Grouse said, grinning. "Guthrie will need something warmer, too."

"It's agreed then. We'll hunt."

Guthrie was easily persuaded, and once again the three of them rode out onto the plains. They located a herd of buffalo, but before they could plan the hunt, a small band of *Wihio* wagon people crossed their trail.

"It's late in the year to be crossing the prairie," Guthrie said, frowning at the small party. There were only six wagons, and each was pulled by a team of four thin horses. Women drove four of the wagons, and only one full-grown man was among the herd of children that plodded along on either flank.

"Don't get too close," Horn warned. "Maybe they've had sickness, and the men are in the wagons, burning with fever."

"No, it's the war," Guthrie declared. "These are the soldiers' widows and orphans. I've heard about such parties from the soldier chief."

"Orphans?" Grouse asked.

"Fatherless children," Guthrie explained. "Women with little ones and no husbands to provide for their care and protection."

"Don't the helpless ones have uncles? Cousins? Aren't there any men of the people to take them in?" Grouse asked.

"The *Wihio* expect them to provide for themselves," Guthrie said, frowning. "It seems odd to you, I know. Remember, I was such a person."

"You could have come to us," Grouse argued. "You probably have relatives in the *Suhtai* camp."

"They have burdens enough," Guthrie insisted. "These others have no one to help, though. They seem lost. I'll ride down and talk to them."

"We'll go with you," Horn volunteered.

"No, stay here," Guthrie urged. "I know these pilgrims. They won't see past the color of your skin and your quiver of arrows."

Buffalo Horn frowned, but he allowed Guthrie to go ahead alone. Guthrie spoke a considerable time with a tall hairy-faced man before the wagon people changed direction. Only then did Buffalo Horn lead Grouse toward the strangers.

Almost immediately a smallish *Wihio* girl screamed and yelled, "Indians!"

Guthrie tried to say something, but the wagon chief drew out a pistol and fired. The second ball struck Grouse in the throat and toppled him from his horse.

"Ayyyy!" Horn shouted, jumping from his pony and hurrying to the young man's side.

"Horn?" Grouse whimpered through a mouth filled with blood.

"Nothing lives long," Buffalo Horn began singing. "Only the earth and the mountains."

Grouse gazed at the sky a moment. Then his eyes lost their shine.

"Horn?" Guthrie called. "Is he . . ."

"He's gone," Buffalo Horn replied as he strung his bow. "Killed by another bad-heart *Wihio*."

"No," Guthrie argued, stepping in front of the wagon chief as the children fled to the safety of the nearby wagons.

"What are you going to tell me, Guthrie?" Horn asked. "That it's another mistake? That you can't blame the *Wihio* for being crazy?"

"No," Guthrie said, taking off his leather hat and throwing it onto the ground. He then stripped his shirt and pointed at his heart. "It's my doing," he said, speaking slowly, using *Tsis tsis tas* words and animating his feelings with hand motions. "I knew better. I should have led you away from here, but I wanted to help. I keep thinking I can prove myself to them, to the *Wihio*. And so I've sacrificed my brother's life!"

Buffalo Horn's anger drove him to notch an arrow, and for an instant he aimed it at Guthrie's exposed chest. The summer sun had turned it brown, though, and it was a white man that deserved punishing. Horn fired the arrow into the prairie and screamed out in a mixture of pain and futility.

Now the *Wihio* cautiously approached Grouse's corpse.

"He's only a boy," one of the women said, shuddering. "Lord, Jacob, what have you done?"

"I didn't know," the wagon chief pleaded. "I only saw . . ."

"His skin," Guthrie said, kneeling beside Grouse's bloody body. "I should have stopped this, Horn. I should have . . ."

"Only Man Above decides what will happen," Buffalo Horn argued.

"We'll take him back to his people," Guthrie declared.

"I'll take him home," Buffalo Horn said, frowning. "You won't be welcome there."

"No?" Guthrie asked.

"As I'll never be welcome among them," Horn said, pointing to the wagon people. "Go away from this country, Guthrie. You'll try to be a bridge between two peoples, but it will only bring you sadness and disappointment."

"Probably," Guthrie admitted. "But if I can't find a path to walk here, I won't find it elsewhere."

"I'm going," Horn announced as he cradled Grouse's thin frame in his arms and lifted it onto his waiting horse.

"I should . . ." Guthrie began.

"I hope you find your way, brother," Buffalo Horn told the young trader.

"I hope you find yours, brother," Guthrie answered.

12

Grouse's death tore at Buffalo Horn's soul like an eagle's talons ripping the soft belly of a river trout. As he broke down his small lodge and packed his possessions, Horn couldn't help noticing Grouse's meager belongings. A man, even one as young as Grouse, should leave more to mark his passing. It was so easy for the *Wihio* to kill!

Twice Buffalo Horn spied Isaac Guthrie watching from the far bank of the river. Anger fueled an urge to strike out at the trader, but what purpose would another death serve? Later Horn considered inviting the trader over to share the grief. Horn knew, though, that they must take separate paths. The *Wu ta piu* would react sourly to Grouse's death, and Guthrie would provide too tempting a target for their anger.

The Horn tied his lodgeskins onto a drag made up of short pine poles and placed Grouse's broken body on top. A red trader's blanket shrouded the unfortunate young man's face, but Buffalo Horn nevertheless felt Grouse's presence. Riding north toward the *Wu ta piu* camps, Horn felt a cold cloud engulf him. Even singing the old *Tsis tsis tas* and *Suhtai* mourning songs failed to ease his gloom. Finally Buffalo Horn reined in his pony and dismounted.

"*Heammawihio*, help me!" he cried. "I've lost my way!"

The wind stirred, and an odd sensation crept up Buffalo Horn's spine. He sank to the earth and buried his face in his hands. The sadness overwhelmed him, and he remained there, numb. So much had happened. Sometimes it seemed to him that every good memory in his young life had been drowned in a sea of death and pain.

Buffalo Horn stared out across the empty landscape. He had only his thoughts for company, and so there was no escaping the sense of hopelessness.

"*Heammawihio*, help me," he pleaded a second time.

An odd calm settled over the land then, and Buffalo Horn gazed at the sky overhead. He saw no ominous hawk. Instead he watched a great white cloud take shape on the eastern horizon. It might have been Bull Buffalo. It had his shape.

"Uncle, what can I do?" Horn called.

"Nothing," the wind seemed to whisper.

"I have to restore the harmony of my world," Buffalo Horn whispered. "I won't find it here, alone. No, I have to go back, deliver this dead brother to his family. Then maybe I can put his ghost behind me."

Horn only half believed it possible, but the notion of returning to the *Wu ta piu*, seeing Otter and Bright Swallow, and speaking of the future with Black Kettle cheered him. Gradually the sorrow flowed out of his soul, and he recovered his senses.

He didn't know exactly where Black Kettle would have taken the band, but something unseen guided him north to the banks of Red Shield River. The *Wu ta piu* had formed their camp circle in that country three of the past four winters, and Buffalo Horn hoped to locate them there. It was a considerable distance, and Grouse's corpse had begun to take on an unsettling odor. The horses grew skittish, and Buffalo Horn reluctantly abandoned his intention of returning his friend's body to his family. Instead Horn chose a high hill overlooking the river. After making the proper prayers, he erected a scaffold and placed the corpse atop it.

"Hurry on to the other side," Horn whispered as he began cutting his hair. "Maybe you can find peace there."

He placed Grouse's weapons at his side, and he cut the tails from two ponies and tied them to the scaffold poles. He then raised the lodge over the scaffold and left most of his own belongings inside.

He remained on the hillside three days, observing the mourning rites. When he finally left, he rode like a dead man eastward along the river. With his hair cut short, he appeared younger, more vulnerable. He ate almost nothing, and his ribs protruded through the bronze skin of his sides. He had left his heavy garments in the burial lodge, and he wore only a plain breechclout.

For two days he saw no hint of life. Then he sniffed the odor of woodsmoke. Slowly, cautiously, he continued. In time he saw the faint plumes of smoke rising from cooking fires. He tensed, knowing he might be approaching a friendly *Tsis tsis tas* camp or a band of Pawnee raiders, or even a camp of *Wihio* wagon people like the ones who had slain Grouse. He threaded his way between rocks and trees, avoiding any wary eyes. He lacked the heart to fight anyone. He only wanted to escape the darkness that choked his world.

"No more killing," he mumbled as he momentarily halted his pony. "No more dying."

Overhead a hawk shrieked, and the dream came back to him. He shuddered as he recalled the bloody massacre. With a shout raised from deep within him, Buffalo Horn slapped his horse into a gallop and raced out from the trees and on toward the waiting encampment.

He half expected to spy columns of bluecoat soldiers surging toward a peaceful camp, but he saw nothing of the sort. Instead he raced by startled pony boys and trotted between racks of drying buffalo meat toward the circle of painted lodges. By then he had recognized the camp as *Tsis tsis tas*. Once the panic engendered by the dream abated, he slowed his mount and caught his breath.

"It's Buffalo Horn!" Otter cried. "Our brother's returned."

Rabbit Foot and Snow Bear were the first to reach him. They virtually tore him from his horse.

"Have you been fighting the Pawnees?" Snow Bear asked.

"What's happened, brother?" Otter called from a stone's throw away.

"Someone's died," Rabbit Foot said, touching Horn's shorn head. "Where's Grouse?"

Summer Cherry Woman raced over, leading her little son. Her face betrayed fear, and Horn read a similar question in her eyes.

"*Na tsin' os ta*, it's good you've come home," Pony Leg said, joining his wife. "But where's our brother?"

Buffalo Horn turned to Summer Cherry Woman and dropped his eyes.

"I was bringing him to you, but it was too far," he explained. "I put him in a high place, two days' easy riding from here."

"He's dead?" she whispered.

"It shouldn't have happened," Horn told her. "He was riding with me and a trader, Guthrie, not far from Bent's Fort. We came upon some *Wihio* wagon people, and the trader thought we should help them. They saw only enemies, and they killed the young man who was your brother."

"Did you punish them?" Rabbit Foot asked, clutching Horn's arm.

"No," Buffalo Horn said, swallowing the bitter taste that filled his mouth.

"It's always the same," Rabbit Foot muttered. "They come into our country and kill us. Nobody does anything. Soon we'll all be dead."

"No," Black Kettle said, making his way through the throng of curious *Wu ta piu* men, women, and children. The chief's probing eyes peered into Horn's soul. Buffalo Horn remained mute. He wanted to speak, needed to explain, but he suddenly lost the power of speech.

"Take our brother's horse," Otter told Rabbit Foot. "He's tired. He looks like he needs to eat something, too."

"We have plenty of food here," Summer Cherry Woman added. "You'll eat with us tonight. Pony Leg, we should have a feast to celebrate your nephew's return."

Horn tried to return her forced smile. He couldn't. He knew she was thinking that her brother should be there instead. He wished it were possible for the two of them to exchange places, but Grouse's pain was over. Horn had the longer, harder climb.

"First I want to talk with him," Black Kettle announced.

"There will be time for that later," Otter suggested.

"The words need to be spoken now," Black Kettle insisted. "There are things I have to know."

"He's right," Pony Leg agreed. "Go with him, Horn. Then come eat with us."

"It's going to be hard," Buffalo Horn objected. "I . . ."

"It won't be as hard as living among the *Wihio*," Pony Leg replied. "Our family has always done the difficult things."

"We're Elks, after all," Otter whispered.

"Yes," Buffalo Horn agreed.

"Let's walk," Black Kettle said, pointing toward the river. Buffalo Horn turned and followed the chief. They walked a short way before halting. A group of pony boys approached, but a stern look from the chief sent them hurrying back toward the horse herd.

"You didn't find any answers?" Black Kettle asked.

"I did as you suggested," Buffalo Horn told the chief. "I walked among the whites."

"What did they teach you?"

"I learned to speak their words," Horn explained. "I learned to treat with them. I know the value of a buffalo hide and a *Wihio* blanket. Both are more valuable than the life of a *Tsis tsis tas* boy."

"You believe that?"

"It's the way they are, Uncle."

"Not all," Black Kettle insisted. "The Bents know us. They've taken our relatives for wives. They . . ."

"They're not the ones who decide what will happen," Horn pointed out. "It's the soldier chiefs. Not all the *Wihio* have bad hearts, but there are enough that do to kill us. Oh, they don't shoot us because they hate us. No, they kill because we're in their way. We matter less than the ants."

"It's not true, Horn. It's sadness and pain that clouds your thinking."

"No, my dreams tell me things," Buffalo Horn explained. "I've seen the bluecoat soldiers killing us."

"They're in the east."

"They'll come back. I know you think you're doing right, but maybe we would do better to fight them. When your enemy gives you a strong fight, you begin to respect him. I don't like the Pawnees, but I don't take them lightly."

"It works with other tribes, but not the *Wihio*," the Kettle argued. "The only peoples who will survive a fight with them are the ones who reach agreements with them."

"We've made treaties before," Buffalo Horn pointed out. "It doesn't change anything."

"Then we'll treat with them again. As long as we talk, there's hope of better relations."

Buffalo Horn doubted it, but he couldn't destroy Black Kettle's hope. The older man was convinced of his path.

"Who am I to say what's going to happen?" Horn finally asked. "You might be right."

"You can help me avoid trouble, Horn," Black Kettle added. "I've been asked to go to Denver, the big *Wihio* town. We'll speak to the *Wihio* chiefs there and share our concerns. That way we can begin to understand."

"I can do you no good," Horn argued.

"You understand their words," Black Kettle noted. "Before we have had to rely on traders or soldiers to make our meaning known. You can be my *Wihio* mouth and ears."

Buffalo Horn started to argue. He wanted to remind the chief of the severed toes, of dead parents, of Grouse, but he swallowed his reply. *Heammawihio* had given him another difficult path to walk, and he had to walk it.

The journey to Denver came later, though. First Buffalo Horn had to reacquaint himself with his relatives. Although he said little about Grouse's death, Summer Cherry Woman sensed Horn's pain and guilt.

"That young man who was my brother was determined to find his own way," she told Buffalo Horn. "You never led him anywhere he wasn't certain to go."

A surer sign that she held no ill feelings was her willingness to allow Horn to oversee his small cousin Mole's activities.

"You should have had younger brothers," she whispered to him one afternoon. "You have a talent for dealing with little ones."

"I can get them killed easily enough," he observed.

"I recall you saved a relative of mine."

"I didn't lengthen his path much."

"You did your best," Summer Cherry Woman observed. "No man can do more. I'm glad Mole will have your attention."

"I owe Pony Leg that much," Horn said. "Mole will have other helpers, too. Otter's brothers are riding Man's Road now."

"I was wrong to think you had no brothers, wasn't I?"

"Yes, there are those three," Horn admitted.

Actually Snow Bear was becoming a regular hunting companion of Buffalo Horn's. Otter remained close to camp because Feather Dance Woman was expecting a child momentarily. Swallow came sometimes, too, but Rabbit Foot stayed away. He rarely said anything, but Buffalo Horn knew the Foot held him accountable for Grouse's death.

Buffalo Horn had also begun walking the river road with Bright Swallow Maiden again.

"I'm surprised you still haven't taken a husband," Horn told her when they spoke after his homecoming feast.

"I'm surprised you stayed away so long."

"Too long," he muttered.

"My father had offers," she explained, "but he likes my cooking. I was in no hurry. I knew you'd return."

"I still haven't regained any harmony," he warned her.

"Maybe you'll find yourself during the coming journey."

"I'm never at peace among the *Wihio*," he told her. "I'm not certain I can find harmony anywhere."

"Maybe I can help," she said, clasping his hands.

"Maybe," he replied.

Actually, he did find a degree of peace walking the river and sharing her company. Part of him was ready to send Pony Leg to White Goose to speak of horses. The pending trip to Denver hovered like a circling buzzard over his life, though, and he resolved to do nothing until the journey was over.

Barely a week had transpired since Buffalo Horn's return when Snow Bear brought the summons.

"Black Kettle asks you to come speak with him," Snow Bear explained. "I'll prepare our ponies."

"Our ponies?" Buffalo Horn asked.

"Otter would go, but his son hasn't yet been born," Snow Bear pointed out.

"He'll need a watcher when he goes to seek a dream," Horn argued.

"Rabbit Foot and Swallow will do it," Snow Bear replied. "I haven't seen a *Wihio* camp before. It will be interesting."

As it turned out, though, the bluecoat leader, a minor soldier chief named Wynkoop, insisted only a small party could go to Denver. Besides Black Kettle, two other *Tsis tsis tas* chiefs were invited. White Antelope and Bull Bear agreed to come. The Arapahoes sent four chiefs. A few younger men came along, but most were sent back to their camps.

"You needn't come," Wynkoop told Buffalo Horn. "I have an interpreter."

Horn translated for Black Kettle, and the chief folded his arms.

"Tell the bluecoats I insist," the Kettle barked.

"My chief wants his own mouth and ears," Buffalo Horn told the soldier chief. "I won't twist his words, and I won't bend yours. Isn't it important we all understand each other?"

Wynkoop asked a few questions, and when Buffalo Horn replied to each, the soldier agreed Horn should come. The following day they started westward.

It didn't take long for Buffalo Horn to discover the

reason for the meeting. The whites were angry because some Crazy Dogs had stolen several *Wihio* women and children. Some of the missing people had probably been taken by other tribes, and Black Kettle had personally arranged for the release of several captives by trading ponies with other bands. The *Wihio* insisted there were more prisoners among the *Tsis tsis tas* and demanded that they be freed.

"They want to punish us for holding *Wihio* children," Buffalo Horn muttered to himself. "What of the little ones they've killed?"

"I didn't bring you with me to talk like that," Black Kettle scolded his young companion.

"I'm only speaking the truth," Horn complained.

"Yes, and if that alone could bring us peace, I would agree to speak it. They only grow angry when I complain, though. Let's hear their words and treat with their big chief, Evans."

In Denver this Evans, governor of the territory, met the Arapaho and *Tsis tsis tas* chiefs at an army camp outside of the town. Evans offered his guests the chance to speak first, and Black Kettle rose to his feet.

The *Wu ta piu* chief explained how he had come with the soldiers, following them blindly. All he wanted was peace. "We come here free," Black Kettle explained. "Without fear. We want to be at peace with you, to understand you."

If Buffalo Horn had not spoken the words himself, he would have suspected the accuracy of the translation. Evans didn't seem to comprehend a single phrase. Instead he accused Black Kettle of starting a war. He shouted angrily that the Indians would soon be sorry for causing trouble. The war over the freeing of the black men was nearly over, and soon the plains would be full of bluecoats.

"My advice to you all is to help the army," Evans added. "Live peacefully, and turn over the other captives. If an Indian steals livestock or kills a settler, turn him over."

The words were hard for Buffalo Horn to utter, but Black Kettle nevertheless agreed to help.

"We only want peace," the chief insisted.

"It's a mistake to speak of peace with a man like that," Horn argued afterward as he and Black Kettle prepared to return to the *Wu ta piu* camp.

"He's an important man," Black Kettle pointed out. "His words carry weight."

"He wants war," Buffalo Horn observed. "Did you see how his eyes brightened when he spoke of the soldiers? We should be very careful."

"It's always wise to be careful," Black Kettle agreed.

Perhaps for that reason Black Kettle summoned the people to Fort Lyon.

"Wynkoop promised to protect us from the other *Wihio*," Black Kettle told the other chiefs. "We can get rations there, too."

When they returned to Fort Lyon, though, Wynkoop had been replaced by a new bluecoat chief. This man, Anthony, agreed to keep Wynkoop's promise, but he warned there was sickness among the bluecoats. He suggested Black Kettle make his camp near Sandy Creek, two days' ride to the east.

The place filled Buffalo Horn with an odd sense of foreboding. It was a poor place to make a winter camp. There were no hills or timber to shield a camp from the fierce winter winds, and no cover against enemy raiders. Nevertheless most of the southern *Tsis tsis tas* and three Arapaho bands erected their camp circles there.

"We have to trust the *Wihio* chiefs," Black Kettle argued. "We can't fight them and survive."

"Perhaps not," Buffalo Horn told Otter when he went to visit his brother-friend's newborn son. "But I would rather put my head in a bear's mouth than make my camp in a place so open to attack as this!"

13

Buffalo Horn had no memory of true peace. All his life one enemy or another had tormented the *Tsis tsis tas*. That autumn was no exception. To the north, along Fat River, *Wihio* soldiers and Crazy Dogs frequently fought. Sometimes the soldiers would be looking for some wandering cow. Another time they would surround a party of *Tsis tsis tas* hunters and demand surrender. Worse, the wagon people shot at anybody wearing feathers or riding a painted pony. Too many young women cut their hair and sang the mourning songs. Too many small children walked the world at their uncles' or cousins' sides.

"It's always the same," Otter grumbled. "They ask everything of us. When they have it all, they will believe we are too poor a people to live. That's when they'll finish killing us."

It sometimes seemed that way to Buffalo Horn, too.

With wary eyes he studied the bands of bluecoats who rode by on the far side of the creek.

"They'll ride out of the mists one morning and kill us," Horn warned Black Kettle. "Just look into their eyes. They're hungry for murder."

"No, only curious," Black Kettle insisted. "They're looking for white captives, too."

"We have nobody like that here," Buffalo Horn pointed out.

"Not here, but some of the young men continue to burn the *Wihio* ranches, and sometimes they take women and little ones. I send those I discover to the fort, but I don't see everything."

"And what about the *Tsis tsis tas* killed by the wagon people?" Horn asked.

"We have to warn the young men to stay away from the wagon roads. Once, not so long ago, the wagon chiefs were smart. They brought along guides who knew the tribes. Now the wagon people are all old men and children. They're too frightened to think."

"They shoot you just as dead, Uncle."

"Yes," Black Kettle admitted. "They're sad later, but they'll kill again the next time one of us comes to treat with them. It's difficult to understand such people, but we have to learn to live with them."

"They'll never allow us to live among them," Buffalo Horn argued. "They'll cut us like oxen and dress us up like Pawnees, in cloth shirts and trousers. Soon we won't be men at all."

"You talk like the Crazy Dogs," the Kettle admonished Buffalo Horn. "They burn some *Wihio* houses and kill some people. We're all blamed for these things. The Lakotas on Platte River take horses and shoot soldiers, so the bluecoats grow eager to kill us.

It has to stop, Frog. We have to stop it. That path will only get us all killed."

"They'll kill us anyway," Buffalo Horn growled.

"No," the Kettle argued. "We have an agreement. So long as we camp in this place, with the Arapahoes, and hurt nobody, we have nothing to fear."

"Don't we?" Buffalo Horn asked. "I've told you about my dream."

"Dreams can advise us, but we have to walk our path. Don't be so concerned, though. There are just a few bluecoats at Fort Wise. This new chief of theirs, Anthony, has hard eyes, but he isn't in a hurry to die."

Buffalo Horn nodded. The words were persuasive. He and the Kettle had recently visited the *Wihio* fort, and neither saw enough soldiers there to endanger a large camp like that of the Arapahoes and *Tsis tsis tas* at Sand Creek, as the *Wihio* called the place.

"You're still worried," Black Kettle observed.

"I remember my dream," Buffalo Horn told him. "And I remember the bad-heart words spoken by the *Wihio* chief, Evans. He wasn't treating us with respect. He spoke like a *Wihio* scolds his children."

"He was angry," Black Kettle said, trying to excuse the governor's actions.

"We should be the angry ones," Horn insisted. "It's our land that's been stolen. It's our young men that are killed."

Buffalo Horn knew in his heart that things would only grow worse. Winter was coming, and that was always a hard time. He wished the people were still camped in the hills beyond Red Shield River where game was more plentiful and bluecoats didn't ride by each day to gaze at the camp with hungry eyes.

He wasn't the only one to sense the danger. Even as

the first snowflakes swirled through the late autumn air, Otter began packing up his lodge.

"Winter's here, brother," Buffalo Horn observed. "It's too late to leave."

"You're wrong," Otter replied. "I've seen the bluecoats' eyes. It's too late to stay here."

"You can't go alone like this," Horn objected, "just you and Feather Dance Woman, your small son."

"His name's Rock Watcher," Otter pointed out. "It might have been something else, but you didn't invite a dream to guide the namers. Brother, I remember the other dream, and so do you. We should hurry away from this place."

"A man of the people has to consider the welfare of the helpless ones," Buffalo Horn argued.

"We're all helpless," Otter said, sighing. "I remember how we stood, waiting for the bluecoat chief Sumner to strike. When the *Wihio* raised their long knives, our power vanished. It will be the same this time. Your dream told you that much."

"I can at least stand and fight them, Otter."

"My mother's three sons are coming with me," Otter said. "I hoped my other brother would also come. He'll be needed."

"A man can only make his stand in one place," Horn pointed out.

"Yes, and you're right. You should stay and defend the helpless ones. Someone should."

"Someone will," Buffalo Horn vowed.

"He didn't help Grouse very much," Rabbit Foot said, joining Otter. "He hears the chiefs and values their wishing words. He doesn't understand what's coming."

"Do you?" Buffalo Horn asked. "Does anyone?"

"We'll go north, to the Lakotas," Otter said, waving Rabbit Foot along. "I've hunted with them. They'll welcome us."

"There are bluecoats riding near Fat River," Horn observed.

"They won't find us," Otter boasted. "We're too few to attract anyone's attention."

"I hope not," Buffalo Horn replied. "Maybe the Lakotas know a path you can walk that's safe from *Wihio* trouble."

"Perhaps," Otter said, clasping his brother-friend's wrists. "It's a hard thought, facing the next fight without Buffalo Horn."

"Harder knowing you won't be there to steady the young men," Horn added. "You're right to keep your son safe. The people will need brave hearts. Maybe we'll be together when it's time to celebrate New Life Lodge."

"Certainly," Otter whispered. "Earth will need our help to become green once more."

Otter's brothers began packing the lodge onto its poles, and Feather Dance Woman spoke farewells to her sister and father. Then the little band started north, and Buffalo Horn walked alone to the river, shivering from a chill far colder than that carried by the wintry wind.

Usually Horn kept his own counsel. After all, he was no chief chosen to look after the welfare of others. He was still a young man, and the young hunters who respected his skill with a killing lance and his courage facing enemies were out riding the north country with the Crazy Dogs. Black Kettle's camp, and the others nestled along Sand Creek, were communities of women and children. Those men who remained were fathers and grandfathers. Even the pony boys appeared to be young for their task.

Horn busied himself tending his horses, crafting bows for youngsters, and walking the creek path with Bright Swallow Maiden. Those walks offered a brief pleasant respite from what was becoming a seemingly endless world of fear and anxiety.

"What's wrong?" she asked again and again. "Did your walk among the *Wihio* blind you to the sacred path?"

"It's not that," he insisted.

"Then it's the dream," she said, gazing deeply into his eyes. "You're afraid."

"Not for myself," he mumbled. "For you. For little Mole. For all the helpless ones. Especially for Otter's small band."

"You dreamed again then?" she asked.

"No, but I see the bluecoats across the creek."

"Everybody does," she noted. "I understand why you worry about Otter. My father warned my sister not to go north alone like that. Bluecoats will mistake their intentions and attack."

"Mistake?" Buffalo Horn muttered. "It won't be a mistake. They'll attack because they see the chance to kill some of us."

"The *Wihio* are only punishing people they think are raiders," Bright Swallow argued.

"So when they charge this camp, it will be because they fear we'll attack their towns?" Horn asked. "With what? A few lances and some old worthless muskets? Can't you see how more and more soldiers camp out there, watching?"

"They haven't hurt anyone."

"What about Summer Cherry Woman's brother?" Buffalo Horn asked.

"That wasn't the bluecoats."

"It might as well have been. Swallow, we should collect our belongings and follow Otter. I have Lakota cousins. We could . . ."

"We're safer here," she insisted.

"Are we?" he asked. "I know they'll come. Soon, when the snows are deeper and we aren't able to run away."

"My father says we're protected here," Bright Swallow argued. "Black Kettle and White Antelope have treated with the soldiers. Everything's agreed."

"What good have agreements with the *Wihio* ever done us? They break their promises whenever they want! Or ignore them. One of us is already gone."

"It's that boy's dying that's troubling you," she observed.

"I should have prevented it," he told her. "I have the far-seeing eyes, but what use are they when I can't change anything? It's the worst sort of torture, standing by and waiting for the dying to begin."

"There's always something you can do."

"What?"

"Seek another dream. Ask *Heammawihio* to show you a way."

"And if there isn't any way?"

"There has to be," she insisted. "A man can do anything if he trusts himself and makes the proper preparations. Ask for another dream. Find a path we can walk."

"I'll invite the dream," he agreed. "But only *Heammawihio* can find a path away from the death that clings to this place."

"Ask him to show you that path," she pleaded. "There are too many helpless ones here for the men to protect."

Horn sighed. That was true enough. There were simply too many mothers, small brothers, and sisters there.

"That's why we must stay here," Black Kettle had explained. "The *Wihio* soldiers have promised us food and protection. The whites will ride out after the ones of us that are camped past Arkansas River or in the north country with the Lakotas."

Buffalo Horn didn't believe that. What hope did a few bluecoats have of catching small bands scattered across the plains? No, if the *Wihio* decided to strike a blow against the *Tsis tsis tas*, there were plenty to kill close at hand.

He searched his heart for a solution to the problem. What could a solitary man do to change the course of events? He might as well try to stop a river from flowing or the sun from coming up! He hoped to find an answer in his dreams, but he saw only a frozen world of snow and mist, even in his sleep.

"*Na tsin' os ta*, I know you're worried, but look how deep the snows have become," Pony Leg told him. "The *Wihio* are crazy, but they're not coming out here when Hard Face Moon is shining. They're a lazy people. They need the sun on their backs."

"You didn't see the ones in my dream," Buffalo Horn objected. "The snow wasn't half as cold as their eyes."

"What do you want to do?"

"Stop it. I don't know how, though. Or even if it's possible. I've warned the chiefs, but they don't hear my words. They believe in the *Wihio* promises."

"No," Pony Leg replied. "They don't. What else can they do, though? It's fine for a few young men like Otter to ride off alone, but someone has to stay and look after the helpless ones."

"It's our obligation," Buffalo Horn agreed.

"You could do something more, *Na tsin' os ta,*" Pony Leg insisted. "Invite a dream."

"Bright Swallow suggested that, too, but it's a hard time to ride off alone into the hills."

"You need a watcher."

"Otter and his brothers are gone. There's nobody to do it."

"You have an uncle here."

"And a cousin," Horn pointed out. "You can't leave Summer Cherry Woman and Mole, not with so much danger near."

"There are many good men here to look after my son," Pony Leg observed. "We'll take a sweat together. Tonight we can cross the creek and find a hill."

"You're certain?"

"I'm not as young as Otter, but I have eyes. A half-blind Pawnee could spot trouble when the world around him's painted white with snow."

"Then it's decided," Buffalo Horn said, sighing. "I'll make my preparations."

"I can help with that, too," Pony Leg said, stepping closer. "You didn't bring much back from your time on Arkansas River. Summer Cherry Woman has some good elk and buffalo hides for us to take with us and plenty of food."

"I'll be fasting," Horn explained.

"Only until the dream comes," Pony Leg noted. "Then you'll need food to drive away winter's chills."

Buffalo Horn wasn't sure whether it was the sweltering heat inside the sweat lodge or riding out from camp with Pony Leg that chased away the gloom that had been choking his world. The bitter cold of the wind and the dampness of the snow-covered ground brought every inch of him to life.

"It will take a big fire to keep you from freezing up there," Pony Leg said as he turned toward a nearby hill. "I wish we could find a cave. It's best to have shelter in winter."

"No, I need to see the stars," Buffalo Horn argued. "How can I invite *Heammawihio* into my dreams if He can't see me standing bare and helpless before Him?"

"I hope He hurries the dream," Pony Leg said, eyeing his nephew with concern. "This is a freezing winter. It's certain to kill a man who forsakes food and warm hides."

"Build up the fire," Horn advised. "It can keep me warm, and perhaps its light will attract Man Above's eyes."

"Maybe so," Pony Leg agreed.

They left the ponies at the base of the hill. The trail beyond was rocky, and ice made the going treacherous. Buffalo Horn and Pony Leg trudged through deep drifts and eased their way along an icy ledge to a small clearing on the bare side of the hill. Horn nodded to his uncle, indicating it was an appropriate place, and Pony Leg began clearing the snow from a small circle. As Horn spread hides a foot away and began painting himself for the singing, Pony Leg built a fire with dry kindling he had brought from the camp. He then cut cottonwood logs so that the dry interior wood could welcome the flame while the wet exterior dried. Soon a smoky fire began warming the chill winter air.

Buffalo Horn had prayed before. He had even invited dreams. That afternoon was different. A sense of dread, of urgency, filled every inch of him. After stripping himself bare, he began singing loudly a mixture of old *Suhtai* prayers and warrior songs he had learned riding with the Elks. He also cut the flesh of his chest and arms so that warm blood trickled down his flanks, ran down his legs, and mixed with the snow below.

"Man Above, show me the way," he pleaded again and again. "Lead me back to the sacred path. Your people need your help. Our enemies are many, and you alone can save us from them."

Most of that afternoon, night, and the following day Buffalo Horn danced and prayed and bled. He shivered as the wind tore at his exposed flesh, but he refused Pony Leg's offer of an elk robe. He intended to attract the dream through his suffering. Even so, he began to wonder if the dream would come before he fainted from loss of blood or simply froze.

He did collapse, but as Pony Leg covered his nephew's quivering body with elk and buffalo hides, the dream was already creeping into Buffalo Horn's mind.

The world was painted white, like before, and the *Tsis tsis tas* lodges stood in their circles beside the icy creek. Dogs yelped, and small boys raced about, gathering sticks for the morning cooking fires. It was as peaceful a scene as Buffalo Horn had ever witnessed.

Suddenly the heavens seemed to explode as thunder roared across the camp. Lodges exploded in great fiery clouds. Women and children ran about, screaming and racing for safety.

On the far side of the stream, not far from the hill

where Buffalo Horn lay at that very moment, Bull Buffalo emerged from a smoky white mist.

"Nothing lives long," the massive creature sang as *Wihio* bullets struck its chest and shoulders. "Nothing."

Horn didn't see the bloody spectacle in the camp. He only heard the screaming and the shooting. He felt the tears in his eyes as familiar voices pleaded with bluecoat soldiers for their lives. He saw Bright Swallow Maiden fleeing for safety. He saw long knives cut the life out of old, respected chiefs. It was more than a man could bear, and Horn screamed out in madness.

"It's all right," Pony Leg said, shaking his nephew awake. "The dream came. It was only that."

"It was enough," Horn replied, gazing wild-eyed at the flickering flames beside him.

"*Heammawihio* showed you a path. Tell me what we can do."

"Nothing," Horn said, hugging himself so that the unearthly chill might lose its grip on his soul. "Everything's gone. We're dying! Even the spirits are helpless to prevent it!"

"Tell me about it," Pony Leg pleaded.

"I will," he promised, hoping that perhaps Pony Leg might be able to convince others of the danger. But even as he related the vision, he felt the emptiness within growing. Before, he at least had seen the hawk. Now there was nothing but the thunder, and it offered no time, no hope of escape.

"We'll be watchful," Pony Leg vowed. "We'll send out scouts to spy on the bluecoats."

"Those are good ideas," Horn agreed. He doubted that any of it would help, though.

14

Each morning Buffalo Horn rose and warily walked out onto the snow-covered banks of Sand Creek. The stream itself was frozen, and an icy chill gripped the land. Horn gazed overhead, searching for a screeching hawk or some other omen of danger. Sometimes he saw ominous black storm clouds, but the soldiers he expected to see failed to arrive. Bluecoats from Fort Lyon continued to ride along Sand Creek, but only a few rode up to the camp itself.

George and Charlie Bent, the *Wihio* trader's mixed-blood sons, came to swap flour and gunpowder for buffalo hides. The Bents were followed a few days later by the bluecoats' interpreter, John Smith. Smith, who brought his Indian wife and mixed-blood son, bartered two wagons of trade goods for a hundred buffalo hides.

"It's a good thing, having *Wihio* with us," Black

Kettle declared. "No soldiers will attack when their friends are here."

Buffalo Horn wasn't certain how much the bluecoats valued the younger Bents or Smith. Horn remembered Isaac Guthrie's tales of *Wihio* prejudice and mistrust. Wasn't it Guthrie's eagerness to win favor with the wagon people that had caused Grouse's death? Many *Tsis tsis tas* considered anyone who worked for the bluecoats to be an enemy. Pony Leg, in particular, suspected Smith of spying on the camp.

"Even so, the bluecoats wouldn't attack with their spies here," Pony Leg observed. "They'll come later, after these traders leave."

Buffalo Horn wasn't half so certain. Why would the *Wihio* send spies into Black Kettle's camp? Any fool knew where the *Tsis tsis tas* were camped, and anyone with eyes could count their number. The snows choked every path of escape, and the ponies were growing thin and weak under the starving moons of winter.

Only two days after Smith's arrival the yapping of camp dogs woke Buffalo Horn from a troubled sleep.

"*Na tsin' os ta?*" Pony Leg called as Horn began dressing.

"It's only barking dogs," Horn explained.

"Is that why you're hurrying out to count the ponies?" Summer Cherry Woman asked.

Little Mole also sat up. The child stared with questioning eyes as his cousin gave him a concerned nod before departing the lodge.

Outside, the sun was beginning to cast a yellow, warming glow across the frozen landscape. Buffalo Horn blinked his eyes into focus and gazed out toward the creek. A heavy mist clung to the creek bank. A figure on horseback emerged from that foggy shroud and splashed into the thin ice coating the surface of the creek.

"The hawk," Buffalo Horn mumbled. Where was the hawk? It should have warned him!

The first thunderous boom erupted from the far side of the creek. The bluecoats were firing off two big cannons, but the first shells fell short of the camp, shattering the silent morning but otherwise harming no one.

"Bluecoats!" Buffalo Horn shouted. "They're coming!"

He raced back to Pony Leg's lodge and found his bow. As he strung it, a second explosion splintered a sheet of ice alongside the creek.

"Here!" Black Kettle shouted. "Come to my lodge. You'll be safe there!"

Black Kettle was running a large rectangular cloth up a rope attached to his lodge pole. It was the striped American flag with the blue corner full of stars. One of the treaty makers had given it to the *Tsis tsis tas*, and it was supposed to show the bluecoats that here was a peaceful camp. The Kettle also raised smaller white surrender flags. He then gathered a handful of women and children beside him. The flags didn't stop the bluecoats from firing off their big guns, though. A whole line of horse soldiers splashed across the creek and turned toward the pony herd.

"The horses!" Pony Leg shouted.

Buffalo Horn also realized the danger. He raced along the creek in an effort to distract the bluecoats, but they were mounted. Buffalo Horn slipped and slid in the snow, and the raiders raced on to the animals and captured the entire herd. George Bent, the young mixed-blood, helped Horn to his feet.

"Maybe we can do something to help the others," Bent suggested.

Buffalo Horn nodded. He could tell Bent's heart was with the horses. He had ten of the best animals in the entire herd, and no one knew better than a *Wihio* trader's son the chance of getting them back from the bluecoats.

Two other big guns opened fire then, and these new guns found the *Wu ta piu* camp immediately. White Goose's lodge disappeared in an inferno of fire and smoke. A second explosion blasted a gap in the camp circle only a stone's throw from Black Kettle's flag-draped tipi.

"No!" Buffalo Horn screamed as he raced toward the fiery remains of the Goose's lodge. His heart ached with the notion of Bright Swallow's broken body lying there. She met him halfway there, though, and pulled him aside.

"It's too late," she said with wide, angry eyes. "He that was my father has gone to join his son."

"You're safe, at least," he said, holding her tightly. "I'll get you to safety."

"You have other obligations," she said, waving toward the bewildered circles of women and children. A few men managed to stumble out of their lodges and locate bows or rifles. It was a world of madness blown apart by cascading explosions.

White Antelope, a famous fighter who had touched the treaty pen, disdained the offer of a rifle. Instead he walked out in front of the camp and called to the bluecoats. The chief wore a peace medal given him by the *Wihio* leaders to guarantee the peace. He hoped he could halt the attack, but a man might as well hope to move a mountain. Riflemen fired a volley, and the chief fell at the edge of the creek. A swarm of bluecoats quickly. surged across the stream and began stripping his corpse.

Buffalo Horn glanced around in hopes of spotting a familiar face. He regretted more than ever Otter's leaving. At the same time, he was glad at least some of the people were safe. Finally he saw Pony Leg and a group of youngsters shielding a party of fleeing women and children.

"There," Horn told Bright Swallow Maiden. "Go with them. I'll hold off the bluecoats."

"Come with me," she argued.

"Go!" he shouted, giving her a rough shove that silenced her resistance. "We'll meet later."

"You'll only let them kill you!" she complained.

"Why not?" Horn asked. "Today's as good a day for dying as tomorrow. If you're right, tell Otter I fought well."

He then notched an arrow and started toward the line that Pony Leg and the others were forming.

When Buffalo Horn reached his uncle, Pony Leg was already bleeding from two bullet wounds. Only two boys of fourteen summers stood beside him. The rest had been swept away by a sudden charge by bluecoat horsemen.

"Save my son," Pony Leg pleaded. "Help him up Man's Road."

"You can do it yourself, *Na khan*," Horn replied.

A pair of grinning bluecoats approached, waving their long knives, but Buffalo Horn fired an arrow into the first man's chest, and the other one quickly turned away. Horn then discarded his bow, caught the dead *Wihio*'s horse, and tore the bluecoat from his saddle.

"*Na khan*," Horn called, holding the skittish animal.

"For my son," Pony Leg insisted.

Buffalo Horn reluctantly climbed atop the saddle and slapped the horse into a gallop. He soon spotted Summer Cherry Woman. Mole was trying desperately to keep pace as she fled.

"Here," Buffalo Horn called, halting the horse and climbing down in a single motion. "Take the horse. Get to Otter."

"My husband . . ." Summer Cherry Woman started to say. Then she hung her head.

"Go," Horn urged.

"It's for you to do," Summer Cherry Woman argued. "You can keep the boy safe."

"I have obligations," he told her. "Take care of my little cousin. You, Mole, look after your mother."

The five-year-old stared up with a mixture of fright and confusion. There was no time to offer comfort or advice. Horn helped Summer Cherry Woman mount the bluecoat horse and then passed the boy up to her. Mole held on to his cousin's hand a moment, and Buffalo Horn managed a brief sour nod. Then Summer Cherry Woman kicked the horse into a gallop.

By the time Buffalo Horn got back to the camp, bluecoat horsemen were everywhere. Lodges were burning here and there. Bluecoats were busy butchering helpless children or forcing their attentions on the women. Black Kettle's lodge was surrounded, and Horn wondered if the chief himself was dead.

Those who could escape trickled back away from the creek and headed off north and east, toward the refuge of the snowdrifts and the emptiness that lay beyond. One group of *Tsis tsis tas* continued to exchange fire with the bluecoats along the creek. Buffalo Horn picked up a discarded bow, located a quiver of arrows, and set off to join the other fighters.

By then it was clear the whole camp was lost. Bluecoats already controlled the pony herd, and two or three hundred horsemen occupied the camp circles. Perhaps that many more were rooting the Arapahoes out of their adjacent camps. A third group of two hundred bluecoats appeared to be circling around to trap the fugitives. All the other *Wihio* were busy with the little band of fighters at the creek.

As Buffalo Horn hurried along, he tried not to look at the bloody scene that met his eyes. Small boys and girls lay everywhere. Most had not even had time to dress. Some had been resting in their beds when cannons tore their lodges apart. Those few men who had managed to arm themselves had never been able to form any sort of organized resistance. Famous fighters lay where they had fallen. Some had already been scalped. Poor old White Goose lay broken and shattered in the smoking remains of his lodge. The *Wihio* had cut two fingers from his right hand in order to take golden rings. Elsewhere men, women, and even little children lay where they had fallen, all victims of *Wihio* rage.

"These aren't men we're fighting," Horn muttered as he raced toward the creek. "They're devils!"

At that very instant a bullet whined past Buffalo Horn's cheek, and he dove to his right as a charging bluecoat slashed at his back with a saber. Horn notched an arrow and braced himself as the bluecoat turned back to try again. The *Wihio* laughed as he quirted his horse. Buffalo Horn took aim, paused, and waited until the bluecoat was less than seven paces away. Horn then released his arrow, and the stone tip sliced into the bluecoat's neck just below the chin and tore up through his brain. Blood trickled out of the *Wihio*'s ears as he fell back, sliding off his pony.

With a wail born of fury and madness Buffalo Horn fell upon the bluecoat's corpse, drew out a knife, and began slashing at the hated enemy's face until all that remained was a mass of gore.

"Horn!" a voice called then.

Buffalo Horn leaped away from the bloody corpse and searched the creek for some sign of a friend. Finally he detected a slight-shouldered young man splashing frantically in the icy stream. Before his mind allowed him to identify the face, Horn raced over and pulled the struggling figure from the water.

"No!" Buffalo Horn cried as he noticed the torn blue shirt. "Not you, too."

"I . . . didn't . . ." Isaac Guthrie mumbled. "Horn, I didn't know what . . ."

"Go!" Buffalo Horn barked, turning away. A moment later a volley of rifle fire swept along the creek, obscuring the scene ahead. Horn could no longer catch sight of the other *Tsis tsis tas* fighters. In desperation he ran along the stream bed, calling for someone, anyone, to respond.

"They haven't killed us yet," Pony Leg shouted from behind a low mound of dirt he and his two young companions had managed to raise a dozen paces from the creek.

"*Na khan*, I was certain they had killed you," Buffalo Horn said, happily crawling over beside his uncle.

"Your wife and son should be safe. I found a horse for them."

"No one of us will ever be safe now," Pony Leg predicted. "We can only put off the dying a little while. There are too many of them out there. We have no food, no lodges, hardly any clothes."

Buffalo Horn frowned. Pony Leg's companions wore no moccasins. They had only breechclouts, which adequately covered them in summer, but were clearly inadequate for winter nights.

"They took the ponies, too," Horn observed. "Everything."

"We have our lives," Pony Leg said, coughing. "At least for a time."

"They won't kill us easily," Buffalo Horn boasted. "They can't get at us from the far side of the creek, and we'll kill some of them if they charge."

"Yes, we'll make it hot for them," Pony Leg agreed. He was clearly more concerned with the welfare of the women and children still streaming away from the creek into the snowy refuge beyond.

"These boys should leave, too," Horn declared, nodding to the youngsters.

"We're Foxes," the older of the two insisted. "Our fathers and brothers have died here. We won't leave them."

Buffalo Horn nodded grimly. He recognized their determination. Hadn't he and Otter made a similar stand against the *Savane*?

"I'm Buffalo Horn," he told them.

"We know," the older boy replied. "I'm called Two Feathers. My brother here's Elk Foot."

"I remember you used to come down and swim Red Shield River with my brother-friend Otter's brothers,"

Horn said, forcing a smile onto his face. "Those were better days."

"Yes," the youngster agreed.

"Otter was right to leave," Pony Leg whispered. "I should have heeded your dreams."

"We should have done a hundred things," Buffalo Horn said, taking a deep breath. "What does it matter now? Nothing lives long. We'll stop them long enough for the helpless ones to get away."

"Yes, we're Foxes," Two Feathers said, notching an arrow. "The difficult things are ours to do."

Four bluecoat horsemen splashed into the creek then, and Buffalo Horn also notched an arrow. He could see seven or eight other riders starting across farther upstream in an effort to break the feeble *Tsis tsis tas* defensive line.

"I have the one on the left," Horn told the others.

"Then I'll kill the next one," Pony Leg boasted.

Two Feathers and Elk Foot vowed to stop the others, but a horn sounded far to the left, and the bluecoats hesitated.

"There," Buffalo Horn said, waving toward a tall, heavy man wearing a thick blue wool coat and brandishing a pistol.

"The bluecoat chief," Pony Leg muttered bitterly.

Horn knew his uncle was right. The other *Wihio* responded to the big man's orders. His eyes were full of fire and hatred. A bluecoat dragged a small child along the creek, but the big hairy-faced man ordered the soldier to throw down the youngster. Another bluecoat shot the child and kicked it into the stream.

"No!" Pony Leg screamed, rising to his feet. Buffalo Horn realized too late how much the dead child resembled Mole. Before Horn could move, Pony Leg,

Two Feathers, and Elk Foot charged toward the blue-coat chief.

The three of them surprised the first bluecoats they met and sent them fleeing back toward the creek. Other *Wihio* soldiers had time to aim their rifles, and they sent a fusillade of lead toward the three defiant *Tsis tsis tas* warriors. Elk Foot was in front, and five bullets struck him in the chest and belly. He fell face-forward whispering his death song with his final breath.

Pony Leg's right arm hung limp at his side, and a second volley shattered his left knee. Two Feathers managed to race on, unharmed, but a bluecoat on horseback shattered the young Fox's bow with a saber stroke before blasting the life from him with a pair of pistol shots.

Buffalo Horn started his second charge as Two Feathers fell into the bloody snow. He sang an ancient *Suhtai* medicine song and fired his final arrow toward the hairy-faced chief. The big man dodged the arrow and laughed loudly.

"This is all the Cheyenne's got left, boys!" the big *Wihio* boasted. "Little boys and lame fools."

It had been a long time since Buffalo Horn had thought about his mangled foot and the *Wihio* trappers who had robbed him of his toes. A fresh fury filled his insides, and he managed to elude the ten bullets that were fired at him as he made his way to his uncle's side.

"It wasn't Mole, was it?" Pony Leg asked as Horn knelt beside him.

"No, *Na khan*," Horn assured him. "I told you that they're safe."

"It's good to know something's survived," Pony

Leg whispered. He then sang the old, well-remembered death song of the *Tsis tsis tas* as Buffalo Horn stared hatefully at the twenty bluecoats that surrounded them.

Horn closed his uncle's frozen eyelids and reached for an arrow from his quiver. It was empty. He discarded the bow and drew out a knife.

"Well?" he called to them in their own words. "Come and kill another one of us if you can. Sons of dogs! Fight a man if you have the stomach!"

"He's mine, Colonel," Isaac Guthrie announced. "I told you I got a personal score to settle with these people."

"Ain't got a scalp yet, eh, Guthrie?" another bluecoat called.

"Just us, Cheyenne," Guthrie said, climbing down from his horse. His tunic was still torn from his earlier encounter with the enemy, but he seemed to have forgotten who had pulled him from the creek. Guthrie's eyes were hungry for killing, and Horn faced his one-time companion as a tremendous weariness swept over him.

"Give me a real *Wihio* to kill," Horn pleaded, using the *Tsis tsis tas* words only the two of them could understand. "I haven't got the heart to . . ."

Guthrie surged forward, blocked Horn's weak knife thrust, and touched his own blade to Horn's neck, drawing blood.

"It's the only way," Guthrie whispered as he clubbed Buffalo Horn across the back of the head. "Forgive me, brother."

15

Buffalo Horn expected to awaken on Hanging Road. He thought he would find Pony Leg and old Two Claws waiting to speed him on his journey to the other side. Instead when he opened his eyes, he discovered Isaac Guthrie's tearful eyes gazing with concern at him.

"I hit you too hard," Guthrie said as he placed a cool cloth on Horn's forehead. "I was afraid the others would suspect. They don't trust me, and I . . ."

"Where am I?" Buffalo Horn interrupted.

"A cave near the creek," Guthrie explained.

"Alive, then," Horn muttered. "It would have been better for both of us if you had killed me."

"Easier maybe," Guthrie replied. "Not better."

Guthrie crawled away a moment. When he returned, he held a water bottle to Horn's lips. The cool liquid revived a terrible thirst, and Buffalo Horn drank eagerly.

"Take it slowly," Guthrie advised. "There's plenty. I'll warm some soup, too. You're probably hungry. It's been two days, you know."

"Two . . . days?" Horn asked. "I've slept that long?"

"I hit you too hard," Guthrie repeated. "I had the devil's own time getting you up here, too. I had to wait for darkness and then slip away unseen."

"The others?"

"A fair number got away. Not all the soldiers attacked. Si Soule and his company held back. He told the colonel right out that he wasn't there to murder women and children. The colonel ordered Si arrested, but . . ."

"This colonel," Horn interrupted. "He was the big man with the hairy face?"

"Chivington," Guthrie muttered through clenched teeth. "He was a sort of hero fighting the southerners. I knew all along he had a taste for blood. We had some rebel prisoners, and he ordered every last one of them shot dead and left for the buzzards. One or two of those fellows hadn't yet shaved. He had orders to protect the prisoners, but he ignored them."

"Why, Guthrie?" Horn asked. "We came here to be at peace. The soldier chiefs told us to camp at Sand Creek. Now there can be no peace. The rivers will run red with blood. No *Tsis tsis tas* or Arapaho will forget this killing of the helpless ones."

"The killing's only part of it," Guthrie said, covering his eyes. He began sobbing, and Horn sensed the young mixed-blood was holding back something dark and dreadful.

"Tell me," Horn urged.

"Your eyes are dark enough already," Guthrie insisted. "I wish I hadn't seen it, and I hope you never do."

"A man must know the truth, Guthrie."

"Truth," Guthrie said, spitting the bitterness from his mouth. "What truth? That you and I are enemies? I can't believe that. You pulled me from the creek. I saved you from the colonel. That makes us brothers, doesn't it?"

"That's nothing," Horn declared.

"Then maybe it's the pain," Guthrie said, gripping Horn's wrists. "Maybe it's being alone, cut off from everything else."

"I'm not cut off," Horn argued. "Otter is out there somewhere. I'll find him, and together we'll punish this Chivington."

"I suppose I'm the only one who's cut off then," Guthrie said, avoiding Horn's questioning eyes. "They'll call me a deserter, you know. Hang me on sight."

"Maybe they'll just think the *Tsis tsis tas* caught you," Horn suggested.

"Either way, that path's closed to me now."

"You can't come with me, Guthrie. The blood's still fresh on your shirt. My people will kill you."

"I suppose, in a way, you're the lucky one then. At least you have a place to go."

"Maybe the Bents . . ."

"George and Charlie are lucky to be alive," Guthrie noted. "Old John Smith's boy, Jack, is dead. The colonel held him captive for a while. Then some hot-bloods decided to shoot poor Jack. We weren't supposed to take captives, you see. The colonel ordered us not to. Day before yesterday some of the men went over the battlefield, rooting out a few boys who'd been hiding. One wasn't more than seven years old. They . . . well, they killed him."

Guthrie covered his face and wept uncontrollably. Horn could only guess at the cruelty the young mixed-blood had witnessed.

"We should take another sweat," Horn eventually suggested. "Cast the evil humors from our world."

"Not even a sweat can do that," Guthrie said, shaking his head. "There's no forgetting this."

Horn knew his companion was right. Too many had died. How could anyone, even Black Kettle, forgive the *Wihio* this time? Brave men were dead! Well, that was expected in a fight. But the helpless ones? Old men like White Goose?

The remainder of that day Buffalo Horn passed in and out of a twilight world of mist, fog, and memory. Sleep might have offered some peace, but his dreams were haunted by visions of the dead friends and relations. He knew he had to regain his senses. He had obligations. Pony Leg's body lay out there, unattended, and as a near relation Horn had to erect a scaffold and place the corpse in a suitable place. The prayers that would hurry the man who had been uncle up Hanging Road and so many more needed speaking.

At first Buffalo Horn refused the soup Guthrie offered, but both knew the weakness would not pass unaided.

"You have to eat," Guthrie scolded. "You have to regain your strength. Now, more than ever, you have to protect the helpless ones. There are so many of them!"

Buffalo Horn sighed. Guthrie had recognized a weakness. Horn could not simply lie in the cave and ignore the other survivors' torment!

"You realize I may grow strong enough to kill you," Horn whispered.

"That would be merciful," Guthrie said, offering a cup of hot soup. "It's hard living with all I've seen."

"What have you seen?" Horn asked as he sipped the scalding liquid.

"You have enough shadows stalking you, Horn. I won't add to them."

Buffalo Horn searched the mixed-blood's eyes and recognized a mixture of torment and anguish. Any hostility that lingered in Horn's mind from Guthrie's part in Grouse's death and the *Wihio* raid on the Sand Creek encampment flowed away.

Why blame him? Buffalo Horn thought. After all, Guthrie already carried a world of guilt in those eyes.

The two of them passed five days in that cave altogether. Of course, Horn only recalled the final three. The morning of the sixth day Guthrie dressed and stepped outside. After walking about a short while, he returned with word that the last of the bluecoats had left.

"We can leave now," he announced. "We'll ride east a day or two. By then we should sight a *Tsis tsis tas* camp."

"I can't leave this place yet," Horn objected. "I have relatives among the dead. I have to tend to their bodies and make the mourning prayers."

"You don't understand," Guthrie complained. "There's nothing left to mourn. The animals have been busy, and . . ."

"It's winter," Horn argued. "The cold will prevent rotting, and most of the animals are sleeping."

"Some animals don't rest," Guthrie said, gazing warily southward toward Fort Lyon.

"The bluecoats marked the bodies," Horn muttered. "Well, it's to be expected. It doesn't relieve me of my obligation."

"You don't want to see," Guthrie said, shaking his head violently. "It's terrible! Hellish! You won't rest!"

"I don't rest now," Horn pointed out. "We'll find Pony Leg and set him at peace. White Goose, too. He would have been my father."

"You don't understand," Guthrie pleaded. "Let's leave this place."

"A man can't turn away from the unpleasant things. He has things he must do."

"I . . . can't . . ."

"Stay here then," Horn said, his disappointment showing. It would be difficult to build the scaffolds and carry the bodies alone.

"You don't know what you're asking, Horn."

"A brother would do it," Horn replied. "I know there are ghosts walking in that place, but I have to help my uncle find peace. Once, when I was little, an older man helped me survive. He, too, may be there. I must help his spirit find rest, too."

"We'll do it then," Guthrie mumbled. "Remember, though. I warned you."

Nothing Buffalo Horn had seen or done prepared him for what he found on the far side of Sand Creek. He expected death. He anticipated destruction. He discovered cruel savagery beyond the power of description.

The camp was a smoldering ruin. The bluecoats had pillaged the place. What they had not carried away they had piled into lodges and set afire.

The looting was nothing compared to what the *Wihio* did to the bodies. The first man Buffalo Horn

came upon was White Antelope. The famous fighter
had refused to break his treaty vow. Horn had seen
the bluecoats fall upon him, but he hadn't witnessed
the true horror. What remained of White Antelope lay
frozen beside the creek. *Wihio* knives had cut off his
ears, his nose, his hair. There was a horrid bloody hole
between the man's legs where some bluecoats had cut
away his manhood.

"Here was a man that only wanted peace," Horn
whispered as he tried to turn his eyes away.

"There's worse," Guthrie said, blocking Buffalo
Horn's path. "Let's leave."

Horn stepped past his companion and made his way
along the creek to where Pony Leg, Two Feathers, and
Elk Foot had made their charge. Elk Foot lay in pieces.
The bluecoats had severed the boy's legs, arms, and
head from the body. Someone had taken pieces of the
young man as trophies.

Buffalo Horn stumbled through the snow, collapsed
to his knees, and vomited. He retched and retched until there was nothing left inside him to bring up. Only
then did he continue to Pony Leg.

The *Wihio* must have grown tired by the time they
reached Buffalo Horn's uncle. Pony Leg's forelock had
been cut away, and he, like most of the others, had
been stripped. Except for the holes left by the bullets
that had killed him, though, Pony Leg's corpse was
unmarked.

"*Na khan*, I'll help you find peace," Buffalo Horn
whispered as he covered the body with a discarded
trade blanket.

A few feet farther on Two Feathers lay beside a willow sapling. An amused *Wihio* had forced a smile
onto the dead youngster's face. Someone had also

folded the boy's hands on his chest. They contained
something, and only when Horn glanced lower did he
realize what it was.

"I pray he was already dead," Guthrie whispered.
"Not all of them were.

"He was just a boy," Horn growled. Even the
Pawnees would have shown respect for the young
Foxes. These devil bluecoats didn't deserve to live!

Buffalo Horn continued. He felt as though he were
following a guide through a nightmare. There were
sixty or seventy bodies scattered about the camp. Only
a few were men. Children as young as a few weeks
had been brutally clubbed to death. Women had their
genitals cut out.

Horn felt something inside himself die. A great chill
formed around his heart, and a hunger for revenge
swelled up until it threatened to explode.

"This isn't the end of our people," Buffalo Horn
told Guthrie. "Those who are still alive will punish the
bluecoats for this."

"And the farmers and ranchers?" Guthrie asked.

"The *Wihio* have made this war," Horn explained.
"They chose to strike our helpless ones. They cut
apart our women and hacked our boys into pieces.
We'll do the same to theirs. We'll kill until the rivers
run with the tears of their weeping women. A people
who could do a thing like this can never belong within
the sacred circle of the world. They disturb the harmony of the land by breathing."

"I knew I should never have let you come here."

"You should have killed me, Guthrie," Horn declared. "That's the only way you could have prevented
it. Then you might have returned to the bluecoats."

"I can never be one of them!" Guthrie shouted,

tearing his blue shirt into rags. "Don't you know anything? Can you imagine you're the only one that's feeling pain?"

"You rode with them," Buffalo Horn reminded his companion.

"Not to do this," Guthrie insisted. "I hoped to prevent it. When John Smith came out to intercede, I stopped the others from killing him. I saved you, too, didn't I? Chivington had a thousand men. They weren't all dark-hearted devils. Si Soule refused to kill helpless women and children, and so did I. We did what we could, Horn."

"It wasn't much."

"Don't you think I know that? Why do you suppose I stayed here? It wasn't for my health!"

"No," Buffalo Horn admitted. "You remained to look after me. You don't deserve my anger, Guthrie, but nobody else is left here. I've become a crazy man. Leave me. Get away before the ghosts twist my thinking."

"I can't go yet," Guthrie replied. "My brother asked for my help. We have a scaffold to build."

"Yes," Horn agreed. "And I have to locate White Goose."

"He's the uncle of that boy that died," Guthrie said, sighing.

"Yes," Horn agreed. "The one that the wagon people killed."

Guthrie nodded. They made their way along the blackened remains of the lodges, avoiding the eerie frozen gazes of the dead until they reached White Goose's lodge. Only ashes remained. As for the Goose, the flames had consumed every bit of him. He might as well have been smoke.

"Man Above's done our work," Buffalo Horn observed. "We should tend to my uncle."

In the end they raised three scaffolds. Guthrie, perhaps to atone for his role in young Grouse's death, insisted they provide a resting place for the two young Fox warriors, Two Feathers and Elk Foot. Buffalo Horn did his best to place the body parts in their proper places, but he suspected neither boy could climb Hanging Road or find peace on the other side. They would haunt Sand Creek forever.

Buffalo Horn placed Pony Leg on the low hill where he had watched his nephew invite that last dream. Although Horn spoke the appropriate prayers and performed each ritual, he found no peace. Perhaps in a world gone mad it was impossible for anyone to find harmony.

Buffalo Horn observed the proper three days of mourning for his uncle. By then word of the slaughter had spread up and down Arkansas River. Horn watched angrily as the bluecoat chief Wynkoop who had promised them safety rode across the corpse-littered scene. *Wihio* farmers from the nearby settlements came to see, too. Some of them found bits of lodge coverings or discarded arrows to carry away as reminders of the place.

"How can they make a game of it?" Horn asked Guthrie when some farm boys dashed about the camp, hurdling corpses.

"They're trying not to think of the dying," Guthrie declared. "It won't help. Nobody will forget what's happened here who's seen it."

"That won't stop them from putting blue coats on when they're older and cutting the life from our people."

"Maybe not," Guthrie agreed. "But even that won't help them forget who died here. They saw the faces. They'll always know."

"It's time we left," Buffalo Horn announced when he had completed the mourning rites.

"Yes," Guthrie agreed. "It's a long walk east."

"Shorter riding," Buffalo Horn observed. "Those *Wihio* camped down there have good ponies."

"They're simple people," Guthrie argued. "They mean you no harm. You can't . . ."

"They're *Wihio*," Horn insisted. "For all I know those ponies may belong to me anyway."

"You don't believe that."

"It doesn't matter. I have to take the ponies because there are no other ones close."

"You have to promise not to hurt those people."

"I should cut them into pieces the way they cut those boys who used to ride with the Foxes."

"I'll stop you," Guthrie declared, pulling a pistol from his belt. "I wouldn't let them hurt you, and I won't let you harm them. The hatred and the killing have to stop."

"Stop?" Horn asked. "It's only just beginning."

"Promise me," Guthrie urged.

Buffalo Horn nodded, and Guthrie put the pistol aside. That night, once darkness set in, the two of them crept past a boy of thirteen and cut two ponies loose. The two raiders then led the animals out of camp, mounted, and began the long ride eastward.

Buffalo Horn led the way, but he really had no better notion of where Black Kettle or whoever was leading the survivors might be taking them. The winds were fierce out in the open, and drifting snow covered any trail the fugitives might have left behind. Eventually, after riding the best part of three days with only the briefest rest, Horn spotted smoke.

"We've found them," Guthrie observed.

"Yes," Horn agreed. "You must go now, my friend."

"Go?" Guthrie asked.

"Can you imagine how welcome I would be riding the streets of Denver City waving a *Wihio* scalp in my hand? That is how it would be for you to go among our people now."

"I'm not wearing my blue shirt anymore," Guthrie pointed out.

That was true. Guthrie had located buckskin leggings and a shirt in the abandoned camp, and if his hair had only been a little longer, he might have passed as one of those *Tsis tsis tas* who hung around the *Wihio* at Fort Laramie on Horse Creek, trading for buffalo hides and chewing army rations.

"You told me I'd only find death when we returned to Black Kettle's camp," Horn noted. "It's all you'll see here, too, but the people who have survived will misjudge your sadness. They're angry, and they'll kill you."

"Where can I go, Horn? What can I do?"

"Try and find a path to walk, brother," Buffalo Horn said, sighing. "It's all that any of us can do."

16

Buffalo Horn waited until Guthrie was safely out of sight before approaching the fugitives' camp. Actually, it was a far cry from a real camp. A few buffalo hides were stretched across frameworks of willow and cottonwood limbs. Snow had been shaped into walls, and three small fires provided warmth.

He approached the pitiful huddle of survivors unseen. Only when his horse snorted did a single slender boy of fifteen years dash out from the makeshift lodge.

"You should be glad I'm no *Wihio*," Buffalo Horn declared. "You should be watchful."

"Watchful?" the boy asked. His face was tense, and his hands trembled with fatigue. He had no bow. His only weapon was a sharpened willow branch.

"What are you called?" Horn asked.

"Dragonfly," the boy said. "My father was Panther Claw. He and my brothers are dead, I think."

"And your mother?" Buffalo Horn asked.

"I saw the bluecoats kill her," Dragonfly explained. "My sister, too, is dead."

The boy turned sideways and rubbed tears from his eyes. Buffalo Horn ached to see his people so helpless, but it wasn't this boy's fault. He had only a length of cloth tied around his waist to cover his nakedness, and the wind attacked the exposed flesh on his arms, legs, and chest.

"I'm sorry I disturbed you, Dragonfly," Horn told the boy. "Go back to your fire. I'll watch for a time."

"I could tend to your horse," a second, smaller boy offered.

"It's generous of you," Horn said, "but I think I'm better dressed to endure the wind."

"Yes," the youngster admitted. He rubbed his bare belly and laughed. "I was sleeping with the pony boys, and they forgot to wake me. If I hadn't found this piece of cloth I would . . . be even colder."

"Yes," Horn agreed. "Go back to the fire. When it's warmer, we'll find you something more appropriate to cover yourself with."

"I can hunt," the youngster boasted. "If I had a bow, I could punish the *Wihio*."

"You'll soon have your bow," Buffalo Horn assured the boy. "How many of you are there?"

"Twenty," the younger boy said, frowning. "We used to be twenty-five. Two died last night, and three others wandered away."

"Men?" Horn asked.

"Dragonfly," the smaller boy said, hugging himself to stay warm. "And me. I know I'm small, but I won a man's name hunting Bull Buffalo."

"I remember," Buffalo Horn said, nodding as he

recalled the naming. White Antelope had conducted the giveaway. This boy was the Antelope's grandson, Fire Lance.

"Did you see my grandfather?" Fire Lance asked.

"He walked out to stop the killing," Horn said, sighing.

"They killed him then," Fire Lance said, staring at his feet. "The *Wihio* will kill us all. Their fevers took my mother, and my father died riding Platte River. I used to have a brother, but I haven't seen him since the bluecoats attacked."

"There's time to consider all this later," Buffalo Horn insisted. "Do you have anything to eat?"

"Nothing," Fire Lance confessed. "We haven't eaten in three days now."

"I'll find something," Horn promised as he dismounted. He waved Fire Lance back to the others, tended to his horse's needs, and then walked out into a nearby thicket to have a look for game. He finally spied a small cottontail and killed it with a stone. It wouldn't feed everyone, but at least they would have something to chew.

Buffalo Horn passed two days with that weary band of survivors. Most of them were White Antelope's people, and some of the women expected the Antelope to arrive any moment with a rescuing force. Besides the two boy warriors, eight women and ten smaller children cowered in the snow shelter. Horn had the only horse, and he decided to ride out and locate help.

"It's a hard thing, climbing Man's Road alone," Buffalo Horn told Dragonfly and Fire Lance as he passed his bow into their hands. "I'll bring help, but it may take some time."

"Not too much time," Fire Lance said, frowning. "The little ones are crying. They're cold and hungry."

Buffalo Horn knew that the children weren't the only sufferers. The women and older children had given their portions of the rabbit to others. Fire Lance seemed so frail that the next wind might blow him across the land like a snowflake.

"*Heammawihio*, watch over them," Buffalo Horn silently prayed as he mounted his horse. "Let me find help soon."

For once Man Above smiled down on him. Horn had only ridden a short distance before spying a swirl of snow dust rising from the valley to the north. He turned in that direction and reached for his bow. He had, of course, left it behind with the others. He had a knife, but it would be of little use in a fight on horseback. He could only hope the approaching riders were from an allied tribe and not *Wihio* cavalry out to finish off stragglers.

He considered hiding in a nearby stand of cottonwoods but decided otherwise. If the riders were bluecoats, at least his suffering would be brief. He nudged his big *Wihio* horse into a trot and shouted a greeting.

The riders slowed their approach. The first four of them fanned out into a line and waited.

"Am I such a fierce man that you should fear me?" Buffalo Horn called first in *Tsis tsis tas* and afterward in English.

"Afraid?" a familiar voice replied. "You look like a beggar, brother. What should we fear?"

"Otter," Horn said, grinning. It seemed as though the sight of his brother-friend warmed his whole being. "You're far from Red Shield River. I thought you would be up there with the Crazy Dogs."

"I was," Otter said, scowling. "An Arapaho brought us word that the bluecoats struck us a hard blow. I heard you were dead."

"It was a close thing. Many of our best men are climbing Hanging Road. My uncle . . ."

"His wife and son are with Black Kettle a half day's ride from here," Otter told him. "You should have come with us. Your dreams told you what would happen."

"I didn't think it possible, though," Buffalo Horn confessed. "There are some of White Antelope's people nearby. They are starving, and most of them need coats to keep off the winter's chill."

"We'll help them, too," Otter promised. "You look exhausted. Snow Bear can take you to our camp. You can rest there."

"You could find them on your own," Horn replied, "but not as fast as if I lead you to them. They have only pony boys to look after them."

"More helpless people," Rabbit Foot said, frowning. "We can't feed them all."

"We have to," Otter barked. "We're Elks, aren't we? We are obligated to help. We've all been hungry. Once other men helped provide for us."

"There are no buffalo to hunt here," Buffalo Horn observed. "We have to find food and clothing elsewhere."

"From the *Wihio*, you mean," Snow Bear said, grinning.

"They took our ponies and burned our winter food," Horn said. "It's only right that we get what we need from them."

"Our brother suggested that to the chiefs," Rabbit Foot noted. "Black Kettle continues to urge peace."

"There can be no treating with anyone this winter," Horn grumbled. "We need to provide warm clothes for the children. We have to fill their bellies."

"Most of all we need ponies," Otter observed. "Without them all we can do is sit beside our fires and wait for the *Wihio* to come back."

"We've found ponies before," Buffalo Horn declared. "There will be plenty of boys eager to go with us, I think."

"Not boys anymore," Otter said, frowning. "Anyone old enough to pluck his chin hairs is a man now. Even so we're only a few."

By then Otter's small band of twenty riders had formed a circle, and Buffalo Horn greeted the others. He then led them south toward the survivors' camp.

When Horn reappeared at the snowy camp, Fire Lance and Dragonfly rushed out to greet him. The other rescuers received an equally warm welcome.

"We have a little food to share," Otter said, passing down to the women a provision bag filled with dry buffalo strips. "Chew some food and prepare yourselves. We have a hard day ahead."

The dazed women barely moved, but as the rescuers draped buffalo and elk hides over them, they began to come back to life. As for the little ones, they eagerly accepted something to eat while the men began disassembling the shelter and making pony drags to carry the fugitives to safety.

The rest of that day seemed to stretch itself into an eternity as the little band snaked its way north through the snow. Buffalo Horn rode beside Otter, but neither of them spoke. They were preoccupied with the suffering of the women and children. Only the youngest of the children and the weakest of the women rode in the pony drags. The older children and stronger women walked. From time to time Buffalo Horn would lift one of the youngsters up behind him and offer the child a brief rest. It was the numbing cold of the snowdrifts that provided the gravest challenge.

"I'm sorry we have to go so far," Buffalo Horn told one of the stumbling women.

"I'm not," she replied. "The farther we are from the *Wihio* fort, the safer my sons will be."

"Of course, she's only partly right," Otter said later. "There are *Wihio* in the north country, too."

It was well past midday before Horn built up the courage to inquire after Bright Swallow Maiden.

"She shares my lodge with her sister," Otter explained. "Don't expect too much of her, Horn. She came to us nearly starved with a bullet in her shoulder and escorting a small army of children. Most have now found relatives to go to, but we still have several young ones with us. Rock Watcher may have brothers and sisters as well as uncles."

"Were all the men killed, then?" Buffalo Horn asked.

"Most of the chiefs got away," Snow Bear grumbled. "Good fighters stayed behind to shield the helpless ones. My friend Elk Foot is missing."

"He's dead," Horn said, sighing. "He and his brother, Two Feathers, died with my uncle, fighting until the end. I put all three of them on scaffolds together."

"Were their bodies badly abused?" Snow Bear asked.

Horn knew from the look in Snow Bear's eyes that

tales of the butchery had reached the Crazy Dogs. He saw no purpose in adding to Snow Bear's loss, though.

"Who would cut up boys?" Horn asked. "I put them in a good, high place, and they are certainly on the other side by now."

"We'll all of us see them soon," the Bear said. He then began singing a mourning prayer.

The sun was just beginning to set when Otter sent Rabbit Foot ahead to announce their return. A short time later Buffalo Horn detected a small circle of lodges through the dim twilight.

"Ayyyy!" a group of horsemen howled as they rode out from the camp. "More of us are here!"

They were followed by a handful of men and women hopeful that their missing children might be among the newcomers. Three were. Others tried to hide their disappointment as they invited fatherless children and some of their mothers to share their lodges.

Only a few of the refugees failed to find a relative or accept such an offer to join a family. Otter insisted Buffalo Horn join him, but Horn declined.

"It would be improper for Bright Swallow Maiden and myself both to share your lodge, Otter," Horn explained. "I'll make a shelter for myself."

"We'll help," Fire Lance announced. He and Dragonfly followed Buffalo Horn into the camp and took charge of the weary *Wihio* horse.

"We have no family left, we two," Dragonfly explained. "We understand that's how it is with you, too."

"I have an aunt and a cousin," Buffalo Horn told them. "My brother-friend . . ."

"You won't go to their lodge, though," Dragonfly

observed. "No, you're like us, a man alone. It's said you are a man without brothers, Horn."

"My father had no other sons," Horn confessed.

"Maybe we can be your brothers," Fire Lance suggested. "We wouldn't disappoint you."

"My path's a difficult one to walk," Buffalo Horn told them.

"What does that matter?" Dragonfly asked. "We should all be dead. Nothing lives long, after all. We'll keep you company."

"Actually I hoped to find someone else to chase the winter's chill," Horn told them.

"I understand she's in Otter's lodge," Fire Lance said, managing to crack a faint smile.

"You'll soon have your own sons," Dragonfly observed. "By then we'll find wives of our own."

"It's a good notion, having more brothers," Horn told them. "I'll soon be taking some men after ponies. Maybe you could come along."

"If someone will offer us horses to ride," Dragonfly replied.

"I'll get the ponies," Horn promised. "You find some hides to make us a lodge. It's best to begin a raid with plenty of rest and a fully belly."

"We have nothing to eat," Fire Lance said, sighing.

"Otter will invite us to share his kettle tonight," Horn assured them. "When we return, we can repay his kindness."

Buffalo Horn then headed for Otter's distinctly painted lodge. He was still a stone's throw away when he spied Bright Swallow Maiden. Her sour face and dead eyes shocked him. Her hair had streaks of white in it, and three small children clung to her dress.

"Well," she said as he reached the cook fire, "I hoped that you had survived."

"It wasn't my doing," he told her. "A man I knew made a mistake and saved my life."

"We have need of men here," she said, holding a small girl tightly. "There are many children in need of a father's guiding hand."

"I've never been a father," he argued. "I haven't even been a proper brother."

"You never accepted the burdens," she grumbled. "My father's gone now. Your uncle, too. There are few left who can lead. You'll have to do it."

"I sought the dream as you suggested, but the warning I expected didn't come. I was as blind as the chiefs to the coming danger. I've always struggled to find my own path. How can I lead others when I'm unsure what's the best thing to do?"

"You must see more clearly next time," she urged.

"Swallow, I'm a dead man clinging to his final breath. Who can tell if any of us will survive this winter?"

"We have to survive," she insisted. "For them," she added, lightly touching the heads of the two boys beside her. "You and the other men with horses have to ride out and hunt. I know it's a bad time, but we're hungry. Many people have no warm clothing."

"I'll do what I can," Horn promised. "I see that you've accepted burdens yourself."

"I have no father to look after," she said, swallowing a sob. "No brother. No husband."

"Your path hasn't been easy," he said, taking her hand.

"Oh, you mean this?" she asked, touching a strand of white hair. "You have a fresh scar yourself," she added, running her finger along the mark left on Buffalo Horn's neck by Guthrie's knife.

"It's little enough when so many are dead."

"Was my father . . ."

"He climbed Hanging Road in a swirl of smoke."

"They burned him?"

"The lodge, Swallow. Considering what the *Wihio* did to some of the bodies, it was his good fortune to be kept safe from the sharp points of their knives."

"I'm glad I saw so little of it," she told him. "I only wish the little ones hadn't."

"Soon the *Wihio* will regret what they've done," Horn said with darkening eyes. The children sensed a change and retreated.

"The Crazy Dogs have brought us enough trouble," Bright Swallow scolded. "Black Kettle hopes to speak with some of the *Wihio* chiefs soon. He's a great peacemaker, and he deserves a chance."

"He's made agreements, but we're the only ones that keep them," Buffalo Horn said. "I'm finished listening to empty talk."

"He values your friendship, Horn."

"He saved my life once, but that was long ago, Swallow. That life he saved he threw away at Sand Creek. The *Wihio* want us all dead, but we'll make them bleed before they finish with us."

"You talk like the bad hearts."

"Maybe they were right all along," Horn said, shaking his head. "Who can say? I only know my heart's full of anger, and I have to strike out at the ones that brought us all this pain."

"You could bring more soldiers down on us."

"None that won't come anyway," he argued. "I'll let Black Kettle and the other chiefs make their plans. I only mean to get some ponies and find something for the hungry people to eat."

"I need you, Horn," she said as he turned to leave.

"I need you, too," he whispered. "Maybe when the madness is over, we can make a new start."

"I hope so," she said, clasping his hands.

That night he, Fire Lance, and Dragonfly shared a scant supper with Otter's family. Horn sat quietly most of that evening. For a time Rock Watcher rested on his lap. Later Otter entertained Bright Swallow Maiden's little brood with tales his grandfather had once told him.

It was later, when Buffalo Horn followed his new brothers to their makeshift lodge, that Black Kettle approached him.

"Have you forgotten your old friends, Frog?" the chief asked.

"I've forgotten nothing," he replied. "I've seen too much death these past few days to trust *Wihio* agreements, though."

"Yes, it's difficult to trust people who are so quick to break promises," the Kettle agreed. "I should have seen the truth in your dream."

"I didn't."

"You're young," Black Kettle said, peering deeply into Buffalo Horn's tormented eyes. The chief appeared to have aged a lifetime. Horn knew he had marked sixty summers of living, but always before, Black Kettle had seemed eternal.

"What would you have me do?" Horn whispered.

"Listen to your dreams," the chief replied. "Help us find a path to walk. And when old men begin to lead their people blindly, tell us. I knew we could never hope to fight all these *Wihio*, but I never wanted us to die in our camps, rubbed out by the dark hearts."

"None of us wanted that," Horn agreed. "We'll try to find a better path to walk."

"There's talk you and Otter will take the young men out hunting," Black Kettle said, gazing at Horn's young companions. "It's true we need food and clothing. Ponies, too. Before you darken your own heart with the blood of the helpless ones, though, consider who's to blame. Too many children died at Sand Creek. It's right the bluecoats should die, but not their little ones."

"I've never been a butcher of children," Horn declared. "I don't wish to be like the *Wihio*. My fight is with the fathers, not the sons."

"Make it a good fight, then, Frog," Black Kettle said, drawing away. "Be careful, too. I would mourn your death."

"As I would yours, Uncle," Horn added.

17

Shortly before first light that next morning a rough hand shook Buffalo Horn to life.

"Bluecoats," Snow Bear whispered. "My brother's readying horses."

Horn shook himself awake and began dressing.

"Where?" he asked Snow Bear. "How many? Are they approaching this camp?"

"They are on the wagon trail to Bent's trading post," Snow Bear explained. "Bringing supplies to the *Wihio* who did all the killing."

"We'll hit them hard," Buffalo Horn vowed.

"Yes, we'll avenge our fathers," Dragonfly added.

"You don't intend to bring these children, do you?" Snow Bear asked.

"You're not so much older," Horn replied. "Who has a better right to strike a blow for our people?"

"They'll need horses," the Bear observed.

"Does Otter have two ponies he can spare?" Buffalo Horn asked.

"I'll ask him," Snow Bear said, sighing.

"Bear?" Horn asked, holding the young man back a moment. "If Elk Foot had survived, wouldn't he want to go?"

"Yes," Snow Bear admitted. "I'll find the horses."

"I don't think your other brothers like us," Dragonfly observed as he slipped his feet into moccasins.

"They've fought before," Horn explained. "They know how hard it is. We all wish you could wait, but Man's Road is no longer a gentle slope. It's a high cliff, and you have to climb it now."

As many as twenty men and boys gathered that morning to form a war party. Fire Lance was the youngest, but there were several others who had seen only fourteen summers. All of them shared a sense of urgency, but Buffalo Horn insisted on making preparations. He performed the pipe ceremony himself, and the leaders touched a pipe to their lips and vowed to look after the younger men. Horn offered each boy an elk-tooth charm, and he helped those who wished to paint their faces. Many of the younger men lacked weapons, and Otter passed from lodge to lodge, collecting spare lances and bows.

"You should wait," an old man named Broken Tooth grumbled. "You don't have enough arrows. Some of those boys have never pulled a man's bow before."

"There can be no more waiting," Buffalo Horn argued. "If the bluecoats get more rifles and bullets, they'll use them to kill the rest of us. We have to show them that we intend to punish liars and child-killers."

"You, boy," the old man said, clasping Fire Lance

by both shoulders. "Wait until you've plucked your chin."

"They killed my mother," Fire Lance answered as he shook himself loose from the old man's clawlike fingers. "They cut my father to pieces! They may kill me before I grow very tall, but at least they'll learn how a brave heart can die."

"Dying's easy," Horn grumbled. "We're not riding out to die. We're going to take ponies and food and clothing for the helpless ones. We're going to punish the *Wihio*. I'm not hungry to kill them, but I want them to be afraid. Let's run them! And if there's killing and dying to be done, we're ready."

The young men howled their agreement, and Buffalo Horn sang a final warrior prayer before climbing atop his horse. The others did likewise. Then Otter motioned toward the south, and the war party started toward the wagon road.

By midday they crossed the road itself. The heavy supply wagons had cut deep ruts in the snowdrifts. Buffalo Horn spotted fresh dung, too. He knew they were close.

"The Crazy Dogs have men watching," Otter told Buffalo Horn. "We'll soon see them. Then we can make a surround and strike them a hard blow."

"It's going to be difficult to make a surround here," Horn argued. "There's nothing in this country but a few rocks and a world of snow. We won't be able to charge them, and they can spot our approach and form a circle. It's hard to get at their wagons when they do that, and they have an easy time killing us."

"What would you do?" Otter asked.

"Wait for the sun to go down. Or maybe for fog. Mask our movements. Then, when we do strike, we come together, like a great strong wind, and we cut off the wagons and take them each in turn. The bluecoats are no good at fighting by themselves. They'll run away, and we'll have the supplies."

"It's a good plan," Otter agreed.

"What does he know about plans?" Rabbit Foot objected. "His ideas usually get people killed."

"You should forgive our brother for the death of that young man the wagon people killed," Otter declared. "No one mourned more than Horn. He would die in your place, Rabbit Foot, and you know it. We must all be of one mind when we make this fight."

"I'll do what I'm told," Rabbit Foot muttered, "but I'll be careful, too."

"We should all be careful," Buffalo Horn insisted. "Enough have already died. We can't afford to lose anyone else."

The raiders moved on then. Gradually they closed the distance until they met the four young Crazy Dogs who were scouting the supply wagons. Otter shared the plan, and the Crazy Dogs agreed to it.

"Our main band's half a day north of here," one of the scouts explained. "If you wanted to wait until daybreak . . ."

"No, they'll be rested and ready then," Horn objected. "They won't expect us today."

Buffalo Horn and Otter then formed their companions into a column and led the way west. Horn anticipated striking the wagons at dusk, but an obliging mist crept across the plain that afternoon, and the raiders decided to take advantage of its cover. They closed to within an easy arrow's shot of the wagons before charging. Then, with fierce screams that terrified the bluecoat horse soldiers who were escorting the wagons, Otter and Buffalo Horn made their charge.

There were seven wagons on the road that afternoon, and a *Wihio* drove each. In addition an escort of twenty men encircled the supply column. Most of the cavalrymen fled, but six of them turned and counterattacked. Their leader, a tall red-haired man with a great hairy mustache, fired two bullets at Otter, but both missed. Snow Bear jabbed a lance into the red-haired *Wihio*'s side, knocking him to the ground. Horn unhorsed a second *Wihio*, and Rabbit Foot shot one of them through the heart with an arrow. The remaining bluecoats made the mistake of turning in the wrong direction. They were simply overwhelmed by the *Tsis tsis tas* and cut to pieces.

Two of the wagon drivers made an effort to resist, but the others abandoned their wagons and ran off into the snowdrifts. Buffalo Horn took charge of one of the wagons, but he was disappointed to discover that it was full of *Wihio* paper money and big round balls for their cannons. Horn cut the horses loose and set the wagon afire. The paper money burned well, and the raiders rode around the bonfire, shouting and singing brave-heart songs.

Of the other six wagons, one was full of powder and lead. Another carried bolts of blue and black cloth, together with thick wool blankets. Two wagons contained salted beef and hog carcasses. Buffalo Horn ordered those four wagons started north toward the starving and freezing survivors of Sand Creek. The fifth wagon was another disappointment. It was full of letters and dispatches, and the *Tsis tsis tas* made a second bonfire of it. The final wagon was the real prize. It contained two precious boxes of new army rifles and a thousand percussion caps.

"We can turn these good guns on the bluecoats," Otter declared. "There are enough here for each one of us to take one. If you don't know how to fire one of these guns, wait until we return to camp. Someone will show you."

Dragonfly and Fire Lance eagerly accepted their new rifles, but Buffalo Horn shook his head in disdain.

"My power comes from the old ways," he explained to his two young companions. "I won't fight with Wihio weapons. Besides, what good is a rifle when you have no more caps? When you run out of powder and have no more lead to make balls?"

"We have plenty of caps and lead for now," Fire Lance insisted. "These rifles can kill a man from a great distance. They've used them on us often. Now we'll be a match for them."

Buffalo Horn could only sigh. Boys had to learn for themselves what was best. He ached to see the youngsters turn to the Wihio way of fighting, but he understood their desire for revenge. He, too, hungered to punish the bluecoats.

"We've done well, brother," Otter observed as he prepared to lead the remaining raiders home.

"We found food and some cloth," Buffalo Horn admitted. "We came to get ponies, though."

"We captured a few," Otter pointed out. Each of the wagons had a team of four, and the raiders had also taken six cavalry horses.

"They can see the fires from the fort," Horn said, gazing westward. "Someone will come back here to see what's burning. We can ambush the bluecoats and take their horses. Then we can sneak in and take others from the farms on Arkansas River. We might even locate our own captured ponies."

"The risk's too great," Otter objected. "As long as we fight the bluecoats near our camps, we have an advantage. We lose it when we strike near their forts."

"And what do we do if they send another army like the one Sumner brought out onto Red Shield River?" Horn asked. "Without ponies we have no chance to escape. Or to hunt Bull Buffalo. We have to take the ponies, Otter."

"We could take some from the Pawnees," Otter suggested.

"We'd never get halfway there. You know I'm right."

"I'll send Snow Bear and the Crazy Dogs back with the cloth and food," Otter said, frowning. "You and I'll stay with a few of the older men."

"We'll need ten to handle the ponies."

"You trust those two children that follow you around like lost ducklings?"

"With my life."

"And mine?"

"Yes, brother, even with that," Horn replied. "They've seen the darkness that is death. They're not afraid."

"They won't run, even when it's the prudent thing to do," Otter grumbled. "We'll get them killed, Horn."

"We'll be careful."

"You can't always be careful, not when you're trying to steal the bluecoats' pony herd. We'll be spread too thin. They'll have to make their own fight."

"You and I once did the same."

"Ah, but old Two Claws gave us strong medicine. We were bulletproof."

"Were we?" Horn asked. "I've wondered about that."

"We believed we were," Otter said, smiling as he recalled the hard fight. "Maybe that was enough."

"Maybe," Horn agreed. "I'll make medicine for them."

"Make it strong, brother. And make some for us as well."

Even as Snow Bear and the Crazy Dogs were conducting the wagons eastward toward the *Tsis tsis tas* camp, Buffalo Horn was mixing medicine powder into a new, powerful paint. He spread the paste under each of his companions' eyes and across their foreheads. In the dying light of the burning wagons, each man took on an unearthly appearance.

"We look like hawks," Dragonfly observed.

"Will the paint protect us, brother?" Fire Lance asked.

"It will unsettle the bluecoats' aim and make them miss," Horn explained.

"You're certain they'll come?" Dragonfly asked.

"It doesn't matter," Horn replied. "If they don't, we'll continue on to the fort and run their horses. It will be easier if we can surprise some of them, but we'll take the ponies either way."

"Have your dreams showed you all this?" Fire Lance asked. "I remember my grandfather talking about you. He said you dreamed of a great attack on our camp. You saw it all, but the chiefs ignored you."

"I didn't see everything," Horn explained. "I never

do. I haven't dreamed about this raid, but I know we must take these ponies. We're helpless without them."

"Lance and I'll help you take them," Dragonfly boasted. "What harm can come to us, painted as we are? Those bluecoats will be surprised!"

As the sun settled into the western horizon, Buffalo Horn began to doubt his plans. He wasn't accustomed to fighting at night, and neither were the others. Taking a few ranch horses or driving off the Pawnee pony herd was one thing. Battling a regiment of *Wihio* cavalry was something else.

As it happened, though, no thousand soldiers rode out that night. Only ten men left the fort, and they made only a halfhearted effort to discover the source of the fires. After all, the escort had reached the fort, and they had surely warned the others about the raiders.

"Shouldn't we run those men?" Dragonfly asked. "There are only ten of them."

"Only ten ponies, too," Horn observed. "No, let them go back and report we've all left. Then we can strike the ponies."

The plan went well in the beginning. The investigating party returned safely, and the bluecoat soldiers reduced their guard. Only three soldiers kept watch over close to two hundred ponies, and Buffalo Horn considered he had a good chance of success. Even as the raiders rode up toward the grazing animals, though, another three guards left the fort. It was the three newcomers who spied Buffalo Horn and Otter. They fired their rifles and raced back to bring help.

The bluecoats' aim was poor, and Buffalo Horn barely twitched as the bullets passed harmlessly past.

He then waved his companions toward the pony herd and charged the three groggy guards.

"Cheyennes!" one of the guards shouted as he threw away his rifle and fled for his life. The second guard fired wildly, but the third took aim, steadied himself, and fired a single shot through Horn's horse's lungs. The animal screamed out in pain, managed another step, and collapsed.

Buffalo Horn managed to free his bow and notch an arrow. He waited for the third guard to begin reloading before taking aim and firing. The silent, seemingly invisible projectile sped across the snow-covered hillside and pierced the bluecoat's side. The guard stared at the arrow as if unable to believe his misfortune. Then he rose and tried to stagger back to the fort. He got halfway before he fainted from loss of blood.

Young Dragonfly raced past Buffalo Horn and clubbed the remaining guard senseless. A shriek from the far side of the pony herd marked the end of the other guard. The raiders then began cutting the hobbles from the army horses and driving them eastward along the river.

Buffalo Horn watched for only a moment. He then removed his belongings from his dying horse and dragged them to where a marvelous chestnut stallion waited.

"He's a tall horse," Otter remarked as he helped his brother-friend prepare the chestnut for their escape.

"He'll run fast," Horn boasted. "Maybe he can run fast enough to keep me from harm."

"Perhaps," Otter noted.

At that moment a volley of rifle fire erupted from the fort. The noise unsettled the horses, and they became difficult to handle. Horn scowled at this new misfortune. They would never be able to cut all the hobbles now. As the bluecoats organized themselves, they would simply overpower the little force of raiders.

"It's time to leave," Otter announced.

"He's right," Horn added. "Get mounted. Let's drive off what we can while we can."

"Ayyyy!" Rabbit Foot screamed as he slapped his pony into motion. A handful of mares galloped along ahead of him.

One raider after another climbed atop a horse and drove a few unhobbled horses along toward the river.

Buffalo Horn was the last to leave the herd. He managed to cut a big black mare and three spotted ponies free before noticing that the firing seemed to be creeping closer.

"Ayyyy!" Horn howled. "Let's ride, ponies!"

An instant later two shots rang out. The first clipped a lock of Horn's hair just below his left ear. The second startled the stallion and forced Buffalo Horn to divert his attention from the fort.

"Brother, are you all right?" Dragonfly called.

"I'm fine," Horn replied. "Drive the ponies, brother!"

A new volley split the evening air then, and Horn instinctively ducked. He turned back in time to see Dragonfly fall.

"No!" Horn shouted, kicking the stallion into a gallop. He raced over to where the boy lay slumped across his pony.

"Hang on, brother," Horn urged as he stuffed a clean strip of cloth into the hole in Dragonfly's shoulder. "We'll get away from here and cut out the lead."

"It will leave a good scar, won't it?" the young man asked with a grin.

"It will," Horn promised. "Now let's hurry before the bluecoats shoot us."

18

The *Wihio* ponies and the wagons filled with supplies restored hope to the *Tsis tsis tas*. Many of the younger men continued to raid the isolated ranches and settlements along Arkansas River or up north along the Platte River wagon roads, but Buffalo Horn set aside his bow. He devoted himself instead to performing a healing cure for young Dragonfly. Later, when the boy had regained his strength, Horn took him and Fire Lance hunting in the thickets south of Black Kettle's encampment.

The hunts were also a remedy of sorts. Buffalo Horn conducted the ancient pipe ceremony and made the appropriate prayers before taking the life of deer or rabbit. The fresh meat revived his strength, and the sharing of the old, traditional ceremonies revived a sense of direction in what had been an aimless bewilderment.

Others saw the change. Bright Swallow Maiden

welcomed him each evening when he, Dragonfly, and
Fire Lance arrived at Otter's lodge. As the worst of the
freezing nights of winter passed into memory, Horn
appeared with a courting flute.

"It's time to set aside the remembering," Bright
Swallow Maiden said, smiling faintly.

"It will be hard," Horn noted. "The people must
continue, though. We have to do what we can."

"It's all we've ever done," she told him. "Perhaps
there can be a moment for us, too."

"Maybe," he agreed.

"I saw you laughing with that girl," Fire Lance
grumbled one morning when he and Buffalo Horn
walked among the ponies. "You won't be sleeping
with us in our shelter much longer."

"We'll be together longer than you imagine," Buffalo Horn assured him. "I'm not a man to hurry
things."

"A good woman like that won't wait forever," Fire
Lance warned. "Brother, she's had many offers. An
old Arapaho brought three ponies to Otter's lodge this
very morning."

"Three, eh?" Horn asked. "Can we spare so many
ponies?"

"Three?" Fire Lance asked, studying the problem a
moment. "We can always take a few more from the
bluecoats. You won't find another woman so easily.
She would accept two, I think. She likes you. Personally, I believe she would have an easier time with the
old Arapaho."

"Probably," Buffalo Horn agreed, smiling faintly.

"She's found a home for those little children, you
know," Fire Lance added. "I think it's time you
should ask her."

"She has no father or brother to speak with," Horn said, frowning. "I have no relative to send."

"You have brothers," the Lance objected. "Dragonfly and I'll speak to Otter. She sleeps in his lodge, after all. Don't worry about the ponies, either. That should be our gift."

"If more than three . . ."

"We'll arrange things," Fire Lance said, brightening at the notion of making the marriage bargain. "I'll find Dragonfly. We can plan the feast tomorrow. Ayyyy! Our brother is taking a wife!"

No sooner had Fire Lance spoken the words than a cold shudder worked its way through Buffalo Horn's insides. He started to call Fire Lance back, but the young man had already dashed off through the snow to find Dragonfly.

"What are you worried about?" Horn asked himself. "You've always known she would become your wife. It's time to walk Man's Road and bring brave hearts into the world to take the place of all the ones climbing Hanging Road."

Saying the words was one thing. Believing them was something altogether different. As he cut a footpath through the snow several paces from the pony herd, Buffalo Horn wondered if it was appropriate for a man with far-seeing eyes to seek the comfort of a wife and family. Old Two Claws had warned that his path would be steep and lonely. Each time people had tried to ease his burdens, death had carried them away.

Horn was still marching around the pony herd when Otter arrived.

"Brother, why do you send these children to speak about marriage?" Otter asked. "We've been like the claws of a bear, part of the same whole. It was for me to do."

"If Bright Swallow had a father or brother to speak for her, I would have sent you," Buffalo Horn explained. "It seemed proper to ask you to speak for her. It wouldn't be appropriate to send you to speak to yourself. I might have sent a blood relation, but Mole's too young. I've hunted and ridden to war with those two. I call them brother in the same way I've always regarded you."

"It would be difficult to treat for both parties," Otter admitted.

"I'm glad that you understand, Otter," Buffalo Horn said, clasping his brother-friend's hands. "Our paths have strayed from the direction we once vowed to follow. I want to make that path straight again and restore the harmony that's left our world."

"There can be no harmony with *Wihio* everywhere."

"It will be difficult," Horn admitted, "but we have to find a way."

"There isn't one."

"We'll look hard for it, brother. And if it's there, we'll set our feet on it."

"If it can be done, we'll do it," Otter agreed.

"Will you also discuss that other matter with my young brothers?" Buffalo Horn asked, grinning.

"We'll arrange it," Otter replied, laughing. "I was wondering if you would take a wife before all our hair was white. Snow Bear suspected he would have grandchildren first."

"I haven't waited so long, have I?"

"Yes," Otter declared. "She's a good woman, and she'll give you strength, Horn. I've watched her with

the children. She'll be a fine mother. You two are part
of the same soul. You notice the needs of the people
and do what you can to lessen their burdens. It's appropriate you join."

"Appropriate, yes," Horn mused. "And necessary."

Otter offered a reassuring nod before leaving. A
short while later Dragonfly and Fire Lance arrived
with word that an agreement had been made.

"Three ponies is a high price in this time of need,"
Fire Lance observed. "Your wife will win much respect when it's known."

"She's the daughter of a chief," Buffalo Horn
pointed out. "Three's little enough payment."

"She's become a wealthy woman," Dragonfly observed. "Even the old Arapaho said so. Be careful she
doesn't take our ponies and put you out of her lodge."

"If she does, that will be your doing," Horn
scolded. "It's not such an easy thing, taking a husband
who brings brothers along."

"We should remain in our own lodge," Dragonfly
suggested.

"If you want to go there when the grasses green, I
think that would be fitting," Buffalo Horn replied.
"Not now. The winds still carry a bitter bite. Bright
Swallow's lived with Otter's brothers, and she's had
little children to look after."

"We're not children," Fire Lance objected.

"No, so she's certain to welcome you," Horn countered. "Let's not worry about such little things,
though. We have a wedding feast to organize."

"Otter will do that," Dragonfly told him. "Already
his brothers are planning a giveaway. This will be a
remembered time, Horn."

"And a better one than we've known lately," Buffalo Horn added. He certainly hoped so.

The wedding feast truly was a remembered time. Otter sent his brothers out to the scattered bands, and many old friends arrived. Horn's cousin, Wolf Running, came south from the Oglala encampments, bringing ponies and many other good presents for the giveaway. In spite of the scarcity of good buffalo hides to keep away the winter chill, the wives and mothers of Elk warriors crafted a brightly painted lodge.

"This is how it was when we were young," Bright Swallow said as she and Buffalo Horn began the dancing. "A wedding feast should draw the people together."

"I wish there were more of us," Horn replied. "More relations," he added, glancing at where Summer Cherry Woman and Mole sat with an Oglala, Storm Eagle. She would soon have a new husband, Horn suspected.

"When we assemble to remake the world, you'll see that there are more of us than you suspected," Bright Swallow remarked.

"It's a good thing with so many trying to kill us all," Buffalo Horn declared.

"This isn't the time for bad-heart talk," she scolded. "We should speak only of beginnings."

"Yes," he agreed, leading her away from the circle of dancers. "Beginnings."

They walked toward their waiting lodge amid a sea of grinning faces and whispered jests. Friends and relatives had provided wonderful things to eat, and between them, Otter and Wolf Running presented seven ponies in honor of the new marrieds.

"We'll watch the pony herd," Dragonfly told Buffalo Horn when he and Bright Swallow passed. "With so many guests here, someone should be watchful."

"Snow Bear invited me to share Young Man's Lodge tonight," Fire Lance announced. "I think you'll have to pass this night alone, brother. Well," he added, "almost alone."

"You do know what should be done, don't you?" Wolf Running asked.

"He can ask Bull Buffalo to show him," Otter suggested.

"Leave it to me," Horn replied. "I have always responded to difficult challenges."

"Difficult?" Bright Swallow asked.

"Yes," he said, sighing. "Like listening to these foolish remarks by men who should know better."

The others laughed, and in spite of his best efforts to paint a scowl on his face, Buffalo Horn grinned back at them.

"Come on, husband," Bright Swallow said, pointing toward the lodge. "I've received my instruction, and I know what to do. Let's enter our new lodge and rest."

"Yes," Wolf Running said. "But don't rest too much!"

The others laughed once more, and Horn produced a true scowl then. He wasn't comfortable listening to such open talk about private matters, and he told them so with a single icy glare. The others then moved aside, allowing Buffalo Horn and Bright Swallow to pass. They walked hand in hand as far as the lodge. Then Horn stepped through the door and held the flap open for his new wife. She crawled inside, and he closed the hide door.

"I'm tired of prying eyes," he told her.

"You're far too sensitive about such matters," she warned.

"Some things are best shared in privacy," he insisted as he added two willow logs to the embers of a small fire.

"And if those boys were here? I arranged for the others to be adopted, you know."

"I do know, Swallow. As for Dragonfly and Fire Lance, they're sensible enough to realize they're not needed here tonight."

"What about tomorrow night?"

"Who can think about tomorrows with you here?" he asked, grinning as he started to remove the beautiful beaded shirt Feather Dance Woman had crafted for the occasion.

"Let me," she offered, crawling over beside him. "My mother always helped my father. It can awaken the senses, she told me."

Buffalo Horn soon understood why. As her light fingers loosened the rawhide strip that tightened the shirt against his neck, he felt her warming closeness. She eased his neck back onto her belly and slid the shirt over his angular shoulders and past his head. She then untied his leggings and eased them down from his hips. Gripping his thighs, she removed his breechclout and let him linger in the warm glow of the flickering willow logs.

Horn felt odd. It wasn't embarrassment. He had never felt the kind of shame *Wihio* experienced when naked. After all, a man was what he was, better or worse, and one was much the same as the next. True, he couldn't help staring at his mangled foot when she removed his moccasins. Bright Swallow had seen the foot before, though, and she hardly seemed to notice the missing toes.

The strange sensation was more a notion of helplessness, of no longer controlling his words or his actions. His body reacted on its own, providing a kind of exhilaration that was both wonderful and frightening at the same instant.

Swallow moved to one side and removed her own garments. Buffalo Horn had often spied maidens swimming in creeks and rivers, but he had never beheld anything approximating Bright Swallow's sculptured shoulders and round hips. Only the bullet scar on her shoulder attested to her physical being. Otherwise Horn imagined her a cloud taking shape in one of his dreams.

"You're beautiful," he whispered.

"You're not," she said, laughing as she traced the many scars on his chest and thighs. "It's a hard thing, suffering for the welfare of the people. I once believed only a woman could understand the pain a new life causes, or how one can welcome it because of the child that follows. A man of the people also undergoes torment for the sake of others."

"Yes," Horn agreed.

"Once, long ago, when you first came to the *Wu ta piu*, my father said to me, 'There goes a man to know.' "

"He did?"

"He also warned me that your face told him you would know a difficult path. You would need help along the way."

"I do, Swallow."

"I believe he also spoke to your aunt's brother. That's why he went to stay with you. *Ne' hyo* knew you could help a boy overcome his anger, and in doing so, overcome your own bitterness. Grief and pain cloud a man's thinking and dim his far-seeing eyes."

"I only got that boy killed," Horn said, closing his eyes tightly as if that might keep the memory from his head.

"That wasn't your doing," she said, nestling in beside him. "Only *Heammawihio* knows everything. I don't think that boy was sorry for going. When he departed my father's lodge, he was lost."

"He found himself on Arkansas River," Horn said, sighing. A chill worked its way through him as he recalled the young man's dying eyes.

"We've done enough mourning," Swallow whispered. "If we start again, the ghosts will drown us with their tears. We're here to begin something, not wonder about what's gone on before."

"It's hard forgetting," he said as he slipped an arm under her shoulders. She rolled against him, and he sighed. The old, dark memories flowed out of him, and he knew only her wonderful warmth. Her hands kindled a fire throughout his being as they helped him maneuver on top of her. It seemed strangely natural, the coupling. He considered himself unskilled at mating. A great longing had taken possession of him, though, and Swallow responded to every movement. They joined in a oneness that was so total, so complete, that Buffalo Horn wondered how he could possibly have survived twenty-four snows as a solitary being.

Afterward they lay there, intertwined, for what seemed an eternity. For the first time since the *Wihio* trap had sliced off his toes, Horn felt truly at peace with himself and his world.

He awoke to the sounds of yelping dogs and shouting children. He rolled away from Bright Swallow and hurriedly dressed. When he stepped outside the lodge, he expected to see bluecoats riding down on the camp again. Instead he saw it was only the wedding guests preparing to leave.

"We didn't expect to see you," Wolf Running said, grinning.

"I have relatives to thank," Horn said, trying to hide the relief that was spreading throughout his body.

"A man with a new wife should leave such matters to his brothers," Wolf said, pointing to Dragonfly and Fire Lance. "I'm camping with the Lakotas now."

"I know," Horn replied. Wolf Running had taken an Oglala wife and gone to live with her people.

"It's safer there," Wolf added. "Your wife has no family to hold you here."

"I have obligations," Horn insisted.

"Your brothers would come," Wolf said, frowning. "Otter's ridden with us. There's no harmony among the *Tsis tsis tas* now. You have Oglala blood. Our cousin Curly's become a famous fighter. He now leads the young men. Come and join us. There's talk of trouble. We can run the *Wihio*!"

"And who would remain to look after the helpless ones?" Horn asked.

"They'll be killed anyway," Wolf Running said, sadly gazing around at the young faces that rushed by on the way to gather firewood or chase rabbits. "This southern country is full of bluecoats, and I understand their war with the gray soldiers is almost finished. Then they'll swarm over this country like grasshoppers, devouring everything."

"I was born in this country," Horn pointed out. "Among these people. My fight's here, helping them. If I'm to die doing it, well, nothing lives long."

"Only the earth and the mountains," Wolf said, adding the last half of the *Tsis tsis tas* death chant. "If you change your mind, ride north. We can always use a man with far-seeing eyes."

"Your dreams tell you more than mine," Horn pointed out.

"No, I only make some sense of it, and my chiefs listen. If yours had, there would be bluecoat bones at Sand Creek. White Antelope and the other good men would still live!"

"We can only walk the path *Heammawihio* puts before our feet," Buffalo Horn insisted. "Congratulate Curly. Maybe one day you and I and Curly can swim together in Horse Creek again as we did at the treaty signing."

"We're finished making treaties," Wolf grumbled.

"To remake the world then," Horn suggested. "We must continue, we two. I saw the stone points on your arrows. Someone has to remember the old ways and show the young men what needs doing."

"Someone will," Wolf vowed.

"Yes," Horn agreed as Wolf Running nudged his horse into a trot. "We will."

Buffalo Horn and Otter remained with Black Kettle until the grass began to green again. Then the brother-friends broke down their two lodges and set off northward.

"What happened to what you told your cousin?" Black Kettle asked. "I expected you to remain and help us with the hunting."

"We'll find meat, and we'll bring some to the camp to feed the helpless ones," Buffalo Horn explained. "We won't be far from you, and we'll return when it's time to remake the earth and organize the hunting. My brothers and I need to find some clear sky and good grass to fatten our ponies. Don't worry. We'll be watchful."

Buffalo Horn's true reason for leaving was a troubling dream that had begun to torment him nightly. He knew his shouts and screams disturbed the camp, and he hoped that solitude might help him discover its meaning.

He had dreamed only a few times since Sand Creek, and that was why the vision was all the more troubling. It began with him riding across the broad, flat seas of buffalo grass. He wasn't scouting, but he nevertheless spotted a dung trail.

"Bull Buffalo's near," he called to three shadowy companions. "Ayyyy! Fresh meat will be welcome."

Buffalo Horn expected he would next see a hunt, but he didn't. Instead he detected a solitary man riding alone across the plains. He tried to identify the man's face, but it wasn't possible. Eventually a disfigured ear provided the needed identification.

"*Heammawihio*, make my bow arm strong," his own voice bellowed. "Give me the heart and the power to find Bull Buffalo."

At that instant the ground shook, and out of the grass emerged a sacred white buffalo.

"I'm here!" the great beast snorted.

"I come in the old way," the hunter announced. "I carry only my bow and stone-tipped arrows."

"Old way?" the beast thundered. "You ride a horse. Didn't the *Wihio* bring this animal into our country?"

"Yes," the hunter reluctantly agreed. "We took it from him."

"You've taken nothing," the buffalo replied. "Even horses came as Sweet Medicine said they would. I've run often through your dreams, and those of others. You see and hear, but you ignore our advice."

"Not me!" the hunter shouted.

"Now that the *Wihio* comes here with his armies to kill you, it's too late to turn him aside. Once, in the beginning, you might have stayed away and been safe. No longer. See how few the people have become? Soon my children, the buffalo, will vanish. You are seeing the last of us. What will the people eat when that happens? What will they do?"

The dream came over and over until Buffalo Horn saw it even when he was awake.

"I must make sense of the dream," Horn told Bright Swallow. "Is it another warning? How will we save ourselves if the *Wihio* strike again before we are able to finish the hunt?"

"You have to search your own life for the answers," Swallow argued. "They're hard to see at times, but a man must find them."

Buffalo Horn also told Otter of the dream.

"It's clear enough," Otter grumbled. "The bluecoats are coming again."

"But what can we do to protect the helpless ones this time?" Horn asked.

"As much as we did the last time," Otter said, sourly gazing at his feet. "*Heammawihio* decides things. How often have you told me that? You have the far-seeing eyes, brother. Try to find a solution. For my part, I expect they will kill all of us."

"And the buffalo?"

"It's true," Otter pointed out. "Already the herds are growing thinner. It's said that some *Wihio* kill the calves and cows for their softer hides, leaving the meat behind to rot."

"Don't they have teeth?" Horn asked. "Chewing makes a coat soft, and a bull's hide is much better for shield making or sewing into a coat."

"The *Wihio* never bother to see our purpose," Otter lamented. "They act out of self-interest. When Bull Buffalo is no more, how will we make lodges? Where will our winter coats come from? They mean to starve and freeze us, Horn."

"Maybe we can talk to them, state our grievances."

"Hasn't Black Kettle tried to walk that path? Have you seen his woman's back? It's said the white devils shot her nine times!"

"We always return to the same question, don't we, Brother?" Horn asked. "What can we do?"

"Walk our path, Horn," Otter replied. "Walk our path."

19

That summer when the scattered bands of *Suhtai* and *Tsis tsis tas* met to remake the earth, Buffalo Horn estimated that a third of the people who had been there the previous summer were gone. Many had died at Sand Creek or starved during the winter, but a considerable number had broken away to join allied tribes. Some of the northern bands performed their own ceremony and stayed in the safer, north country.

"We're a people broken apart," Black Kettle told Horn. "We can't come together even to pray and hunt!"

"It's a far way to come," Buffalo Horn observed. "Bluecoats ride along the *Wihio* wagon roads, hunting our people. It's dangerous to move camps full of women and children so far."

"We came," the Kettle pointed out.

"We're in no greater danger here than where we

were," Horn said. "There's no place south of Platte River where the bluecoats don't hunt us."

"They'll soon grow tired of this war," Black Kettle declared. "The people in the East don't like it."

"Uncle, they've been fighting each other five summers. It's said that's over now, and they have a thousand times a thousand soldiers to send after us."

"You don't yet understand the *Wihio*, Frog. They grow sick of war. They're good at sending hardhearted murderers out to kill little children, but they have no real stomach for fighting a long war. While you and Otter were out hunting, messengers came to us from the Bents. The *Wihio* wish us to make peace."

"They want us all dead," Horn growled. "Or with our manhood cut away like White Antelope. Don't trust them."

"Frog, you said it yourself. There's no safe place. We can't hide seventy lodges of helpless women and children."

"The Crazy Dogs won't agree to any peace until they've satisfied their thirst for revenge."

"Are they willing to see us all dead?"

"They think it will happen anyway," Horn said, frowning. "They may be right."

The chief had heard such talk from others, but Buffalo Horn immediately regretted speaking the words. Black Kettle winced, and Horn saw that such dark notions tore at the old man.

"You've had another dream?" Black Kettle asked.

"One that I don't understand," Buffalo Horn replied. "It keeps coming, but I don't understand what it means."

"You're no longer a boy, Frog. There's no one here to explain it. The answer . . ."

"I know," Horn interrupted. "It's for me to find within myself."

That summer as the men hunted buffalo, parties of *Wihio* treaty makers often met with the chiefs. In spite of threats from the soldier societies, particularly the Crazy Dogs, Black Kettle smoked with the *Wihio* messengers and guaranteed their safety.

"We should kill them," Rabbit Foot declared. "Punish them for all the killing they've done."

"They're not the ones that did it," Buffalo Horn countered. "I know. I was there. As long as they're talking to us, they're not shooting bullets into little children. Besides, Black Kettle pledged their safety with his life."

"He's an old man," Rabbit Foot grumbled. "He doesn't know anything."

"He's let men make him promises," Horn said, sighing. "Does that make him weak? He's lost no honor that I can see. His body shows the marks of his suffering. When these last treaty people came, Black Kettle instructed his wife to show the scars left by the bluecoat bullets. Nine of them! I could never ask Bright Swallow to show herself to strangers that way, but the Kettle set aside his own feelings and hers because he knew the people would benefit from such a demonstration.

"Black Kettle was once a man wealthy in horses," Horn continued, "but no longer. All he's had he's given to people who needed it. If you don't like his path, don't follow it. That doesn't mean you should dishonor him by making a lie of his promises. That's what a *Wihio* would do."

Rabbit Foot turned and walked away.

"He hasn't been the same since your aunt's brother

died," Otter told Horn. "The Crazy Dogs have invited him to ride with them. He'll be leaving us soon. Sparrow, too."

"And Snow Bear?"

"Is walking the river road with a young Arapaho. Soon they'll all be gone."

"It's hard to believe, a camp without Otter's brothers stirring up trouble."

"Our sons will take their place," Otter vowed. "Rock Watcher's getting bigger."

"I may have a son myself before winter is over."

"It's good to hear. I thought Swallow looked swollen."

"The child will probably be born this winter," Buffalo Horn said, gazing skyward. "It's a hard time to greet the world. I wish I had considered that, but . . ."

"I know," Otter said, laughing. "I tried to wait. I had my brothers to chase up Man's Road. A man may control himself when he's riding his pony across a snowbound valley, but when he sees his wife bare that first time, there's no holding back."

"It just isn't possible," Horn agreed.

"You weren't with me when it was time to name my son," Otter observed. "I'll be your watcher, and you can invite a dream. Maybe you'll find names for both our new children."

"You, too, are expecting a son?"

"Perhaps this time it will be a girl. I hope so. Rock Watcher resembles his mother, so a girl would, too. She would bring me many horses one day."

"It's good to know my brother knows what's most important," Buffalo Horn said, laughing.

"I'm glad you're with us, Horn," Otter said, growing serious. "With my other brothers gone, I'll want some company when the fighting resumes."

"Maybe it won't."

"We know better," Otter objected. "It's fine for the chiefs and the young men to say what they want, but we're the ones who will do the fighting."

"Why us?" Buffalo Horn asked.

"We're the ones with wives and little ones. We can't run away like the pony boys or ignore what's going on the way the old men do. I hear the talk that's going on. Some say the Elks will offer you a chief's bonnet."

"They'll choose an older man," Horn insisted. "I'm no soldier chief."

"You've led raids, brother. Who captured the blue-coats' ponies?"

"It's too much responsibility," Horn said, staring at his feet. "My dreams trouble me enough. Try not to expect more from me than I've given already."

"We do expect more," Otter replied. "We know you. Your father was a great man. Old Two Claws valued you. Who am I to challenge what they've said about you?"

"I'm lost myself!" Horn complained. "How can I show anyone a path when I can't find one?"

"They already follow you," Otter said, waving toward a nearby boulder where Dragonfly and Fire Lance sat, watching.

"Yes," Buffalo Horn admitted. "I wish it were otherwise."

"I believe a wise man always feels that way," Otter remarked. "He leads even though he doesn't want to. You'll do it again, too."

Buffalo Horn knew Otter was right. Horn wasn't comfortable leading, though. He didn't want the glory, and he surely didn't desire the blame. He might easily have let Otter plan and direct the pony raid, but Horn hadn't. There was no denying the tendency of certain young men to follow him. But a soldier chief? No, he could never be that!

The buffalo hunt was a great success that summer. The people's need was great, and Bull Buffalo offered up his sons to feed the starving and leave enough to be dried against winter's need. The women worked tirelessly at curing hides and sewing lodges so that the meager shelters that had sufficed after Sand Creek gave way to tall new lodges.

The *Wu ta piu* sent a party up north to cut pines for lodge poles, and Buffalo Horn was only one of several men that joined. Dragonfly and Fire Lance naturally went along. Otter also rode north, as did his brothers and several Crazy Dogs. In the beginning the journey was peaceful, but at Platte River a patrol of *Wihio* soldiers briefly gave chase. Some of the young men suggested turning and offering the bluecoats a fight, but Otter reminded them that they hadn't started north to kill bluecoats.

"If we killed them all, would it change anything?" Otter asked Rabbit Foot in particular.

"We would at least know those *Wihio* would kill no more of us," Rabbit Foot replied.

"Afterward we would devote our time to healing the wounded or mourning the dead instead of providing the needed lodge poles. Would you be the one to explain to a freezing child that he has no warm lodge because you busied yourself counting coups instead of cutting pines?"

Rabbit Foot hung his head, and there was no more talk of fighting bluecoats. After appropriate poles were cut and tied behind ponies brought along for the task, the Crazy Dogs broke away.

"Now we can strike the bluecoats," Rabbit Foot boasted. "Our obligation is met."

Otter started to remind the Crazy Dogs, or simply Dog Soldiers as they had started calling themselves, that the poles were little use north of Platte River, but Buffalo Horn interceded.

"Let them go," Horn urged. "They will anyway, and any harsh words you speak now will make for hard feelings later."

"And if we have trouble getting back?" Otter asked.

"There are the two of us to deal with it," Horn observed. "It's time my brothers were your brothers," he added, waving to Dragonfly and Fire Lance, who were riding up ahead with Snow Bear. "So we're five, after all."

They continued for a time. Then the sound of a rifle shot echoed through the quiet morning air.

"Horn?" Otter cried out.

"I heard it," Buffalo Horn said, scanning the nearby hills. "Did anyone see a flash? Powder smoke?"

"The shot came from the river, behind us," Dragonfly announced. "Brother, we should have a look."

"It's for me to do," Otter declared. "Bear?"

Snow Bear turned his pony and started toward his brother, but Horn waved him back.

"I'm still your brother," Horn explained. "Snow Bear should stay with the poles. His eyes are better than mine for spying trouble."

"The trouble's back there," Snow Bear said, pointing past a low hill toward Platte River.

"If there's a fight going on, we'll send for you," Horn promised.

"We'll save some bluecoats for you," Fire Lance boasted.

"You're staying, too," Horn barked at the Lance. "It was probably just a *Wihio* from one of the wagon bands shooting at a prairie chicken."

"Probably," Otter agreed, laughing. A gun would turn a plump prairie chicken into a mass of feathers and lead pellets. A child armed with a few flat stones knew enough to stun the birds and then wring their short necks.

The brother-friends made their way toward the river with rare caution. Buffalo Horn recalled Grouse's death all too vividly. He wouldn't risk Otter's well-being. They eventually descended a small hill and found themselves viewing a confused scene full of swirling powder smoke and wild firing. One *Wihio* wagon lay on its side in the river, and a small party of mounted Dog Soldiers struggled to get at it. The rest of the *Wihio* wagon people worked themselves out of the river and up onto the bank.

"Do you see anyone hurt?" Horn asked.

"At the river," Otter observed. Apparently the wagon people had been camped there. Some of the younger ones had gone in swimming, and when the Dog Soldiers arrived, someone had fired in panic. Now three pale bodies rested on the bank, lined up elbow to elbow like grain sacks at Bent's store.

"Our people are unhurt," Horn observed.

"Then we should leave," Otter suggested. "I don't want trouble with the Dog Soldiers, and I'm afraid I would say something ill-tempered about killing swimming children."

"Yes," Horn agreed. As he started to turn away, though, the air below filled with terrifying cries and shouts. He and Otter both turned at the same instant. Brightly painted *Tsis tsis tas* broke through the line of wagons, shooting at everyone with a white complexion. Finally the wagon people started answering the attack, and their determined firing emptied several horses.

"We have to get back," Otter urged.

"Not now," Horn said, sadly shaking his head. "We have to make certain your brothers are well."

"If not, what can we do?"

"Perform a medicine cure," Horn replied. "Coming?"

"You're leading again," Otter observed, grinning. The two of them hurried down to the scene of the fighting. By then the wagon band had passed out of view. Two more wagons remained, abandoned. A woman's body lay in the back of one wagon. Two young men and a small child lay in the rutted road. Bullets had chased the life from their chests.

"Ayyyy!" the Dog Soldiers shouted as they raced beside the derelict wagons, driving several captured ponies. "We've counted coup."

Rabbit Foot galloped past and raced to the river. When he got there, he jumped from his horse and cut away the forelock of one of the dead swimmers. Sparrow followed and likewise scalped one of the corpses. Other Dog Soldiers then fell on the dead and began cutting pieces off them.

"You can't blame them," Horn muttered as he read the rage in Otter's eyes. "They heard all the stories."

"Black Kettle will never be able to make a peace when there are so many bad feelings between our peoples," Otter observed.

"No one will know about this butchery," Horn declared. "Birds and wolves will chew up what's left. If soldiers come along, they'll see only bones."

"I hope you're right," Otter said, doing his best to avoid retching. "Didn't the bluecoats do these same things to our relatives at Sand Creek?"

"All this and worse," Horn said, shrinking from the question. "They're *Wihio*, so we expect such odd behavior from them."

"My brothers have been taught to behave," Otter grumbled. "But they walk their own paths now. It's not for me to say anything."

The killing didn't end with the wagon people, though. Twenty horses were taken from a small ranch a few miles farther west. A *Wihio* who walked out to speak with the Dog Soldiers was cut to pieces. Afterward his sons had begun demanding that the guilty Dog Soldiers be punished.

Buffalo Horn and Otter only learned of that second fight much later when they returned to Black Kettle's camp with the poles.

"That doesn't sound like our people," the Kettle told Horn. "It must have been Lakotas."

"We saw the wagon fight," Horn told the chief. "It was probably the Dog Soldiers."

"It was a bad time to do something so stupid," Black Kettle muttered. "The bluecoat chief who led the attack against our camp has been punished, and the government has offered us presents. Now the *Wihio* are angry. These boys have been showing the soldier chiefs the mutilated body of their father. I'm afraid the bad hearts will take control again."

"They have one dead man to talk about," Horn said, frowning. "It's sad, but does it erase Sand Creek?"

"It excuses it in their eyes," Black Kettle explained. "A people capable of butchering a father in front of his sons is past helping."

"So the *Wihio* will punish us for doing to this man what they've done to us?" Otter asked. "We should all join the Dog Soldiers then. If we're to die, we can at least find honor fighting to the last breath."

"Is that how you hope your son will die?" Black Kettle asked.

Otter trembled, and Horn had to steady him.

"No one wants these things to happen," Black Kettle added.

"They will, though," Horn noted. "In spite of everything."

Not everyone was bothered by the killings at Platte River, though. When Rabbit Foot, Sparrow, and the other Dog Soldiers visited Black Kettle's camp the following week, they were welcomed as heroes.

"Look, brother," Rabbit Foot said, jumping down from his horse and displaying the yellow hair taken from one of the swimmers. "I've counted coup."

"He must have been a fierce fighter," Otter observed, touching the fine, silken-like hair. "Was he older than Rock Watcher at least?"

"He was old enough to shoot a rifle," Rabbit Foot replied.

"Did you help cut the rancher, too?" Otter asked.

"No," Rabbit Foot said, frowning. "That was a bad thing."

"How was it different from what you did at the river?" Buffalo Horn asked. "We saw it, Otter and I. What did you cut besides the scalp, Rabbit Foot?"

"I'm not called that anymore," the young man replied. "I won a new name by killing the *Wihio* at Platte River."

"Do they call you child-killer?" Otter asked. "Ear-taker?"

"Thunder Cloud," Otter's brother explained. "Sparrow, too, won a name. They call him Little Thunder."

"Good names," Otter confessed. "I never enjoyed taking my enemy's hair," he said. "It keeps his ghost close."

"Yes," Thunder Cloud agreed. "Some of the others aren't sleeping well. I cut the yellow-haired one's ears, but they began to smell, and I buried them."

"You've made it hard on the peacemakers," Otter said, "but I understand your intentions. It's important now that you're walking Man's Road that you consider the consequences of your actions. A few men can avoid the bluecoats and raid the *Wihio*, but what does that matter if they send an army here? They'll kill us all!"

"No, that's not how they'll do it," Horn said, vividly recalling his dream. "They'll kill Bull Buffalo. They'll shoot all the game, and we'll have to hang around their forts, eating the scraps they throw us."

"Kill all the buffalo?" Thunder Cloud asked. "No, Horn, not even the *Wihio* can manage such a thing. There are simply too many of them."

"I hope so," Horn replied. "I'm beginning to wonder, though."

20

The first breath of winter found Buffalo Horn on Red Shield River. The autumn buffalo hunt had also been successful, and the chiefs deemed it wise for the southern bands to break apart into smaller encampments. Horn, Otter, and ten other *Wu ta piu* lodges formed one such winter camp. A larger band of Dog Soldiers was a short distance upriver, and beyond them were some Arapahoes.

The plan suited Buffalo Horn. He was anxious to enjoy the peace and tranquillity of a small camp. Everyone there had plenty of ponies, food, and clothing. Each lodge was strong, and its poles were heavy enough to withstand the strongest wind. When fresh meat was wanted, there were deer nearby.

"I always liked this place," Bright Swallow Woman told him. "I can remember the many good times our people camped here."

"Yes, but there were also dark times," Horn observed. Grouse's scaffold was but a short ride away.

"Those recollections will fade when our child is born," she assured him. "It's appropriate that a new life should greet the world here where once you helped another find his peace."

"Do you believe he did find his peace?" Horn asked.

"You're not the only one to walk the medicine trail," she pointed out. "I've stood in the high places overlooking this river, and I know *Heammawihio* watches over us. We're never far from Him."

"Do you think our pleas reach His ears?"

"I refuse to consider otherwise. Horn, you must invite a dream again. Our child will need a name, and your family has a bad habit of steepening the paths its sons and daughters must climb by giving them names like Mole and Frog."

"I'll go into the hills whenever you think it's time," he promised.

"You should leave when I go to Woman's Lodge," she said. "It will be soon."

The approaching birth of his child filled Buffalo Horn with anticipation. The shadows left by death and violence had too often choked the good from his life, and he hoped the little one might help him find a new and brighter path to walk. He recalled the difficulty and disappointment that had haunted his uncle, Raven Heart, though. Three times Raven Heart's wife had brought dead children from her womb. That was why Horn hovered near the lodge every waking moment, making certain that Bright Swallow did nothing to endanger the birthing. Eventually his nearness overwhelmed her, and she drew him aside.

"I know you're only doing it out of concern, Horn, but please stop," she told him. "I'm afraid to walk anywhere because you'll be blocking the path, trying to help."

"Aren't I right to be worried?" he asked. "It's winter, after all. Everyone knows a child born after the first snow has a difficult time."

"I would agree if the mother had passed her fortieth winter, but I'm young. I have nothing to do but wait for him to come out and see his father."

"That's all I want," Horn insisted.

"Good. Be patient. Children have been born before, even in winter. And take those other two with you. They're almost as bad, always whispering and rushing over here to help me stoke the cook fire or bake bread."

"Someone ought to remain to . . ."

"I have a sister here," she interrupted. "Horn, what will need doing none of you are prepared to do. Dragonfly is sincere, and Fire Lance is becoming like a brother to me, but recently they have become more bother than help. Go out and hunt. Invite a dream. But let me have some peace."

Buffalo Horn found himself laughing. She was serious, of course, but as he thought of all the foolish things he had done the previous week, he could not resist laughing.

"I'll behave myself," he promised, "and I'll speak with the others. We can hunt a deer."

"Fresh meat would be welcome," she observed.

"Then we'll do it," he volunteered.

Actually Buffalo Horn waited two days before departing the camp. It was difficult even then. He ached to pass every moment with Bright Swallow, but he trusted her to know what was best. She would soon be going to Woman's Lodge for the birthing, and he would have time enough to fret then.

Otter, Dragonfly, and Fire Lance went along. The two younger men were eager to leave. The monotony of winter was hardest on young people. Buffalo Horn was naturally concerned about Bright Swallow, and Otter was worried about his brother-friend.

"This time it's best if I lead," Otter said, riding out in front. The hard-face winds were yet to arrive, and a bright sun burned overhead. There was only a finger's depth of snow on the earth—hardly enough to notice. It made the tracking easy, though, and Otter soon located a deer run. Just as he was about to wave the others along, though, Buffalo Horn saw other tracks a stone's throw farther along.

"Wait, brother," he called to Otter. "There's something we should examine."

"More deer?" Fire Lance asked.

"No, something else," Horn said, sourly studying the tracks as his companions turned their horses and trotted over.

"Shod horses," Otter said, frowning. "Big horses, too. See how deep the tracks are?"

"That or heavy men," Horn observed.

"Not bluecoats, though," Dragonfly said, rolling off his pony and picking up a scrap of paper from the trail.

"How do you know that?" Otter asked.

"They're all bunched together," Dragonfly explained. "I've watched plenty of bluecoats. They ride in orderly lines, spaced out like on parade. These people follow no particular order. See how they carelessly leave things behind to mark their passing? These aren't any real *Wihio* soldiers. Maybe some graycoats from the south. More likely trappers or hunters."

Horn winced. The recollection of the steel trap and his severed toes overwhelmed him. He stared angrily at the tracks and then turned to Otter.

"What do you want to do, brother?" Otter asked. "They're too close to our camp. Should I go over and get some help from my brothers in the Dog Soldiers' camp? Maybe we can run these people."

"You won't have to ask for help," Horn replied. "These tracks lead to the Dog Soldiers. The *Wihio* will get there first."

"They'll be sorry they raided those men," Fire Lance declared. "They won't be fighting women and children there."

"There are plenty of helpless ones in the Dogs' winter camp," Otter pointed out. "We have to hurry."

"We'll never beat these *Wihio* there," Horn noted. "But we may not be too late to help if there's fighting."

Buffalo Horn then took the lead. He rode with all the haste prudence would allow. The trail across the intervening ridge wound through several treacherous notches. Stationed there, a well-armed trapper or two could have easily killed any pursuing party.

A short distance from the Dogs' camp Buffalo Horn heard the first of several shots echo across the far side of the ridge. More firing followed, and Horn threw caution to the wind. He sensed the anxiety in Otter's heart. Horn was determined not to fail another friend.

By the time they got within sight of the Dog Soldiers' camp, two lodges were already in flames. A handful of *Wihio* dressed in buffalo hide coats were shooting pistols into the camp and doing their best to capture women. Horn pointed to one of the trappers, and Otter pointed to another. The brother-friends then charged.

It wasn't an equal fight. The two *Tsis tsis tas* seemed to appear from nowhere. By the time the first trapper realized he was in danger, Horn had notched an arrow. It flew off his bowstring and pierced the *Wihio*'s chest just below the breastbone.

"Dan?" the man called out. The jagged stone point of Horn's second arrow cracked the trapper's skull, and he slumped across his horse's neck.

Otter killed the second man with a heavy war club. The stone head of the club simply caved in the whole left side of the trapper's skull.

Dragonfly and Fire Lance hesitated a moment before joining in. They had their bows and plenty of arrows, but they worried about striking their companions instead of the raiders. Finally they tied their ponies to a cottonwood and went ahead on foot.

"There!" Buffalo Horn shouted, pointing to a half-naked *Wihio* who was dragging a young woman into a stand of bare oaks.

"Ayyyy!" Fire Lance shouted as he tossed his bow aside and drew a knife. The Lance was only fourteen, and small for his age, but the recollection of his mother's death at Sand Creek drove him mad. He found the trapper cowering behind a rock and plunged the knife into the *Wihio*'s middle. The trapper stared at the blood spreading across his white shirt and gasped. Fire Lance then yanked the knife out again, leaving a terrible bloody hole.

"Lord Almighty!" the *Wihio* cried.

The trapper was still alive, and Fire Lance laughed as he began cutting. Everything the bluecoats had done to his grandfather Fire Lance then did to the dying trapper.

Buffalo Horn would have stopped that, but his attention was drawn by a cry for help. On the far side of the camp three raiders had a pair of *Tsis tsis tas* pony boys cornered. Horn recognized Little Thunder, as Sparrow was now called, as the one on the left.

"Brother, you're needed!" Horn called to Otter. The two of them shouted furiously as they slapped their ponies into a gallop. The *Wihio* spotted the onrushing rescuers, but they had no choice but to press their attack. They needed horses to get away.

The young Dog Soldiers held their ground, and it seemed at first as if they had escaped unharmed. The trappers finally retreated from the ponies. Horn killed the first one with a single arrow through the heart. Otter clubbed a second man, and Dragonfly, who was following on foot, shot the third man twice through the back.

"*See' was sin mit*, that was a brave-heart stand!" Otter exclaimed as he rolled off his pony and embraced his youngest brother.

"Sometimes it's all a man can do," Little Thunder whispered.

"Otter?" Horn called in concern as Thunder fell to his knees.

"See to the other one," Otter suggested as he cradled his brother's head in his hands.

Buffalo Horn knelt beside the second pony boy, who appeared to be resting beside a boulder. The boy's eyes were frozen, though, and when Horn touched the youngster's shoulder, the pony boy tottered off one side of the rock and lay on the ground, his whole side blown apart by bullets.

"Why?" Horn asked as he closed the boy's eyelids. "What made those trappers come here and bring about so much death?"

"I hoped the next time we would make prayers on a hillside, it would be to invite a naming dream," Otter said as he stepped over beside Buffalo Horn. "Instead we will be speaking the mourning prayers for my brother."

Horn took a quick glance, noted Little Thunder's bloody back and side, and frowned.

"It's always the same," Horn mumbled. "Where are the watchers? How could a camp be left so unprotected?"

"Come here," Otter shouted to a small boy who was helping his mother rise to her feet. "Where are the men?"

"You killed the last of them, there," the boy said, pointing to the dead trapper at Otter's feet.

"Not *Wihio* men," Otter said impatiently. "Our men. The Dog Soldiers."

"Raiding," the child explained as he drew out a small knife and cut a piece of a trapper's forelock away. "They'll be back."

"They left the camp like this, unguarded?" Otter cried.

"We considered it safe," the boy's mother explained. "We had plenty of food, but one of the men traded half of it to one of these traders for good rifles."

"The rifles proved expensive, didn't they?" Otter growled.

"We also thought we were safe," she replied. "There are Arapahoes to one side and *Wu ta piu* on the other."

"You were safe," Otter noted bitterly. "It's my brother they've killed."

The woman offered comforting words to ease his sadness, but Otter was beyond that. He began cutting his hair and screaming warrior songs.

"I should never have let him leave," Otter said. "It's my doing."

"A brother can only do so much," Horn argued. "If you hold a man back forever, he has no chance to grow tall or strong."

Otter only shook his head in dismay. Later, when the Dog Soldiers returned and discovered what had happened, Thunder Cloud sought out both Otter and Buffalo Horn.

"It's my fault," Cloud told them. "I should never have left him behind. He wanted to come, and he should have. He was no child. A man of seventeen summers, even one short of stature, should ride with the men."

"He fought well," Otter observed. "His was a brave death. I would rather he had run away, but that's a brother's heart speaking. He was, as you said, a man."

"Even so, I . . ." Thunder Cloud began.

"Life is a sacred circle," Buffalo Horn explained. "No man chooses the moment of his birth. Only a few select the moment of death. The important thing is to walk your path as a man, in the old way of our grandfathers' grandfathers. *Heammawihio* decides things. Not you. Not I."

"I blamed you for my friend's death," Cloud said, frowning. "I knew it wasn't your doing, Horn, but I was angry."

"Sometimes it helps to blame someone," Buffalo Horn said, clasping the younger man's hands. "The dead are still gone from us, though. It's better if the living don't cut themselves off."

"You'll help us make the proper prayers?" Otter asked.

"I was his brother, too," Horn insisted. "It's my place."

They set Little Thunder in the high rocks within sight of the scaffold holding the bones of young Grouse. The burial lodge had collapsed, or perhaps been torn down, but Horn was glad that the platform remained. Perhaps Grouse could help Thunder up Hanging Road.

They never did shoot a deer. After the killing, Horn had no heart for hunting, and Otter was too distraught to even ride. Fire Lance was trying to regain his senses after cutting up the *Wihio*, and Dragonfly had seen all the blood he could bear.

Following the three-day mourning period, the four of them returned to their meager camp. They discovered the women had welcomed Bright Swallow into Woman's Lodge.

"I expected you back yesterday," Feather Dance Woman complained when Horn and Otter sought her out. "You must hurry and make your prayers. She'll be popping soon."

"Can I see her?" Horn pleaded.

"You know it's the worst kind of misfortune for a warrior to be around a woman who's bleeding," Feather Dance explained. "I'll tell her you asked about her. She was concerned because someone died in her dreams."

"She saw things more clearly than I did," Horn muttered.

Otter then explained what had happened, and

Feather Dance Woman stood in reverent silence a moment.

"Go and invite your dream," she then told Buffalo Horn. "You don't have too much time."

"And your child?" Horn asked.

"Dream for him, too," she said, forcing a tired smile onto her face."

"Her," Otter insisted.

"I have another moon before my time's here," she told Horn. "I'll be able to tend my sister. Don't worry. I've done it all before."

And so they paused only long enough to pack some hides and food onto a pony and exchange their mounts for fresh ones. Otter led the way, and for a time Buffalo Horn suspected they might return to the burial place. Instead Otter located an even higher cliff that looked out across Red Shield River and onward for an eternity.

"It's a good place," Horn said when he dismounted. "I feel the spirits here. I can open my heart and invite the dream."

"Do you dream with your heart, Horn?" Fire Hawk asked.

"You dream with your whole being," Horn explained. "You must open your heart first, though. Hold nothing back."

"We should have taken a sweat," Otter remarked.

"If there had been a lodge ready, I would have suggested it myself," Horn replied. "As it was, there was no time. We'll use sweet grass and cedar to do the purifying."

Dragonfly and Fire Lance appeared mystified, but Horn explained it as he prepared each ritual in turn. He intended to perform the purification rite on himself, but the others asked to join in. Each of them helped build up a fire. Then Horn prepared a stack of cedar bark and sweet grass. He removed his clothing and stood before the fire as he added the aromatic strips of bark and plant. Using an eagle-feather fan, he forced the smoke from the fire around his body until it appeared as if his body had been enveloped. Horn whispered three old *Suhtai* prayers before satisfying himself that he had set the past behind. He repeated the ritual for each of his brothers.

Buffalo Horn next began his fast. He ate nothing and drank only a little water. That afternoon he sang and chanted and cut the flesh of his arms and chest. As the blood flowed, he prayed for a vision of the future. "Show me what's coming, *Heammawihio*," Horn pleaded. "I need to prepare myself and my people."

More than even that, he wanted to see what future lay ahead for the children Bright Swallow and Feather Dance would introduce to the world.

As had so often been the case, the dream appeared reluctant to come. As he sang and danced and cut his flesh, he induced a fever. One whole day he suffered, but no spirits entered his head. It wasn't until late afternoon on the second day that exhaustion overpowered him, and he collapsed. Otter hurried over and covered him. Then he and Dragonfly eased Horn over beside the warming embers of the fire.

Horn saw many things. It appeared as if his eyes were being bombarded with sights and his ears with sounds. In the end he glimpsed a lovely green land full of tall willows and gurgling streams. Bright Swallow was there, and at her side walked the loveliest of children. The little girl was as graceful and serene as a prairie flower.

He also saw a red-tailed hawk soaring over a territory unfamiliar to his eyes. In that same country coyote raced along, as did a rampaging bear.

Later the hawk flew overhead in slow, methodical circles. It screeched out a warning of some sort. Then Horn found himself once again in a winter camp. Lodges spread out in circles beside a river, and all seemed well, when lines of bluecoats charged out of a mist and attacked the camp.

The dream became a nightmare, and he screamed out into the night. He saw Sand Creek all over again— the death, the suffering, and the anguish. He wanted to run away, but he was frozen there.

Otter roused him and broke the dream's hold. Horn pulled a heavy elk robe around himself and shivered.

"You found the names?" Otter asked.

"I saw a daughter," he said, grinning. "Mine, not yours. She'll be called Prairie Flower. I saw nothing that would give an appropriate name to your child, brother."

"What did you see?" Otter asked.

"The same hawk as before," Horn explained.

"The one that warned of Sand Creek?" Fire Lance asked. "What did it warn us of this time?"

"I only saw Sand Creek again," Horn replied. "It made no sense at all."

"Certainly it did," Dragonfly said, sighing. "The bluecoats will come again. This time they'll finish us."

"Not if we're watchful," Horn insisted. "We must be."

By the time they returned to the camp, Bright Swallow had brought the child into the world of light.

"My daughter will be called Prairie Flower," Horn

announced. "She'll grow tall and wise under the guidance of her mother."

Later, when he had finished overseeing a giveaway, he spoke softly to Bright Swallow.

"We'll nurture this lovely child," Horn promised. "We'll make her world one fit for her to walk. She'll know better days than we have."

"Then we'll have better days, too, husband," Swallow replied.

"I hope there are many of them," he added softly. "Many."

21

Buffalo Horn had always regarded winter as a season of death. Bitter cold choked all the life from the earth and left it barren and cold. Even deer and buffalo appeared to vanish. His dreams were usually full of haunting voices and the stark outlines of burial scaffolds.

That winter was different, though. Prairie Flower bloomed like a summer rose, and she magnified the love of her parents. Horn saw a renewal in the child's face, a revival of lost hope. He was equally cheered when Feather Dance Woman and Otter announced the birth of their second son.

"We'll call him Sparrow," Otter explained when he came to invite his brother-friend to help with the give-away.

"It's a good name," Horn observed. "Someone should carry it."

And so as the snowdrifts deepened, and the icy

winds tightened their grip on the land, Buffalo Horn concerned himself with his new daughter and the welfare of the small band of *Wu ta piu* who continued to follow their old chief Black Kettle.

As spring greened the earth, the chief and his people faced new trials. The younger men flocked to the Dog Soldier camps, and it seemed sometimes to Buffalo Horn that only old people, women, and children remained with the Kettle. Bluecoats rode the valleys, hunting any band of *Tsis tsis tas* they could find. Peacemakers came among the people, promising presents and new treaties, but up in the northern country whole armies of *Wihio* soldiers were carving roads through the best hunting grounds. New settlers built towns where Buffalo Horn had ridden as a boy, and the *Wihio* began laying down the iron rails that always brought more towns and more white people.

Thunder Cloud carried a pipe to Otter, inviting his brother to join their northern relations in a final fight to save the north country.

"You could come, too," the Cloud told Horn. "Your relatives are fighting already. I rode with your cousin Wolf Running when he took the bluecoats' ponies near Crazy Woman's Creek."

"You're certain that there will be fighting?" Buffalo Horn asked. "It wasn't so long ago that Wolf and I raced ponies along Horse Creek. At the treaty signing."

"Treaties," Thunder Cloud muttered. "The *Wihio* sent chiefs to talk with the Lakotas about a new treaty. Already bluecoats were building roads. Red Cloud, who stands tall with the Lakotas, scolded the treaty makers. 'Do you think we're children?' he asked. 'You talk about peace while you steal our land.'

Red Cloud's got many good men up there. We'll make a good fight."

"Red Cloud's a man to follow," Horn observed. "He knows the medicine trail. He'll make his preparations and keep the helpless ones safe."

"That's not what's needed," Thunder Cloud argued. "We have to punish the *Wihio*."

"So more of us can die?" Otter asked. "Once our mother had four sons. Our camps spread through all this country. Now look at us."

"They'll kill us all if we don't punish them soon," Thunder Cloud argued.

"It's easy for a man without children to talk that way," Otter said sourly. "Horn and I've counted more coups than most, but what does that matter? If we have no children to follow us, there will be no *Tsis tsis tas*. If we kill a hundred times a hundred bluecoats and all the helpless ones die, what will it gain us?"

Buffalo Horn sighed. Black Kettle had often used those same arguments in his efforts to dissuade his people from joining the Dog Soldiers. Buffalo Horn had heard the old man speak more forcefully to the *Wihio* peacemakers.

"I've done everything you've asked," Black Kettle had recently told a *Wihio* delegation. Horn knew because he had translated the words for the white men. "We gave up our guns and turned away from the soldier roads," Black Kettle had continued, "but this man Chivington came and killed us at Sand Creek. He took most of our ponies and other possessions. He murdered the children. He cut up our men and women. You ask me to trust you, but each time we've done what you asked, and what has it brought us? Only death and sickness. Now our young men say it's better to fight you and die like warriors. What can I tell them?"

The *Wihio* agents had listened, and they had even provided gifts. The Bents even acquired some horses for the *Tsis tsis tas* to replace those stolen at Sand Creek. A new treaty council would soon be held.

"Promises," Thunder Cloud muttered when Buffalo Horn explained. "What power do words on a paper hold? They can tell us the words say this or that. How can we know? We can't read their scratches."

"The Bents can," Horn explained. "We have other friends who have learned the *Wihio* ways."

"You lived among them," Thunder Cloud reminded Buffalo Horn. "A young man I knew followed you, and he's no more."

"I remember," Horn said, trying to shake off the recollection.

"The *Wihio* like to talk of treaties," Thunder Cloud noted. "They're great men at making promises. They vowed never to come into the Powder River country, but they're there now, building roads and putting up forts. There's no trusting them, brothers. If you stay here so close to the soldier forts and the wagon roads, be watchful. I'm going north to die like a warrior."

"It's a path others have taken," Buffalo Horn observed. "It's a road where a man has simply to turn his horse and ride. Your brother and I can't make such an easy choice. We've vowed to put the welfare of others before our own."

"We have to stay," Otter said.

"I see that," Thunder Cloud told them. "I understand. We would have welcomed you, but you have your path to walk, and I have mine. I'll mourn you."

"It's a comfort knowing someone will," Otter declared as he clasped his brother's wrists. "If you're the ones who survive, don't forget all of the old ways."

"I'll forget nothing," Thunder Cloud pledged.

The trouble up north kept the *Wihio* army busy, and for a time there were fewer bluecoats to bother the southern people. When word came south that Red Cloud and his Lakotas, aided by some of the northern *Tsis tsis tas* bands, had punished the bluecoats, killing hundreds of them, the white peacemakers spoke with new fervor.

"It's time to put an end to the killing," a tall man in a fine black hat told Black Kettle. "You bury sons, I bury sons, and what have either of us won?"

"Only tears," a shaggy-haired young man at his side added.

Buffalo Horn recognized the voice even before the buckskin-clad *Wihio* translated his thoughts into *Tsis tsis tas* words.

"How do you come to know our words?" Black Kettle asked.

"A friend taught me," Isaac Guthrie explained, nodding silently to Buffalo Horn. "Not to speak them. I already knew that," Guthrie added. "To understand them."

"What are you talking about?" the tall *Wihio* asked Guthrie.

"How I came to know the language," Guthrie explained in English.

"You're here to talk for me," the tall man insisted.

"I'm here to help peace get made," Guthrie replied.

"I pay you . . ." the tall man began.

"Want your gold back?" Guthrie asked. "I owe these people something."

"Something?" Black Kettle asked after Buffalo Horn translated.

"A life," Guthrie explained. "One at least. More maybe. I was raised by people who insisted that a man pay his debts, and I expect to do just that."

Buffalo Horn had great difficulty translating those last words for his *Tsis tsis tas* companions.

"Do you know this man?" Black Kettle asked.

"He lived at Bent's Fort when I was there," Horn explained.

"I saw him there," Dragonfly remarked. "And at Sand Creek."

The mention of that place brought a chill over the *Tsis tsis tas*, and Guthrie explained it to the *Wihio* delegates.

"I'll send him away," the tall man offered. "I didn't know. We aren't soldiers, you understand."

"I understand," Horn replied, speaking his own thoughts for once. "None of your treaties consider what the soldiers will do, so they're worthless. We make agreements, and we keep them, but you allow the soldiers to come and kill us anyway."

"We try . . ." a *Wihio* woman began.

"Maybe Guthrie's the only one among you who *can* understand," Buffalo Horn said. "Only someone who saw the dying at Sand Creek can know why we don't trust you."

"I've been there," the tall man said, fighting to steady his trembling hands. "Only last month I walked among the bones that still lie there, unburied. Not men's bones, mind you. They're too small. Children, I suppose."

Buffalo Horn translated, and Black Kettle rose.

"You see bones and feel sad," the Kettle told the *Wihio*. "We see the faces of those sons and daughters in the night, and our dreams give us no peace. The little ones are gone now, and we won't speak their names. I'm concerned for the ones that remain alive. We can't have empty words from you this time. The words must be like iron, and the bluecoats must honor them."

"Yes," the tall man agreed. "But you must promise to control your young men. The raiding and stealing have to stop."

"I can't hold back anybody," Black Kettle replied. "Only a fair agreement will silence the rage among the young men. If they kill, most times it's because someone's chasing them. If they take horses, it's because Chivington and his bluecoats took all of our ponies. Talk straight to us, and we'll cause you no trouble. Don't blame us for this war, though. We didn't start it."

"I didn't start it, either," the tall man declared. "I plan to end it."

Buffalo Horn read a rare determination in the peacemaker's eyes, and he told Black Kettle afterward that he believed this *Wihio* truly wanted to bring peace to the plains. Whether it was the treaty makers' determination, guilt over the Sand Creek killings, or the failure of the bluecoats to defeat Red Cloud that led the *Wihio* to invite the scattered bands of plains people to treat with *Wihio* delegates at Arkansas River, Buffalo Horn didn't know. He didn't care. Three summers had come and gone since Sand Creek, and at no moment in all that time had any *Tsis tsis tas* man, woman, or child felt safe in the southern country. Even Prairie Flower, born after the massacre, hugged her mother's leg whenever a bluecoat rode near the camp or dogs barked out a midnight warning that an intruder was approaching.

By then it was autumn, and the grasses were yellow. Black Kettle had moved his camp to Medicine Lodge Creek near the *Wihio* soldier post called Fort Larned. It hadn't been easy. The Dog Soldiers objected to making any peace, and throughout the summer they had threatened to kill any chief who attempted to touch a pen to a treaty paper.

"I never imagined the road to peace could be so dangerous," Buffalo Horn had observed once when he, Black Kettle, and three other chiefs avoided a party of Dog Soldiers sent to intercept them.

"Nothing important's ever easy," Black Kettle had replied. "I've prayed and sought a vision, though. *Heammawihio* knows what must be done. He determines what will happen."

So it was that Black Kettle met with the *Wihio* delegation at Medicine Lodge Creek. It wasn't like earlier meetings, though. A soldier chief, General Harney, was there with a small army, and the Dog Soldiers who were camped nearby spoke of attacking the bluecoats. Harney had killed many Lakotas when he struck their winter camp on Platte River several years before, and the chance to avenge that slaughter appealed to the Dog Soldier chiefs.

"You have enemies among my people," Black Kettle warned the *Wihio* chiefs. "Hundreds of them. They're hot to fight you. They say I should come among you and promise peace so that you will call in your scouts and make it easy for your enemies to kill you. You know me for a man who speaks the truth. I won't lie to you. We can talk some, but I won't keep you here once there's danger. Another fight won't bring us closer to making peace."

"No," Harney agreed.

Those first meetings brought Buffalo Horn and many others great anguish. By meeting with the *Wihio* and revealing the plans of the Dog Soldiers, Horn wondered if he and the others weren't betraying their brother *Tsis tsis tas*. Black Kettle assured his party that he had seen everything in his dreams and that all would be fine. The Kettle's clever game of brokering peace between the bluecoats and the Dog Soldiers then began. In the end the old chief managed to lead the great majority of all the southern people, Dog Soldiers included, to Medicine Lodge Creek. No one made an accurate count, but Horn was certain there were two thousand at least. It was an imposing sight, so many *Tsis tsis tas* riding their best ponies, dressed in their finest clothes.

"But will we have peace?" Otter asked.

"I hope so," Buffalo Horn replied. "If Black Kettle can't arrange it, then war's all that's left to us."

Horn himself sat in the council with the peacemakers. An important *Wihio* official, Senator John Henderson, did most of the talking for the whites. When he read a proposed new treaty, Horn scowled. It gave away most of the land previously promised to the southern peoples and forced them south into unknown country.

"We'll never give up our buffalo-hunting country," the leader of the Dog Soldiers, Buffalo Chief, insisted. "How would we live? There are no ponies to chase in that other place. Bull Buffalo is almost dead there. You promised before that we would always have the land between Platte River and Arkansas River. Now you take back your word and leave us nothing!"

Even the moderate chiefs were upset. Buffalo Horn tried to explain the sense of betrayal he and the others felt. Henderson finally shook his head.

"Friends, let's reconsider what this paper says," the senator began. "You'll have a place in the Indian Territory that will be yours and yours alone. No white people will bother you there. The government will supply your needs. There will be food and trade goods. All you have to do is wait for them to arrive."

"That's fine for old women," Buffalo Chief grumbled. "Men have to hunt."

"We understand that," Henderson said, laughing. "The treaty doesn't limit your hunting. There are few white people in that country. Just don't bother the ranchers when you do your hunting. We have no quarrel with hunting parties."

The *Wihio* delegates even promised to supply lead and powder. None of that was written down, though, and it worried Buffalo Horn.

"It should be added to the paper," he told Black Kettle.

"The paper's nothing," the Kettle replied. "We've had papers before, and they never saved us from war. It's what a man carries in his heart that will give us peace or war."

The Dog Soldiers, who previously had opposed any agreement, echoed Black Kettle's sentiments.

"We'll remain strong," a Dog Soldier named Broken Tooth said. "If the *Wihio* keep their promises, we'll keep ours. They'll bring us good guns and powder. They'll feed the helpless ones. We'll grow strong again and wait for the day."

"The day?" Horn asked warily.

"The day when they change their mind and no longer keep the promises," Broken Tooth muttered. "We all know that day's bound to come. When it does, we'll punish the liars."

The Medicine Lodge Treaty, as it came to be known, was praised by the *Wihio*. Chiefs among the others bands, particularly the Arapahoes, deemed it a fair agreement. After all, they had already left most of the surrendered territory. The *Wihio* made a great show of giving away presents, and the people danced and celebrated. The Dog Soldiers broke away, though, and many among the *Wu ta piu* followed them.

"What's wrong?" Isaac Guthrie asked when he visited Buffalo Horn's lodge the last day of the gathering.

"The treaty," Horn explained. "It takes from us again, and what do we gain in return?"

"Peace," Guthrie answered. "You and I both know your people can't hold on to that Colorado country. The whites are already there, and more are coming."

"We bled and suffered at Sand Creek," Horn observed. "Now it seems as if the *Wihio* have forgotten that."

"No one's forgotten *that*," Guthrie insisted. "This peace will help you grow strong, though. The treaty goods will prevent starvation."

"You believe that?" Horn asked.

"I do," Guthrie replied. "As much as you want and need this peace, the white people need it more. They've fought a terrible war against themselves. Up north Red Cloud humiliated the army. They're sick in their hearts, and they want the bleeding to stop."

"I'm afraid it will be like all the other treaties," Horn grumbled. "Broken into pieces."

"If you really believe that, why do you remain with Black Kettle? You have relatives up north."

"My wife's people are here. We're not like *Wihio*, blown from place to place, alone in our hearts. We need to be among our relations. My daughter needs an aunt's guidance."

"But you believe that there will be trouble."

"Isn't there always?" Horn asked.

"I won't believe that there has to be another war," Guthrie declared. "It's why I agreed to help Senator Henderson and the others. You and I, together, insured that both sides understood what the other meant."

"Understood?" Horn asked. "Do you believe there can ever be understanding? I don't. I remember riding among the *Wihio*, greeting them as brothers, when they killed a young man who intended no harm."

"That was a long time ago," Guthrie said, frowning.

"It was yesterday," Horn argued. "It happens all the time. The peacemakers make promises, but can they make their brothers obey? Can anything change the bad blood? You saw the Dog Soldiers. You heard their words. Do you think they will be content to sit beside a fire and wait for the giveaway?"

"No," Guthrie confessed.

"And the bluecoats? Why were they even here? It's to show us how they'll punish us. The ashes in our fires haven't yet cooled, but a rancher was here, claiming we have his small son in our camp. Do the soldiers believe us when we tell them we don't? No, they come into our camp with guns and search our lodges."

"Did they find the boy?"

"No," Horn said, sighing. "You see? You yourself have doubts, Guthrie. There's no trust among us. Without trust, there can be no peace. Will this treaty bring peace? No, it will be like the others."

"What will you do?" Guthrie asked.

"What *Heammawihio* determines," Buffalo Horn answered. "I'll rely on my dreams to guide me, but they're no longer clear. I will respect Black Kettle's word. In the end, I can only hope to see my daughter climb Woman's Road. It's the young that matter most."

"Yes," Guthrie agreed. "Maybe I'll come and hunt with you in the spring."

"White men may not be welcome here then," Horn warned.

"I'm not . . ." Guthrie began.

"The *Wihio* consider you white, and that will save you," Horn insisted. "Leave this country and find a place of peace. Raise your children. Tell them sometime about the people you once knew."

"I can do some good here," Guthrie protested. "I know your language, and I can help the soldiers understand."

"They do understand," Buffalo Horn said, staring at the smoke rising from the cook fires in the nearby bluecoat camp. "They know that if they kill us, all of us, there will be no need to build new forts or make yearly giveaways. They don't try to see the world through our eyes."

"You think I'm a fool to expect peace?" Guthrie asked. "Is Black Kettle also a fool?"

"I hope not," Horn replied. "If he is, you won't see me again on this side of the great mystery."

"I wouldn't see you again if I went east."

"No, but that's what you should do. Soon. Before the dying resumes."

22

Although many doubted that the treaty would bring peace to the plains, it did. For once Buffalo Horn enjoyed a peaceful winter. Each time a rider approached Black Kettle's camp, Horn expected news of bluecoat raiders or intruding settlers. Every visitor proved to be some relative down from the north or else a party of young men returning from a morning hunt.

"Horn, why can't you believe we're truly at peace?" Bright Swallow finally asked.

"I would like to," he answered. "Winter's never been a good time to fight a war, though. Maybe the bluecoats are just lazy."

"You're worried about more than that," she insisted.

"I am," he confessed. "I've seen it in my dreams. Bluecoats charge out of the snow and kill us."

"The snows will be melting soon," Bright Swallow observed.

"They'll come again, and so will the bluecoats. I know it in my heart."

"Have you warned the chiefs?"

"Who listens?" he asked. "After all, they can't prevent it."

"Maybe you should go north and join your relations," she said, clasping his arm.

"No, our friends and your family are here," he told her. "If there's trouble, I should also be here."

Bright Swallow then spoke of having another child.

"A warrior should have sons to ride at his side," she argued. "My sister has brought two boys into the world. Surely our next child will be a son."

"Trouble's coming," Buffalo Horn replied. "It would be hard for a small child to survive."

"Survival's always a challenge," she countered. "Our daughter is getting older. She'll be able to help a brother."

"She hasn't yet counted her third summer, Swallow. What can she do to help?"

Bright Swallow would not let the matter rest, though. She oiled her body so that it glistened, and each night she drew him close. Finally she announced happily that a child was growing inside her.

"It will be a boy," Otter told his brother-friend. "All of the old women say so."

"And how would they know?" Horn growled.

"You're not the only one who sees things," Otter explained. "Feather Dance Woman says it has to do with the way a woman sleeps. On her back means it will be a girl. On either side, and it's a boy."

"And if the mother sleeps sometimes on her back and sometimes on her side?" Horn asked.

"I don't know," Otter confessed. "Perhaps a he-she like old Broken Shell."

Buffalo Horn laughed at the notion. But while the brother-friends could amuse themselves discussing the birth of a child, other more serious matters soon drew their attention.

Following the signing of the new treaty, Black Kettle had kept his band far to the east and south of their traditional home. As winter lost its grip on the land, Buffalo Horn realized how much he missed the northern country, with its tall hills and raging rivers. The southern country given to the *Wu ta piu* by treaty was flat, and the rivers were little more than shallow, muddy streams. There were few tall trees to cut for lodge poles, and although game remained abundant in many areas, Bull Buffalo no longer ran there.

Worse, it was an area frequented by *Wihio* whiskey traders and all manner of thieves. The bluecoats had forts scattered through the country, but their soldiers lacked energy. Some of the bluecoat chiefs appeared to be cooperating with the whiskey peddlers. The first traders Buffalo Horn encountered wore soldier coats. Horn and Otter located them the same morning they had discovered three drunken Dog Soldiers lying beside the ashes of a cook fire near the Cimarron River.

"We didn't know we weren't supposed to be here," the older of the two traders claimed. "I've got supplies bound for Fort Cobb."

"You're a long way from that place," Horn replied.

"Maybe it's some other fort," the second *Wihio* suggested as he eased a pistol out of its holster.

"Don't waste words with them," Otter suggested. "I recognize the ponies they have tied to their wagon."

"Where did you get those horses?" Buffalo Horn asked.

"Well, that's a strange thing," the younger *Wihio* answered. "I just saw 'em running free along the river. They belong to you?"

"You know it's a bad business, selling spirits to our people," Horn said, laughing. "You never know what a drunken Indian will do. He might be foolish enough to let you steal his ponies. Or maybe he will become crazy and cut off your ears."

The second *Wihio* tried to point his pistol at Buffalo Horn, but Otter had an arrow notched and ready. It flew off his bowstring and shattered the peddler's right arm.

Dragonfly and Fire Lance, who were no longer boys, had concealed themselves in a stand of oaks. They also fired arrows, and both struck the first trader in the chest.

"Bob?" the dying man muttered as he tumbled from the wagon onto the dusty ground. The surviving trader clasped his pistol, but he couldn't steady it with his broken arm. Otter killed him with a second arrow.

The whole business left Buffalo Horn sad and sour, but it failed to drive off the peddlers. Drunken young *Tsis tsis tas* and Arapaho warriors became a serious problem, and the chiefs seemed unable to deal with the problem. Women complained that their husbands would sell their ponies, clothing, even their daughters to acquire the *Wihio* whiskey.

"It's not the young men's fault," Otter argued when the Elks met to consider what to do. "When I was a boy, I occupied myself hunting and raiding Pawnee ponies. Now the bluecoats bring us wagons of food, and there's nothing to do but sit with the old men around the cook fires and recount coups. The young men grow tired of all that talk. They need something to do."

Buffalo Horn agreed. The treaty warned against raiding settlements or taking horses off ranches, but it seemed less mindful of old animosities with other tribes. Early that summer an Arapaho carried a pipe among the nearby *Tsis tsis tas* camps, inviting warriors to join a raid against the Kaws camped in eastern Kansas. It would avenge an old wrong, and most of the younger men eagerly joined the raiders. The Kaws owned many good ponies, and there weren't too many soldier forts in that region.

Even Black Kettle thought the proposed raid was a good idea.

"Why, Uncle?" Horn asked.

"Listen to what the young men are saying," Black Kettle advised. "They've chewed the treaty meat and eaten bread made of treaty flour, but are they content? No. All they can see is that the promised guns and powder have not arrived."

The Dog Soldiers in particular claimed that the *Wihio* had broken the treaty by their failure to provide new rifles. When the raiders returned from striking the Kaws, they boasted that they had acquired the promised rifles and many good ponies in the old, traditional manner. *Tsis tsis tas* warriors took both from the Kaws.

Colonel Wynkoop, who had so often treated the people fairly, promised to address all *Tsis tsis tas* complaints, but the Dog Soldiers condemned the new treaty as another *Wihio* lie and refused to take a share of the annuity goods distributed that summer.

"It's hard to give you guns after all the trouble you've caused," a soldier told Buffalo Horn.

"So long as you don't trust us, there can be no true peace," Horn retorted.

It was later that same summer that Black Kettle finally decided to move his dwindling camp north. The oppressive heat dried up creeks and turned even the rivers into sandy bogs. Memories of cool nights north of Arkansas River and the plentiful game there lured the chief from the treaty country.

Buffalo Horn and Otter were among the men chosen to ride ahead of the main body. Altogether there were perhaps a hundred and fifty men, women, and children in the *Wu ta piu* band. It was a pitiful remnant of the great camp that had spread across the hills at Sand Creek just four summers before.

"We're alive, though," Buffalo Horn declared. "There are children here."

"My sons and your daughter," Otter added. "Soon we'll be riding into the hills so that you can seek a name for your new son."

"They make me hopeful," Horn confessed.

"Yes," Otter agreed. "I think even the grandfathers enjoy hearing the children laughing."

Buffalo Horn was also cheered when he looked out at fine young men like Dragonfly and Fire Lance. Dragonfly was marking his nineteenth summer. When he wasn't riding with Horn, the young man was walking the river trail with one of several young maidens. Fire Lance, now seventeen, had grown tall. He rode with a chief's bearing, and when he had returned from fighting the Kaws, a seventh feather in his hair marked yet another brave-heart deed.

The journey north from Indian Territory began well, but once the band crossed into Kansas, that changed. *Wihio* farmers had broken the soil in the southern part of the state, and the appearance of even one Indian could still spread panic through the settlements. It wasn't long before a bluecoat captain appeared with orders to escort Black Kettle's band to Fort Hays, a bluecoat post located a day's ride north of Smoky Hill River.

Buffalo Horn considered it fortunate that the soldiers directed the band there. The *Wihio* who had settled nearby treated the *Tsis tsis tas* with respect, and the fort's commander dealt with his uninvited guests fairly. The bluecoats even shared their rations. A post trader provided stick candy for the children. The only quarrel concerned a light-skinned child.

"He's been stolen from his unfortunate family," a *Wihio* woman declared. "We should take him in and see he's returned to his home."

Buffalo Horn, having heard the child screaming on the steps of a stable, hurried over. He discovered two soldiers dragging the boy from his mother, a young woman known as Red Clay Woman.

"What's happened?" Horn asked, placing a hand on the child's shoulder and silencing the screams.

"This one speaks English," one of the soldiers observed.

"I've learned," Buffalo Horn told them. "What's this boy done? Has he stolen something?"

"He's white," the *Wihio* woman said. "He's probably one of those captives taken from the ranches out West."

Buffalo Horn translated, and Red Clay Woman hung her head in shame.

"Only half white," she explained. "His father was a soldier. He made this baby in me."

"He didn't offer your father presents, though, did he?" Horn asked.

"He shamed me," Red Clay Woman mumbled. "Some of my cousins said that I should leave my child outside of camp for the animals, but he's my blood, too."

Buffalo Horn turned to the growing crowd of *Wihio* and shared the girl's story.

"Sure, I see now," one of the soldiers admitted. "He's browner than I first thought. See how dark his eyes are."

"He still looks white to me," the woman declared. "Henry, offer her that bay horse for him."

A smallish *Wihio* with two yellow stripes on his blue shirt led a good bay horse out from the stable and offered it in exchange for the child. The boy resumed his bawling, and Red Clay refused.

"He's my son," she insisted. "We're poor in ponies, but I won't give him up. He's too young."

"She won't agree," Buffalo Horn told the whites. "See for yourselves. This little one's light in color, but I have cousins who aren't any darker. The mother herself is pale. This boy knows none of your words, and he'd only run away at the first chance. Would any of you take him into your lodge?"

Even the woman who had started all the trouble remained mute, and the soldiers stepped away. Buffalo Horn returned the boy to his mother, and one problem was solved.

Rumors that other white captives were with the *Wu*

ta piu brought about a brief inspection by a handful of soldiers. The bluecoats went from lodge to lodge, satisfying themselves that no white child hid in a *Wu ta piu* tipi. Afterward their commander sent baskets of fruit and vegetables to the camp and expressed his regrets for investigating.

"I don't care myself," he told Black Kettle through Buffalo Horn. "There are many Kansas families whose children were taken captive, and I have a pile of sketches on my desk. We all know any child gone very long is lost to white society. You give 'em too free a rein. I'm paid to look, though."

Black Kettle made little of the inspection, but Horn knew it hurt the chief.

"No *Wihio* ever completely trusts me," the Kettle remarked. "And still they expect me to trust the safety of all our people to their promises!"

The brief stay at Fort Hays had another consequence. Many of the young men watched in dismay as bluecoats brought kettles full of hot soup and baskets of hot bread to the band.

"Once we were a proud people," Otter told Buffalo Horn. "Now look at us! We're no different than camp dogs eating scraps."

"At least a dog barks," Dragonfly complained. "Here we stand like rocks on a hill while the *Wihio* steal our manhood."

"I still have mine," Buffalo Horn said, trying to lighten his companions' mood.

"Are you certain?" Fire Lance asked. "When did you last take up a lance and hunt Bull Buffalo? Are we men if our enemies can ride in and search our lodges? Isn't it our obligation to feed the people? How can we let the bluecoats shame us in this manner?"

"I'm not ashamed," Horn insisted. "I've eaten no soup, and I've chewed no bread. I feed my family. You asked when I've hunted. When haven't I hunted?"

"You understand what we're saying, Horn," Otter argued. "We've come to a fork in the trail. Should we follow an old man who's content to sit beside the fire with the old women, remembering past glories? Or should we ride out like warriors and lead those who still have something more than memories between their legs?"

"We're going!" Fire Lance shouted. "Ayyyy! It will be good to feel like a man."

"Horn?" Otter asked.

"I can't always choose for myself alone," Buffalo Horn told his brother-friend. "Long ago I chose my path. Look around you here, brothers. What do you see? Women. Children. Men? Very few of those. You asked me if I still carry a lance. I do. Because of that I'm pledged to defend the helpless ones. You talk about manhood. What man ever rode away to hunt and left the little ones to face the enemy? Otter, isn't that what the Dog Soldiers did when that boy who was your brother climbed Hanging Road?"

"It's a hard thing, deciding whether to go or stay," Otter confessed. "Too much remains unseen, unknown. I honor you for your vow, brother, but I can't remain. You can speak for our people when the *Wihio* come. Your dreams can help the chiefs see what's to come. I'm only a warrior. I can't be anything else, and I can't be even that in this camp."

"It's the same with us," Dragonfly added as he glanced at Fire Lance. "We owe you everything, Horn. If you insist, we'll stay. But we'll be less than nothing here."

"Lance?" Horn asked.

"The *Wihio* geld a stallion they can't manage any other way," Fire Lance noted. "They haven't used a knife on us, brother. Instead they kill off the game and force us into a valley where we can no longer feed ourselves. They bring sickness to steal the lives of the children. They give the men whiskey that robs their souls."

"I've spoken against drinking spirits," Buffalo Horn pointed out. "We're riding north soon to hunt Bull Buffalo."

"Are we?" Otter asked. "I've heard some of the older men talking. They say the *Wihio* can provide everything we need. Why go north?"

"Their days are growing short," Fire Lance said, wiping sweat from his forehead. "I'm young. I need to prove myself."

"Seven feathers aren't enough?" Horn asked.

"I want to have a son one day," the Lance added. "How can I teach him what it means to walk Man's Road when I haven't walked it myself?"

"I showed you that much," Buffalo Horn declared. "Soon I may have a son at my side. I hoped you, my brothers, would accept an uncle's obligation."

"We will," Otter pledged. "Just as I must now ask you to accept that same obligation. Look after my family, Horn."

"You won't take Feather Dance Maiden and the boys?" Horn asked.

"They're safe here," Otter replied. "I know that. It's a heavy burden you're accepting, Horn, and I know I'm making it heavier. I can't stay, though."

"Then you must go," Horn told his brother-friend. "Let *Heammawihio* guide your feet. Don't forget the old ways, and if the worst comes to pass, know that I did my best."

"We'll meet again," Fire Lance vowed.

"Yes," Horn agreed. But he wondered if it would be on the other side.

23

The defections of so many good men weighed heavily on Buffalo Horn. He felt for the first time in his life as if he were utterly and hopelessly alone. Even Prairie Flower's smile and Bright Swallow's consoling words failed to cast the gloom from his thoughts. Black Kettle, too, was shaken by what appeared to be the disintegration of his band. Disheartened, he allowed the bluecoats to persuade him to turn south toward Fort Larned. There, only a few days later, he received from Wynkoop the long-awaited new rifles, together with supplies of lead and powder.

"Finally," Buffalo Horn told Bright Swallow Woman. "If they had only come earlier, we might have kept the young men with us."

"Maybe," she said, frowning. "Young men are eager to chase glory, though. You were no different at that age yourself. Fire Lance and Dragonfly would have left to take wives soon anyway."

"And Otter?"

"My sister won't be lonely for long," Bright Swallow assured him. "Otter's too much like you. Once he misses his wife and sons, he'll return. Maybe he'll bring us some buffalo meat. I'd welcome it."

"Should I ride north and kill a bull for you?" Horn asked.

"You know better than most the danger of going into *Wihio* country," she grumbled. "I'll have to content myself with smoked venison."

"Rock Watcher killed two prairie chickens yesterday," Buffalo Horn pointed out. "I'll get him to show me how he did it."

She laughed at the notion of a child showing Buffalo Horn how to throw stones at birds. Prairie Flower heard and toddled over, cackling in her birdlike voice.

"And what do you know, daughter?" Horn asked as he lifted the girl onto his shoulder. "Maybe your dreams are clearer than mine."

Prairie Flower smiled a reply. She had not yet begun to talk so that adults could understand. Rock Watcher and Sparrow sometimes made sense of the words, but they refused to share the secret of Flower's language.

Bright Swallow's prediction that Otter would return soon came true. A weary band of riders entered the *Wu ta piu* camp from the north, and Otter was at their head. His brothers, Thunder Cloud and Snow Bear, flanked him. Dragonfly, Fire Lance, and several other younger men followed.

"Brother, you're back!" Buffalo Horn said as he rushed to greet his brother-friend.

"My family?" Otter asked anxiously.

"All well," Horn assured him. "The boys are growing. Feather Dance Woman only gets prettier."

"You've enjoyed better fortune than we have," Otter said, sighing.

"What's happened?" Buffalo Horn asked. "Your brothers appear well."

"Oh, we're safe enough," Otter agreed. "No good's come of our journey, though."

"Tell me," Horn urged.

"Ask the others," Otter suggested. "I must see to my family's needs."

The words alone were cause for concern because Buffalo Horn couldn't recall a time when Otter had ever held anything back. Even as boys they had shared every thought. And now?

"We've had a long difficult ride," Fire Lance confessed after turning his ponies over to an eager boy.

"We never found Bull Buffalo," Dragonfly added. "I wish that we had."

"What have you done?" Horn asked.

"We met a band of Dog Soldiers," Fire Lance explained. "Broken Tooth led them. They planned to strike a Pawnee camp and take horses. We agreed to go along."

"To take horses," Dragonfly insisted. "You know yourself we need ponies."

"I don't count any new animals," Buffalo Horn said, glancing past his young companions. "I suppose the Pawnees were more careful than usual."

"We never reached the Pawnee camps," Fire Lance confessed. "We saw thirty good ponies grazing on a hill, and we took those instead."

"Tried to, anyway," Dragonfly added.

"They weren't Pawnee ponies," Horn said, dropping his eyes to the ground. "Did they belong to the bluecoats?"

"No, but they were *Wihio* ponies," Fire Lance admitted. "A big herd of cows was there, and the men who guarded the cows owned those ponies. They were careless with them, we thought. Broken Tooth said it would be easy. Instead, the *Wihio* cowboys made a fight. We killed three of them, but Broken Tooth's brother died. Another, older man, too, and several of us were shot. We took no ponies, and we suffered greatly."

"It's worse than that," Buffalo Horn told them. "You broke the treaty. The bluecoats may chase you here."

"They may," Fire Lance agreed. "But not for raiding a pony herd."

"There's more?" Buffalo Horn asked.

"Broken Tooth became crazy after his brother was killed," Dragonfly said, taking a deep breath. "He vowed revenge. Treaty or not, he was bound to make war. We would have left, but Otter's brothers were there, and we considered ourselves obligated to stay with our brother's brothers."

"So you fought the *Wihio*?" Horn asked.

"Not soldiers," Fire Lance said, scowling. "Broken Tooth led us south, among the farmers. We killed people. We took a few ponies, and we burned several lodges. Some of the Dog Soldiers abused women, but I didn't."

"Nor I," Dragonfly insisted. "We remembered Sand Creek."

"We spared the helpless ones," Fire Lance said, shuddering. "The children. The youngest ones we left with an old woman on Arkansas River. The older ones we brought along."

"Here?" Buffalo Horn cried. "Not here!"

"We couldn't trust Broken Tooth," Fire Lance explained. "I know he would have killed them."

"Otter promised to take them into his lodge," Thunder Cloud said, joining the conversation. "It's my doing, this trouble. My brother would never have come if I had turned back."

"How many captives did you bring here?" Buffalo Horn asked.

"Six," Otter announced as he stepped past Thunder Cloud and greeted his brother-friend. "I left the two women with Black Kettle. Also a small girl. The oldest boy is in Young Man's Lodge."

"He's known twelve summers," Fire Lance declared, "and his hair's dark. His parents are dead, and we promised him he could stay with us."

"The other two?" Horn asked.

"Fair-haired and younger," Otter answered. "They've said nothing. I believe they saw their mother killed. If they were Crows or Pawnees, I would keep them and try to help restore the harmony of their world, but it's impossible. We'll have to take them to the bluecoats before anyone sees them here."

"It may be too late already," Fire Lance grumbled. "I spied soldiers when we crossed Cimarron River. If they saw the yellow-haired boys, we'll be blamed for the raid."

"Why not?" Otter asked. "We were there."

"The Dog Soldiers . . ." Dragonfly began.

"It doesn't matter," Horn said, gazing into the distance. "What one *Tsis tsis tas* does, all will be blamed for. I'll find Black Kettle and discuss it with him. Maybe he knows something we can do."

"We shouldn't have returned here," Otter said. "If anyone tracked us . . ."

"It doesn't matter!" Buffalo Horn shouted. "When did the *Wihio* need a reason to punish us? I've known all along the soldiers would come. It's never done any good to worry yourselves over what's been done. We have to guard against tomorrow."

"I'll see to it that guards are sent out," Otter promised.

"The bluecoats won't come now," Horn assured the others. "No, they'll have to make plans. Summer will be long past by then. It will be like at Sand Creek, after the snows begin to fall. And it will be the helpless ones again who die."

If Buffalo Horn was alarmed by the news of the trouble up north, Black Kettle was appalled.

"Don't they see that they've assured the death of us all?" the chief exclaimed. "We must talk to the bluecoat chiefs before they send their men against us."

"Will they listen?" Horn asked.

"Maybe," Black Kettle replied. "It will be your obligation to make our words known to them."

"What will you say, Uncle?"

"I dare not go myself," Black Kettle insisted. "They know me. If I remain here, among my people, they may hesitate to attack. Many of their important people in the East have promised me there will never be another attack on my people. So long as I remain, we have hope that promise at least won't be broken."

"Who will you send?"

"Little Robe," Black Kettle explained. "Wynkoop knows him. His words will hold power."

"What can you tell Wynkoop that can hope to restore peace?" Buffalo Horn asked. "We can't make the dead return to life."

"We can return the survivors," Black Kettle suggested. "Not now, of course. If a *Tsis tsis tas* rides to Fort Larned with captured white women and children, he will only anger the *Wihio*. But Little Robe can assure the return of these people, and he can also bring with him some of the ones who are responsible."

"What?" Horn asked. It seemed as if cold fingers had clasped his insides, and he shuddered from head to toe.

"We have to send the guilty men to Wynkoop," Black Kettle explained. "That way he'll see we aren't responsible."

"Did the *Wihio* send Chivington to us?" Buffalo Horn asked. "What *Wihio* was ever punished for killing a *Tsis tsis tas*?"

"It must be done," the Kettle argued. "Otherwise we'll all perish."

"So now we will help the *Wihio* murder our people?" Horn cried. "No, I won't do it."

"Frog, you know the *Wihio* way. Will anything else satisfy them?"

"Nothing ever satisfies them, Uncle. I expect them to attack us. There's no dishonor in dying in a remembered fight. I would never ask more for myself. Maybe the Dog Soldiers are right. We should set aside the treaties and fight as long as we can. Then, when it's over, we'll fade from sight like the Mandans, like Bull Buffalo himself."

"You would let even the children die?" the chief asked.

"I would fight to protect them," Horn insisted. "But

if they are to die, isn't it better that they die as part of a proud people? Would you turn us into Pawnees? Into dogs who run around naked to amuse their masters?"

"You of all people know better," Black Kettle replied angrily. "You've walked at my side, spoken my words for me. You know my heart."

"I do," Buffalo Horn agreed. "The men you want to give up are my brothers, though. Those men would die in my place. I can't give them over to the *Wihio* to punish, to cage, to taunt and torment. If you feel bound to turn them over, do it without me."

"I need you," Black Kettle insisted.

"So do they," Horn replied. "So here I am, a drowning man in a deep river who is unsure which bank to turn toward."

"Even he has to choose," Black Kettle said, clasping Horn's hands. "We all do. It's a terrible thing to give up a part of yourself. I remember a boy once whose foot was caught in the jaws of an iron trap. He lost two toes that day, but he remained alive. Isn't it better, Frog, to sacrifice a few men so that the people may live?"

"Maybe," Horn admitted. "But I could never make that choice. If they decide to go in, I'll respect their decision. You know Broken Tooth will never give himself up, though, and he'll be the man the *Wihio* want."

"We could speak with the Dog Soldiers about it."

Buffalo Horn sighed. Didn't the old man understand anything? The Dog Soldiers wanted a fight! They would never give up a chief in order to save the peace.

As summer passed into memory, Black Kettle continued his efforts to preserve the peace agreement. Little Robe returned to share Wynkoop's stinging words. The *Wihio* believed the raiders were the very same *Tsis tsis tas* warriors who had received new rifles at Fort Larned.

"Did he agree to accept the captives?" Horn asked Black Kettle.

"Little Robe was afraid to admit we held any prisoners," Black Kettle explained. "I'm told there are many bluecoats at Fort Cobb. I'll speak to their chief and see what can be done."

But although Black Kettle himself spoke with bluecoat chiefs assigned to the Indian Territory forts, he found no reason to celebrate.

"They don't believe you," Buffalo Horn said after interpreting one bluecoat's replies to Black Kettle's pleas. "He says he has no authority over most of the bluecoats."

"Then he and I are much alike," Black Kettle noted. "I have little authority over the Dog Soldiers, and he can't tell the bluecoats what to do."

Black Kettle seemed amused at the notion, but Buffalo Horn saw a darkness creeping into the old man's eyes. Hope was fading.

That autumn the *Wu ta piu* hunted Bull Buffalo with the Comanches and Kiowas. The hunting filled Black Kettle's camp with food and new hides to be worked into lodgeskins and heavy coats. More importantly, the young men had a chance to win honor and count coups.

Afterward Buffalo Horn accompanied Black Kettle on a journey south to Fort Cobb. Horn saw many bluecoats there—more than were needed to supervise the giveaways or protect parties of travelers. Black Kettle met their commander, an important bluecoat chief named Hazen, and the two men assured each other of a mutual desire for lasting peace.

"It's all we want," Horn told the *Wihio* general.

"I've been told you have captured white children in your camp," Hazen responded. "That doesn't say much for your peaceful intentions."

"We're often blamed for what others do," Buffalo Horn explained. "If we find such people, captured whites, can we bring them to you? Will we be punished if we help you find these lost people?"

"Only if you held them yourselves," Hazen replied.

"How can we bring them to you without taking them ourselves for a time?" Horn asked.

"It's a problem," the general admitted. "Maybe it would be better if you simply told me where I could find the men who killed the settlers and dragged off those helpless women and children."

Buffalo Horn eyed his chief anxiously, and Hazen frowned.

"Do this," the general advised. "Come south. Camp near the fort. We can help meet your winter food and clothing needs, and you'll be treated as peaceful people. No harm will come to you."

It was Buffalo Horn's turn to frown. Hadn't the bluecoat chiefs suggested the same thing four years before? Wasn't that pledge what had brought the *Tsis tsis tas* to Sand Creek?

"Tell him that we'll do as he says," Black Kettle told Horn. "We have few choices."

Buffalo Horn did as instructed, but during the homeward journey he argued against making camp so close to an army of bluecoats.

"We should remain close to our friends," Horn argued.

"It's probably wise," Black Kettle agreed. And so the *Wu ta piu* erected their camp circle of fifty lodges on the banks of the Washita River. Larger camps of Comanche, Kiowa, Apache, and Arapaho bands also nestled beside that winding river. Black Kettle met with his fellow chiefs, and it was agreed that all would aid each other if the bluecoats came.

"They won't, of course," Otter told Buffalo Horn. "I smell snow. The *Wihio* are soft. They don't like to fight when it's cold."

"I saw snow in my dream," Horn warned.

"You've had that dream many times, brother," Otter pointed out. "It hasn't happened yet."

"That doesn't mean that it won't," Horn argued. "You didn't see all the soldiers crowded into that fort. Be careful, brother. Be watchful. I expect trouble."

24

The first snowfall eased the anxiety of many in Black Kettle's camp. Scouts who had recently reported soldiers in the area relaxed their vigil.

"No one makes war when snow chokes the earth," Fire Lance told Buffalo Horn. "Besides, you know how bluecoats travel. You can smell and hear them days away."

Buffalo Horn shared none of his young friend's confidence. Bright Swallow was heavy with child, and when Horn had followed Otter into the hills to invite a dream, the old nightmare had come instead. It was just as before except for a mysterious silver glow in the sky. The hawk had appeared out of that glow, screaming its warning. Then the killing began.

Horn had gone to Black Kettle to repeat his warning, but the chief had nothing new to say.

"I worry about soldiers, too," Black Kettle explained. "I have no son trying to be born, but I do have a whole people to keep safe. I've spoken to the other chiefs, and we've decided to surrender if soldiers come. We'll set aside our weapons and allow the blue-coats to take us to the nearest fort. It will be hard for the men, but the helpless ones will be safe."

"They won't allow it," Horn tried to explain. "The bluecoat chief in my dream has heartless eyes. He hungers to kill us."

"Not Chivington again!" the Kettle cried.

"No, this man's younger and smaller. He's just as crazy, though."

"We'll keep the scouts out," Black Kettle vowed. "We won't be surprised again."

Only two nights later, twenty horsemen galloped right into camp without the slightest warning, though. Fortunately for the *Wu ta piu*, these visitors were young *Tsis tsis tas*. Like Fire Lance and Dragonfly they had followed Broken Tooth. They, too, had killed *Wihio* settlers and stolen ponies.

"Go," Otter told them. "You're not welcome in this camp."

"Who are you to say who can stay?" one of the raiders asked. "I have relatives here. I came to trade for a good rifle and some powder."

"You'll acquire neither here," Black Kettle announced. "Rest. Eat. Then go back to the Dog Soldiers. You bring us only trouble."

"Horn, look at what we've become!" Bright Swallow exclaimed that night. "We're a people torn by our fears. When did we ever turn away relations in the winter?"

"Those raiders left a clear trail in the snow," Horn

explained. "If there are any soldiers nearby, they'll ride right into our camp."

"You're still worried about our son," she said, holding his hand to her belly. "I'll be going to Woman's Lodge soon, and you'll have fewer worries."

"What about Prairie Flower?" Horn asked.

"My sister will keep her," Bright Swallow explained. "Feather Dance Woman will also cook food for you to eat."

"Will the child arrive soon?" Horn asked.

"Soon enough," she replied. "Another winter child! I hope he's as strong as his sister."

"I pray that he also has his mother's eyes," Buffalo Horn told her.

He took to his bed earlier than normal that night. It seemed as if a great weariness had taken possession of his body. Once asleep, though, the dream returned, and he awoke shivering.

"Horn?" Bright Swallow asked as he rolled away from her.

"I saw it all again," he told her. "This time, though, it seemed different. I wasn't watching. I was feeling it."

Buffalo Horn managed to dress himself before stepping out into the snow. A swirling white mist enshrouded him, and he realized it was well before dawn. Then a bright silvery circle of light appeared over the trees.

"The dream," Horn mumbled. "I saw it in the dream."

Now, though, he recognized the source of the light. It was the morning star, that sacred symbol of the day's renewal. The light snow falling from high clouds cast an amazing glow to the star. It was both beautiful and terrible to behold, for Buffalo Horn knew from his dream that the attack was coming.

"Yes, I expected you," Horn remarked as a large red-tailed hawk flew past, screaming out a warning. "I saw everything, but it wasn't enough. No one believed it possible."

Horn hurried back toward his lodge. Once there, he removed his shield from its cover and grabbed his bow and a quiver full of arrows.

"They're coming!" he shouted to the sleepy camp. "Get up. Arm yourselves. Don't let these bluecoats boast of how they killed the *Tsis tsis tas* without bleeding."

Others in the camp did begin to rise. Then a dog began barking. The animal was silenced by a piercing rifle shot. Another shot splintered a barren willow limb behind Horn's back.

For an instant Buffalo Horn wanted to believe the *Wihio* attack would be halfhearted. Horn longed to see the bluecoats stand around, uncertain what they should do. Instead, the dark-eyed bluecoat chief barked orders, and horsemen charged the defenseless camp.

Black Kettle was among the first to emerge from his lodge. Buffalo Horn saw the old man, but the burdens of leadership seemed to float away into the snowy mists. The Kettle was once again the lithe young warrior who had saved a maimed boy those many years before. Black Kettle fired his rifle into the air to alert his people. Then he and his wife mounted a pony and tried to escape.

The chief and his wife headed toward the river, but the *Wihio* chief had placed a number of well-concealed riflemen there. They fired a volley that killed the chief's pony and struck both him and his wife. The two of them fell together in the snow, and although a few men tried to reach them, no one survived more than a moment or two.

"Form a line," Buffalo Horn urged as the other warriors stumbled out of their lodges. Otter hurried to his brother-friend's side, but Horn only shook his head.

"Take our wives and the children," Horn pleaded. "Away from the river. Into the hills where there's cover. Find a cave to hide them."

"I, too, am an Elk," Otter insisted. "I should stand here with you."

"I didn't see you here in my dream," Horn argued.

"No one can see clearly all the time," Otter replied.

Dragonfly appeared then. He was already bleeding from where a *Wihio* bullet had passed through his left thigh.

"Find our horses," Otter told the young man. "Get my family to safety."

"Mine, too," Horn added.

"I'm no use in a fight," Dragonfly said, holding up his right hand. Blood was leaking from a buckskin binding.

"Take care of them," Otter whispered.

"I'll shield them with my life," Dragonfly promised.

Otter's brothers, Snow Bear and Thunder Cloud, raced over to offer their help.

"It would be a fine notion to die here together," Otter told them, "but you're needed elsewhere. Dragonfly will need help with your nephews. Protect the white boys, too."

"We should kill them first," Thunder Cloud argued.

"No, they can't be found in this camp," Otter objected. "It will give the bluecoats an excuse to kill our children."

Thunder Cloud sighed and dashed off to Otter's lodge. A moment later the firing along the river stopped. Then, shrieking like demons, horsemen charged from seemingly every direction at once. Pistols spit flame, and men fell bleeding into the ivory white snow. The few *Tsis tsis tas* who had located horses tried to make their escape, but most were cut off and killed. The bluecoats raced among lodges, firing blindly at anyone they saw. Sometimes little children no older than Prairie Flower were cruelly clubbed to death. Most of the women and children hid behind iron kettles or in the ruins of their lodges.

Buffalo Horn organized a weak line along the eastern fringe of the camp, and for a short while it held. Twenty-five people followed the limping Dragonfly out into the hills while the Elks shielded them from the attacking bluecoats. Then the line wavered and broke apart.

Horn was burning with anger as he watched good men die fighting desperately to protect their families. When three bluecoat horsemen swept around the far end of the camp and charged the fleeing women and children, a solitary figure appeared out of the mist to stop them.

Fire Lance had performed seven brave-heart deeds in his seventeen years of life, but nothing compared to the fight he made that morning. He had fled Young Man's Lodge at the sound of the first rifle shot, not bothering to dress himself. Instead he had wrapped a red blanket around his waist, and the garment gave his bare chest an unreal quality. The blanket also startled the bluecoat ponies, and they balked at continuing their charge.

Fire Lance notched an arrow and fired his first shot through the left eye of the lead bluecoat. The man shrieked as he toppled off his horse, and his companions had difficulty controlling their horses. That provided Fire Lance a chance to notch and fire a second arrow. This time he fired at a heavy man with a great hairy face. The arrow struck him in the side and pierced a lung. The heavy man fell into the snow and began coughing out his life.

The third horseman kicked his pony and tried to escape. Fire Lance's third arrow struck him squarely between the shoulder blades, and he, too, rolled from his horse.

"Ayyyy!" Fire Lance screamed as he counted coup on each rider in turn. He then cut away their forelocks and screamed defiantly toward the bluecoats gradually working their way from lodge to lodge.

"What now?" Otter asked. Buffalo Horn tried to decide what to do. The camp was already burning. Bodies littered the earth. Instinctively he wanted to charge, to kill, to punish the bluecoats for the death they had brought, but he also hoped to survive, to see his little son born, to give away ponies in honor of his daughter when she took a husband.

"We can't stay here," Otter whispered. Horn nodded somberly. The fight was nearly over. The few remaining *Tsis tsis tas* warriors were melting into the snowdrifts and wooded hills. Bluecoats were herding frightened women and terrified children toward the river. Others were stripping *Tsis tsis tas* corpses and looting the captured lodges.

"Follow me," Fire Lance said, hurrying over and grabbing Horn's arm. "Now!"

The confidence in the younger man's voice set Buffalo Horn's feet in motion. He stumbled toward the trees and huddled between Otter and Fire Lance. The mists and the rocks joined with the trees and provided a fair degree of shelter. Horn's heart warmed when he spied Bright Swallow holding Prairie Flower on her lap. Otter's brothers guarded their nephews and Feather Dance Woman.

"What are they doing?" Fire Lance asked, pointing toward the captured camp.

"They've taken the pony herd," Horn muttered.

"What do we do now?" Otter asked.

"I have two horses tied to an oak," Fire Lance whispered. "I can get more."

"We'll need more," Otter replied, "to get all these people safely to the next camp."

"I'll get some," the Lance declared. He set down his weapons and removed the red blanket. "Don't worry," he told his surprised companions. "I'm used to the cold."

The near-naked young man then crept to the icy river and slipped beneath its surface. It chilled Horn to imagine Fire Lance swimming through that frigid water, making his way past an army of enemies. The young man was gone for what seemed like an eternity, but a startled cry and three frantic rifle shots attested to his successful arrival among the captured ponies. Fire Lance climbed atop a large spotted stallion and drove twenty others ahead of him, past several bluecoats, and along to where the survivors sat cowering in the rocks.

"Get as many as you can mounted," Buffalo Horn

urged. "Lance, ride to the next camp and summon help."

"I can't," Fire Lance said, reluctantly sliding down from his pony. He was shivering with cold and hopelessly exhausted. Buffalo Horn rubbed the moisture from the young man's tormented flesh and wrapped the blanket tightly around his trembling frame. Only then did the shaking stop.

"Take care of him, Otter," Horn said, reluctantly climbing atop a horse. "I'll bring help."

"I'll get as many of us as possible headed east," Otter promised. "Take someone with you."

Horn glanced past Fire Lance to Dragonfly. Neither appeared up to a hard ride.

"It's for me to do," Thunder Cloud volunteered. "I'm as responsible as anyone for this."

"It would have happened anyway," Horn said as he waited for the Cloud to mount a waiting horse. "I'm glad of the company, though."

They headed off together then, but they managed to get only a short distance from the camp when a rifle shot split the air behind them. Twenty bluecoats raced after them, and Horn urged his horse to new effort. The animal seemed to sense the urgency of its flight. It stretched itself out and literally flew across the snow-covered prairie. Thunder Cloud galloped alongside, and the two of them began to pull ahead of the bluecoats. The *Wihio* soldiers fired pistols and carbines, but the range was too great and their aim was poor. The shooting had the effect of alerting the neighboring camps, though, and when Buffalo Horn and Thunder Cloud topped a low ridge, they discovered a hundred mounted Arapaho and *Tsis tsis tas* warriors hurrying to their aid.

"Behind us," Horn explained, and the warriors fanned out across the ridge. By the time the bluecoats realized what was awaiting them, it was too late. A mixture of arrows and bullets emptied half the saddles immediately. The remaining ten men dismounted and formed a circle. For a moment or two they made a fight of it, but they were too few to blunt a concerted charge, and the warriors swept down on them like a prairie fire. Only one man survived that charge, a hairy-faced *Wihio* who shouted defiantly and fired his carbine until he had no bullets remaining. Then he drew a saber and challenged his tormentors.

"We won't kill him," the Arapaho chief declared. "He's a brave man and has made a good fight."

"They've killed hundreds of my people and destroyed an entire camp," one of the *Tsis tsis tas* argued.

"Broken Tooth," Thunder Cloud muttered. "Make your charge, but remember this *Wihio* may fight back."

"I'll enjoy killing him," the Tooth said, whipping his pony into a gallop.

The bluecoat was bleeding from several wounds, and he had dropped to his knees by the time Broken Tooth arrived. The Tooth raised his lance, but the *Wihio* merely smiled and held his saber out as if to surrender it. Broken Tooth grinned, threw away his lance, and reached out to take the saber. The bluecoat then turned the weapon and rammed its point up through Broken Tooth's belly and out through his back.

The Dog Soldier chief managed only a little whimper as he died. Afterward the remaining Dog Soldiers charged down the ridge and cut the surviving bluecoat to pieces.

"Why?" Thunder Cloud asked Buffalo Horn. "He was being spared."

"He didn't believe it," Horn explained. "He didn't trust us to leave him alone. Or maybe all the killing made him crazy. Who can know for certain?"

"It's justice, Broken Tooth dying like he did," Thunder Cloud declared.

"Justice?" Horn whispered. "No, I wouldn't call it that. There's nothing about this day that resembles justice."

Epilogue

It was as bitter a winter as the plains ever knew. Black Kettle's death cast a shadow across the earth itself, and no *Tsis tsis tas* spoke for renewing the peace. The captured *Wu ta piu* remained at the soldier forts, shivering and starving while Indian agents and army officers tried to decide what to do with the pitiful people.

The leader of the bluecoats that frigid morning called the fight the Battle of the Washita, as if it was somehow a clash of great armies instead of a surprise attack on a sleeping camp. He built a reputation for himself and his Seventh Cavalry on that day. The *Tsis tsis tas* who stared in disbelief as the bluecoats burned the camp and shot hundreds of ponies remembered his name. They would meet George Armstrong Custer another day.

Buffalo Horn and Otter, together with their families and friends, formed their own small band that winter. They camped with the Arapahoes until the snows melted, sharing makeshift lodges that they crafted from the ruined lodges and bloody buffalo hides. Then they turned north and joined the northern bands camped in the Powder River country.

Buffalo Horn's heart was torn with grief for the many dead friends and especially for the man who had tried so hard to find a harmonious path through a violent age. In the midst of tears and suffering, though, the piercing wail of a newborn son brought the promise of rebirth, of revival.

"What will you call him?" Otter asked when they met to plan the naming.

"I had no new dream," Horn confessed. "*Heam-mawihio* whispered nothing to me this time. I remember the old dream, though, and its warning."

"The hawk," Otter said, nodding with approval.

"This time the hawk flew out of the glow of the morning star," Buffalo Horn explained. "I'll call my son Morning Hawk."

"Perhaps it should be Mourning Hawk," Otter suggested.

"No, it's time we put the past behind us. We'll help renew the earth this year, and I'll take a sweat and try to revive the harmony I once knew."

"We'll help you," Bright Swallow said, leading Prairie Flower along before her. "Together we can manage it."

"Together I believe we can manage anything," Horn declared. He fervently hoped that the dark times were behind him and that the little ones would enjoy better days and a brighter future.